Praise for Annie Sanders

'Kitchen knives and forks are very much on the table in Annie Sanders' latest comedy, *Busy Woman Seeks Wife*' *Mirror*

'A curl-up-and-read-in-front-of-the-fire tale that has it all – jealousy, heartache and humour' *Sun*

'You'll enjoy [*The Xmas Factor*] long after the last Christmas cracker has been pulled' *Choice*

'A heart-warming and sparkly comedy – ideal for the time of year' *Woman's Own*

'Lighthearted, witty story about family life' *Woman's Weekly*

'Annie Sanders' *Warnings of Gales* is a riot ... This is a must read for anyone planning a trip with friends ... the perfect escape' *Bookseller*

'A hilarious and moving novel about an unlikely friendship'
She

'This sharply observed tale of domestic dispute will strike a chord with the thousands who have endured and enjoyed shared vacations' *Express*

'One of our picks of the year ... poignant, funny and well-observed' *Bella*

'They bring all the wit, charm and sparkle of their debut novel to this entertaining sequel' *Belfast Telegraph*

'So charmingly engrossing that you may well forget to unload the washing machine' *With Kids* magazine

Meg Sanders and Annie Ashworth have written ten successful non-fiction books together. Both have families and live in Stratford-upon-Avon. *Busy Woman* is their fourth novel. Their first three novels, the bestselling *Goodbye, Jimmy Choo*, *Warnings of Gales* and *The Xmas Factor* are also available in Orion paperback.

By Annie Sanders

Busy Woman Seeks Wife
The Xmas Factor
Warnings of Gales
Goodbye, Jimmy Choo

BUSY WOMAN SEEKS WIFE

Annie Sanders

An Orion paperback
First published in Great Britain in 2007
by Orion
This paperback edition published in 2008
by Orion Books Ltd,
Orion House, 5 Upper Saint Martin's Lane
London, WC2H 9EA

An Hachette Livre UK company

1 3 5 7 9 10 8 6 4 2

A CIP catalogue record for this book
is available from the British Library.

ISBN 978-0-7528-9352-5

Typeset by Deltatype Ltd, Birkenhead, Merseyside

Printed in Great Britain by Clays Ltd, St Ives plc

The Orion Publishing Group's policy is to use papers
that are natural, renewable and recyclable products and
made from wood grown in sustainable forests. The logging
and manufacturing processes are expected to conform to
the environmental regulations of the country of origin.

www.orionbooks.co.uk

To Men in Marigolds

Acknowledgements

We can't pretend to know the first thing about life as a marketing executive – that's why we write novels – so we had to turn to a few people for help. Massive thanks to Caroline Whaley, a very special friend, for all her advice about life in the sportswear fast lane. We couldn't have done it without her. Thanks also to Jill Stanton, Alex Fraser, Anthony King, and Adrian McLoughlin, and not forgetting Jane Wood, Sara O'Keeffe and all at Orion for their enthusiasm and gentle handling.

Chapter 1

'In my bed! They were at it in my sodding bed!'

'Never!'

'Yup. Right there. Big hairy bum in the air and Manuela's legs ... oh God, I don't even want to think about it.'

'You must have given her the fright of her life!'

'Well, I think I've probably rendered him impotent for life. Ugly sod. Oh God, Saff ... I feel so dirty, like I've been violated or something.'

'Want to come over?'

'Can I? Will Max mind?'

'Course not. He loves ya. Anytime – though I'll have to sort out the kids.'

'I'll bring a bottle. I need anaesthetic. I'm in shock.'

Saffron laughed. 'Stay calm.'

Alex put down the phone and turned back to the chaos in her room – her cushions strewn everywhere, a bowl of foreign change smashed on the floor, the blanket from the bed hurled into the corner. She wanted to throw up.

She'd heard the strange noises the minute she'd shouldered open the front door, back home earlier than anticipated with an overnight bag in one hand and a laptop in the other. Dumping them in the narrow hallway, she'd thought Manuela might be moving furniture in her bedroom to clean behind it. Though that would be a first. Her Spanish cleaner didn't move anything if she could help it and struggled at the best of times to figure out the workings of a can of Pledge – oh, the irony. Alex had purposely thumped about the flat a bit so as not to give the poor woman a fright, and called her name before opening the bedroom door.

For a moment she hadn't quite been able to work out what was going on, and had said 'sorry' as if two people screwing in her bed at 2.15 on a Wednesday afternoon was normal. Then the horror of the situation dawned on her, not to mention the wobbling nether regions. The man's suit on the floor – tartan boxers off, shirt and socks still on – and Manuela's red stiletto shoes were discarded. The woman herself appeared to still be fully dressed, and not for cleaning.

'What – the – fuck – are – you – doing?' Alex's screech sounded loud even to Alex and the couple's heads shot round, their expressions freezing for one blissful moment in total dis-belief. 'Get – out – of – my – bed!'

If it hadn't been so disgusting, the scramble that ensued would have been funny. The man, grey-haired, bearded and overweight, reversed out of Manuela and off the bed, frantically searching for his underpants whilst holding his shirt-tails over his genitals in some ridiculous attempt to preserve his remain-ing dignity. Manuela pulled down her dress and tidied her hair with her hands as she pushed her feet into her shoes. Clearly knickers were not a consideration.

'So sorry …' he puffed as he struggled with his trousers. 'Didn't know, you know … we were …'

'Get out,' Alex hissed through her teeth.

'Yes, yes of course.' Stuffing his feet into shoes – quite smart brogues, Alex noticed – he shrugged on his jacket, his face red and sweaty, his neck thick where it was stuffed into the collar of his shirt. He appeared to be about fifty, perhaps fifty-five, a wedding ring on his podgy finger. He made towards the door and Alex stood back to let him through. Then he stopped suddenly, putting his hand inside his jacket and fishing out his wallet. He pulled out some notes and it wasn't until he turned back towards Manuela that Alex twigged.

'I think *I'll* have that, thank you.' She snatched the notes from his hand before Manuela could take them. 'It'll go towards some new sheets. Now get out!'

He bolted like a rabbit, slamming the front door of the flat behind him. Alex turned to Manuela, so angry now she could hear the blood pounding in her ears. The little Spanish woman was straightening the sheets and puffing up the pillow. Lunging forward Alex grabbed her thin brown arm. 'Get out, you bitch. You whore,' she shrieked. 'Get out of my flat. Get out,' and as Alex wrenched at the bed sheets, Manuela tottered to the door.

'But señorita.' She turned to Alex, her face outraged as if it was her who had been wronged. 'What about my pay? I've done the bathroom …'

It was all Alex could do not to thump her. 'And it looks like you've well and truly done the bedroom too. How dare you! Get out. You're fired!'

As if possessed, Alex continued to pull off the sheets. Bundling them up into a ball, she hurled them with all her might out of the room, followed by the pillows and duvet, then, opening the flat door, kicked them down the communal stairs to the hallway below, narrowly avoiding Manuela as she bolted out of the front door. Grabbing her overnight bag to prop open the flat door, Alex turned back to her bedroom and pulled on the mattress, her hands struggling to find a grip and slipping painfully. It was heavy and she had to push hard against it to squeeze it through the door. Her tight jacket didn't help and she could feel herself sweating. She was aware she was grunting inelegantly, but eventually she managed it, and pushed it to join the sheets below. Throwing her jacket back into the hallway, she followed her bedding downstairs, clambering over it to open the front door of the building and, in two journeys, dumped it all in the builders' skip outside the house opposite, her duvet cover joining brick rubble and broken plasterboard.

It was then that she'd phoned Saff.

What now? She slowly began to straighten the chaos in the room, picking up the shards from the broken bowl carefully, before scooping up the coins and dropping them into a drawer in her dressing table. She must have knocked the bowl as she struggled with the mattress.

In her room. They'd done it in *her* room and in her lovely bed that she'd bought the day she'd completed on the flat. The lovely bed with its pretty bedding where she and Todd made love and read the papers together on a Sunday morning. Well, she read them anyway while he usually did his hundred press-ups before going on a run. She'd have to call the cleaning agency, of course, and get Manuela struck off, but as Alex folded up the bed quilt, piling it up with the cushions on the bare divan, she realised that wouldn't go any way to ridding her of the suspicion that today's liaison was probably not the first.

Changing out of her work clothes, crumpled from the horrendously early start in Stuttgart and the flight, she purposely turned her back on the denuded bed as she slipped into joggers and her favourite T-shirt. Comfort clothes. Of course, she'd have to sell the flat, that was obvious. Heaven only knew how many sexually frustrated, overweight married men had been entertained by Manuela over the weeks she'd worked here. No wonder the place was never very clean. The tart was too busy turning tricks.

Gathering up her clothes and stuffing them in the washing

machine, Alex could feel her blood pumping loudly again. She tore open the fridge, knowing full well there wouldn't be anything in there to eat – there rarely was – but there wasn't even the measly pint of milk she'd asked Manuela to get. The request had been written on the same note about putting the bed sheets through the machine; clearly another thing that hadn't been done. Alex grabbed her purse, fishing out a few quid, and, locking the flat door behind her, dashed downstairs and to the corner shop.

'Hello there, Alex girl.' Rajesh's toothy smile peeked out from behind the counter piled high with displays of chewing gum and chocolate bars on special offer. 'Where have you been? Off on your travels again?'

'It's been a bit of a marathon,' she sighed, picking up a basket. 'Geneva, Amsterdam, Frankfurt, Stuttgart. I think.' She picked up a few things, including a paper which she knew she wouldn't have time to read, but it was a nodding attempt to keep up with world affairs, and handed over the money to Rajesh.

'Oh, it's no good. A lovely girl like you shouldn't be off on a plane every minute. You should be at home with babies.'

Alex rolled her eyes. 'You are as bad as my mother, Rajesh.' Laughing, she left the shop, as the little shopkeeper shook his head and went back to reading the local paper.

As she elbowed open her door a few minutes later, a rather tired bunch of daffs, a warm bottle of Chardonnay and a loaf of sliced white under her arm, which had been all that was left on the shelf, she could hear her mobile ringing. By the time she'd dumped her shopping it had stopped. The office.

'Yup, Camilla? I'm back now.' Alex tucked the phone under her chin as she leant into a cupboard for a vase. 'Sorry I missed your call. I managed an earlier flight so I'm home.'

'Oh, that's great,' her assistant's soft voice cooed down the phone. It was as pretty as she was, but Alex was grateful that despite her petite frame and doe-like blue eyes, she was awesomely efficient and a rock in Alex's choppy seas. 'It's good to have you back. Just a few things to keep you up to speed. Tetril's factory are happy with the samples date you suggest, the twenty-fifth is fine for the ice hockey and the shoe people want to talk to you about the colour range.'

'OK – can you put something in my diary for a meeting? But, Camilla, tell them I haven't got long or they'll have me there all day and I haven't got time.' Their footwear team put as much dedication into the construction of a trainer as scientists had into the Stealth Bomber and talked with such passion about aerodynamics, cushioning and arch supports, it was almost kinky.

'Oh, and your Yankie dreamboat called by the way. He couldn't get you on your phone – you must have been on the plane – but says he'll be landing at Heathrow after his stop-off in Paris.'

Alex felt a tingle of anticipation at the news of Todd's arrival in the country until she remembered she'd have no bed for him to climb into. Not when the mattress was in the skip, and there certainly wouldn't be room for his muscle-bound body in the tiny single in the spare bedroom where she'd have to sleep. It would have to be the Holiday Inn for him. Hanging up the call, she scanned over her notes quickly. Things were looking good for the next few weeks. Product launches always got her excited; massive build-up, even more massive preparation, then the nail-biting wait to see how the product was received by press and public.

Bread with some cheese she'd found loitering at the back of the fridge, in one hand, and laptop on her knee, Alex now scrolled through the plethora of email messages, chewing absent-mindedly. Everything seemed to be going smoothly in the office. Camilla had held the fort pretty well while she'd been away and Alex sent her an email saying as much. Then she turned to the pile of post on the table. All the envelopes had windows, except for one reminding her of the date of her next dentist appointment – which would have to be changed. The only other uncontroversial-looking one turned out to be from her neighbour in the flat below complaining that unless she did something about her leaking shower and the water coming through his ceiling, he'd issue legal proceedings. Alex stuffed the letter behind the microwave, where she filed everything she couldn't handle immediately, and her eye was caught by the flashing light on the front of the washing machine. It was stuck in the middle of the programme, and no knob twiddling would get it to move on. Damn. She scrabbled in the kitchen drawer to try and find the instruction book. Where was it? All she could find was 'giblets' – plastic bags of Allen keys and screws, the extras from gadgets and appliances she'd bought when she moved in two years ago. She'd look again later. Then she dialled her mother's number and with shoulder scrunched up, phone to one ear, she pulled out bedding from the tiny airing cupboard and began to make up the single bed.

'Hi, Mum, I'm back.'

'Hello daaarling,' her mother's sultry tones came down the line. 'Good trip? I don't know how you put up with all that filthy travelling.'

Alex sighed silently. 'Cos I have to. Can't talk for long, how's things?'

'Busy busy, you know. And now I'm about to tackle the ivy on the front of the house. It's gone mad.'

Alex sighed audibly this time, stuffing a pillow into a pillow case. 'Oh mum, can't you wait? I said I'd do it. I'll come over at the weekend.'

'Well, sweetie, you've been saying that for a while. Do you really think you can this time?'

Ignoring the tone of disapproval, Alex did a mental scan. 'Er, hang on, actually, I'm off to Toronto on Sunday afternoon but—'

'Quite. I'll be fine, darling, up my little ladder.'

Alex had a vision of The Bean, as everyone called her, demure little hat on her head and the most elegant and unsuitable of gardening gloves bought through one of her gardening catalogues, teetering on the step ladder clipping at the ivy. 'No, Mum, wait. I'll come over on Saturday. I'll have an hour or so then. That ivy needs a serious assault.'

'Well, dear … I don't know …' And The Bean went off on some diversion involving her oldest friend Ursula and some blazared lothario who was wooing her at the Arts Club.

Alex pulled up outside Saffron's an hour later than planned and it was already dark. Camilla's call, which had come through just after she'd shaken off her mother, had put everything else on the back burner. Apparently Gavin, her boss, could not now get to Toronto before the key presentation meeting next week. Could Alex do the business for him with the clients over there? So, with assurances from Camilla that she'd help out with preparing notes and the audio visual, Alex dropped everything to begin trawling for information to persuade the sceptical Canadian sales team that the cutting edge properties of their new range were vastly superior to anything the industry had yet been able to offer.

Max opened the door. 'Hello stranger. Glad to see you've

dressed up as usual.' Alex playfully punched his shoulder. 'How vos der trip, ja?'

'Oh tedious.' She returned his warm hug. 'Those Germans have no sense of irony and every hotel looks exactly the same.'

'I get it.' He lead her through to the bright, warm kitchen. 'If it's Tuesday and the bathroom's on the right, must be in Baden-Baden.'

'Something like that.'

Max took the bottle of minimart Chardonnay from her, looking suspiciously at the label and, clearly revolted, put it away in a cupboard to join her other dodgy offerings from the past. 'God, I hope you know more about sportswear than you do about wine,' he'd teased her once, and she now took perverse pleasure in finding a bottle that would guarantee to make the affable TV executive wince. He put a glass of something dark and red in front of her at the kitchen table and she took a deep gulp, comforted now by the flavour as it ran over her tongue. There was a delicious smell wafting out of the oven. Max and Saffron's kitchen was like a security blanket to her – the bright, hand-painted mugs on the dresser, the apron on the back of the door, the children's pictures on the fridge. To Alex it felt like the home she'd never managed to achieve, the only normality in her mad world.

'Saff's just turning off Oscar's light. There's been a home-work drama but she's soothing frayed tempers,' said Max. They then chatted briefly about work; they were both absorbed by the totally different but equally challenging worlds they moved in – media and marketing from two opposing directions.

Eventually footsteps came down the stairs and Saffron entered the room, her neat little frame in a white linen shirt, green checked capri pants and pumps. Alex felt herself begin-ning to relax from the day.

'Hi, good to see you, sweetie.' Saffron kissed her friend warmly on the cheek. 'Have you got a drink? How's the Spanish scrubber?'

'Oh Gawd, Saff.' Alex put her head in her hands. 'It's so vile! I've chucked all the bedding into the skip. The nasty little creep who was giving her one even pulled out some cash to pay her! In front of me! Can you imagine?'

Saffron looked suitably shocked as she bustled about putting on her pinny and preparing the French beans to cook. She placed a bowl of crisps in front of Alex. Max, already informed about the day's outrage and suspecting shrieked outpourings of grief, scooped up a handful and escaped the room for his study.

'You have to admire the woman's business acumen,' Saffron said, tying her wavy blonde hair into a ponytail on top of her head. 'With you away so much, she didn't let the grass grow under her feet, did she?'

'Little slapper,' Alex replied through a mouthful of crisps, realising how hungry she was. 'And now I've got to get a new mattress or I'll never see Todd. Not that we have time to see each other anyway. And my neighbour downstairs is getting nasty about the leak in my shower. But I just don't have time to get someone in to sort it. I *can't* take a day off, and I've got a pile of stuff to get to the cleaners or I'll have nothing to wear in Toronto. Oh, and the sodding washing machine is on the blink, again, and then there's the little matter of work. Bloody Gavin can't make Toronto, so rather than spending the time I should be to consolidate all the information from the last few days and preparing for the launch, I've got to put together a huge presentation which is critical – it's *critical*, Saff. If I get this wrong, it's going to affect how we are perceived in Canada and then—'

Saff put her hand on Alex's arm. 'Hey! Calm down, love. Stressing isn't going to help.'

'But it's *all* stress. There's just no time to do anything, even to buy milk, for heaven's sake. And I haven't managed to see Mum for ages. And now she's threatening to—' Alex was cut off by her mobile buzzing in her bag. 'Hello?'

'Alex? It's Letitia, dear. From next door to your mother.'

Alex could feel her anxiety rising.

'Sorry to bother you, dear, but it's your mother. I think she fell off her ladder. Anyway, I'm here at the hospital with her.'

'Oh, bloody hell. Oh no, is she all right?'

'Don't fret. It's not too serious but they think it's her arm. The thing is, she won't be able to go home tonight. They said something about having to reset it and I'm afraid I'm off on a cruise to the fjords tomorrow first thing or I'd gladly help.'

'Oh, thank you, Letitia. Please don't worry. You've done more than enough. I'll be right there.' Finding out exactly where her mother had been taken to and thanking her again profusely, Alex clicked off her phone and looked across at Saffron's concerned face.

'Is she OK?' she asked cautiously. 'What do the doctors say?'

Alex relayed what Letitia had said, her heart sinking at the implications. 'Oh Saff! What the hell was she doing cutting back the ivy at this time of night? She was bound to fall! I told her I'd do it. I should have been more insistent. Oh God, what am I going to do?' Alex rubbed her eyes, smearing the remaining mascara over her cheeks. 'Who's going to look after her? I can't have her come and stay with me. I mean, how can I? I'm never there ...'

'Well, it might not be for long. She might be able to go

home again by the time you go to Canada. At least you'll be there at night and she can watch TV—'

Alex sat bolt upright. 'But there's no bed for her!'

'I've got a camp bed?' Saff tried to look helpful.

Alex stood up. 'Bless you. Can I let you know? Oh, why couldn't she have waited for me?'

Saff looked up at her friend and laughed ruefully. 'Come on, Alex, you know how stubborn she can be. She's always done exactly what she wants. Why don't you have some food before you leave?'

'Thanks, Saff, but I'd better go and see her straight away – much as I'd love your yummy supper. I seem to have had nothing but airline meals and packet soups lately. Soon I won't be able to cope with anything that doesn't come on a plastic tray. All I wanted to do was talk to you.' She suddenly felt very weary.

'What you need,' said Saffron, standing up and rubbing Alex's arm comfortingly, 'is someone to take away your worries, someone to cook you lovely meals and deal with all the boring details of life.'

'But I've got a bloke already,' protested Alex. 'When he's in the country at least.'

'No, no!' replied Saffron. 'I mean, what you need is a *wife*.'

Chapter 2

Saffron climbed down from the ladder and admired her morning's work. The turquoise-blue paint had definitely been the right choice. She glanced at the swatch of purple-blue floral fabric draped over the chair, the result of a wonderful hour and a half at the interiors shop trawling through the sample books – her favourite pastime second only to having her nose in a cook book. Millie would love it. What nine-year-old girl couldn't? How excited she'd be when she came home from school.

Absently pushing away the hair that was tickling her nose, she wiped the excess paint from her brush onto the edge of the tin. Slipping off her flip-flops on the dust sheet so as not to risk walking paint over the new landing carpet, she carried it downstairs, careful not to touch the newly stencilled walls. She looked at them with immense pride as she passed. Who needed Jocasta Innes when, with a two week course and the right kit, she could do it herself?

She'd washed the brush and was putting on the kettle and thinking about what she could do for the next few hours, and what to make for the children and Max for supper, with half an eye on the dramatic purple tulips in the tubs outside the back door bobbing about in the brisk wind, when the phone rang.

'Saff?' Alex sounded breathless. 'Look, I'm about to go into a meeting but—'

'And hello to you too!' Saff smiled.

'Yeah, sorry. I'm a bit rushed.' Wasn't she always? 'I've been thinking about what you said last night – you know that wife thing you mentioned? We didn't really expand on it. Did you mean like a housekeeper?'

'Well, I don't know really. I was sort of joking.' In Alex's haste to leave to see her mother, Saff had thought her ridiculous remark would have been forgotten. 'It just seems to me that you needed someone like – well, me, really. Someone who does all the things Max doesn't have time to do. Making dentist appointments, letting in the washing machine man, taking clothes to the cleaners, cleaning the loo. Oh, I don't know.' The more she thought about it, the more stupid an idea it sounded. 'I don't suppose there's really enough that you need doing to keep one person busy. Not when you are away such a lot of the time.'

'No,' Alex paused. 'The thing is, when I was at the hospital ...'

'Yes, of course. How is she? Is she out yet?'

'No, not yet. They had to reset her arm under anaesthetic. It's not a very nice break and she's going to take a while to recover but she's the same old Bean.' Alex paused. 'She even told me off for not having any make-up on! Oh Saff, I hate to sound uncaring and I want to make sure she's OK, but this is when being an only child is so difficult. I've never been so busy at work and I just can't get away. The point is, the doctors don't think she should be at home on her own at the moment.'

'Oh.' Saffron didn't need the issue spelling out. 'Well, sweetheart, I can't have her here – much as I love her. We're off skiing next week, don't forget, though I suppose we could have her when we get back. I have to say, though, Max's mother staying for that week here last Autumn nearly precipitated a divorce.'

'God no, I'm not asking that!' Alex laughed. 'Though come to think of it, The Bean would love it. You are much more the sort of person she'd have liked as a daughter. A proper girl. No, what I wondered – gosh, I have to rush – could you possibly put an ad in the local paper for me? I think they publish on a Friday so we might just catch it. Nothing fancy, just a "sits vac". I'll leave it to you – just tell them it's starting immediately. And Saff, could you put in both our numbers? Yours and mine in case I'm tied up? Lord knows what Mum will think – whoever gets the job had better be resilient. But what can she expect if she goes climbing ladders when I tell her not to?' Alex blew Saff a kiss before cutting off the call and dashing off to yet another meeting.

Saff poured the boiling water into the spotty teapot and took down the matching cup from the dresser. They were her favourite set, made by a little potter they had discovered in Norfolk whilst staying with friends. She tutted, smiling to herself – there was she, thrilled by a piece of china. Small pleasures compared to the corporate whirlwind that made up the framework of Alex's day. But then Alex had never been interested in frippery. She'd always been destined for big things and her marketing position at Zencorp, one of the world's biggest sportwear companies, fitted her ambitions as neatly as Lycra running shorts. Tall, athletic, though unenviably flat-chested, Alex could be a man with the men, especially with her font of locker-room knowledge on just about every sport.

Saffron took down the floral biscuit tin and fished out one of the flapjacks she'd made yesterday. There were only a few left since the family had swooped.

She'd seen the corporate woman in action at a promo event that Alex had invited them all to a couple of years ago – Saff, Max, Oscar and Millie. In her company T-shirt, shorts, and ID tag, Alex had stridden about the stadium, utterly at ease in her role and frighteningly efficient. So, what Saff was doing writing an ad for her when Alex prepared global advertising campaigns all the time she wasn't quite sure, but if it helped her oldest friend, then she'd have a go. She had nothing better to do today. So, picking up a pen and paper from the side, padding back to the table with her steaming cup and savouring the sweet oatyness of her flapjack, she began to jot down ideas.

'Busy Woman seeks Wife.' Would that sound like she was looking for a lesbian lover? Though on second thoughts, that might solve Alex's problems! 'Efficient and capable person needed to make a working woman's life easier, including caring for a convalescing relative.' That didn't sound right. Saff drew a line through the last six words. That would attract some psycho who might do something awful to The Bean. The one and only time Saff had considered a nanny, a woman like that had answered the ad. She'd had a manic look in her eye and kept asking to see the children's rooms. Saff had given her short shrift and had vowed that she'd never leave the kids with anyone. No, Alex didn't want one of those. Or a Mrs Danvers-type who'd be all starchy. The Bean would hate that. What they needed was a bright young thing who could be stimulating *and* listen to the reminiscences of Alex's mother – a fascinating pastime for anyone – whilst still managing to run the domestic side of Alex's chaotic life. The more Saff thought about it, the more she knew a wife would fit the bill. Max always said he couldn't function without her running his life – though Saff wasn't that stupid. A kiss on the forehead and the flattery were just a man's way of saying 'I won't bother learning so long as you are there to do it for me'. She sometimes wondered what would happen to the family if she disappeared into thin air. How long before they were eating pasta out of a tin and wearing the same underpants until they could stand up on their own? Saff shivered. Right.

'Busy Woman seeks Wife ... To put her house in order.' She decided not to mention the bit about caring for The Bean and see who turned up. 'Are you capable and efficient?' Obviously. 'Self-motivated?' They'd have to be because Alex would never be there. 'Are you able to combine the skills of gourmet chef, top PA and chambermaid?' Did that sound patronising? Please apply etc. etc. Immediate start.

Saff read it back, then she called the small ads section of the local paper.

Chapter 3

'Mmmmakes you feel f-f-f-fruity!!!'

Frankie waited rigidly in front of the microphone until the recording light went off, then sighed deeply. How many times was that now? He'd lost count somewhere around twenty-eight. He was pretty sure that one thing a banana should not sound was desperate. The voice of the director, ever so slightly impatient, came over his earphones.

'Still not quite there. Could you make it a bit – a bit more yellow? You know – a really ripe banana, but not one that's started to go brown yet? No brown patches at all. All right? Nice and firm but soft as well. You know. Not just out of the fridge. Go again.'

Frankie nodded slowly, trying to take in the flow of information. What the hell was he doing here? 'Fruitacious Yoghurt. Take thirty-seven,' came the bored voice of the technician. Damn it! He was too good for this. But why couldn't he even get a sodding banana right? It was now or never. He called on his years of training.

Frankie closed his eyes tight and saw – nothing but yellow. He dredged yellowness up from the pit of his soul. Yellow. Ripe. Not brown. Zingy. Soft, yet firm. Right. His eyes popped open and he focused, like a Zen archer, on the screen in front of him showing an animated banana tap dancing along a spoon into a yoghurt pot. I *am* the banana, he breathed, I *am* the banana.

'MMMMMakes you feeeel f-f-f-f FRUUUIIIITY!!!!!' he intoned.

It had been his best take yet. A triumph. He knew it. And from all sides, out in the darkened studio, he felt the stunned admiration of the crew.

'That's it!' exclaimed the client, over the earpiece. 'That's our banana. Fantastic. What's his name again? Frankie? Thanks, Frankie. Tremendous. I think er ...' There was a muffled conversation and then the director's voice came over the earpiece.

'Yes, I'm very happy with that. Sweetie, thanks very much indeed. That was tremendous. You can leave any time you like, as far as I'm concerned. We'll be in touch. We've got the raspberry next. What's her name again? Can we have the raspberry?'

So that was it? A whole morning, only to be dismissed in favour of a raspberry? Frankie straightened up from the banana-like curve he'd found himself adopting over the course of the last couple of hours and stood tall, holding the door for the terrified-looking raspberry. 'You were great,' she whispered. 'You really took his direction well. We were all listening.'

'All? Really?' In spite of himself, Frankie felt a surge of pleasure as he looked past her at a collection of other actors, a few of whom he recognised, sitting huddled round a speaker.

'Yes, Adrian – he's the mango, Fliss, kiwi fruit, and Germaine – she's the friendly bacteria.' The raspberry couldn't disguise the envy in her voice. 'She's worked with the director before, so ...'

Frankie nodded his understanding. 'Ahh. Right. Well, thanks. Break a leg.' He joined the others. Glancing around, relatively relaxed now that his work was over, Frankie was relieved that he hadn't gone for the tropical fruit look he'd briefly considered that morning. You could take a thing too far.

He conversed, briefly, with them – a studiedly casual chat about who was doing what and where, who'd got telly, who was spending the summer at Scarborough, who'd changed their agent. But when raspberry girl started, all pretence at disinterest ended and they listened, avidly, as she delivered her lines again and again. There was no more conversation to be had now, so Frankie mouthed his farewells, shouldered his way out through the double doors into the corridor, down the stairs and out into the sunny springtime of Covent Garden, busy as ever with the usual mix of shoppers, gawkers and office workers trying to get a quick sandwich.

He hopped off the tube at Brixton, a copy of *The Stage* already scoured and marked up, tucked under his arm. There were a few castings but nothing really inspiring. He'd have to steel himself to call Marina – again. But meanwhile, the market on Electric Avenue beckoned. Sprawling along both sides of the road, the stalls had the best range of fruit and veg he'd found yet and Frankie roamed happily along, comparing prices, filling up his backpack with the ingredients for a menu he was inventing as he went. Roasted aubergines with some of that nice fat garlic – no castings tomorrow. Maybe some red pepper soup. Frankie hummed contentedly as he stopped into the corner shop for washing-up liquid, a floor cloth, some rice crackers. Was that everything? He was almost out of cash, so it would have to be.

Letting himself into the flat without dropping everything took some doing, particularly as the door was sticking again. Frankie made a mental note to speak to the landlord again and shoved his way in. The sound of Radio One, turned up that bit too loud, made his heart sink. He'd been counting on a little time to himself before Ella got back.

'S'at you, Frankie?' she trilled.

He shouldered open the sitting room door – pointless asking

her to help with the bags – and got his usual view: Ella's bare feet crossed at the ankles, poised on the back of the sofa he'd bought with the proceeds from a couple of lines in *The Bill*. He took the bags into the white-painted kitchen hung with strings of dried chillies and ropes of garlic, and looked around in disbelief. How had she managed to make so much mess in so little time? He'd left that work surface immaculate before he'd left – now it was ringed with sticky brown coffee residue and slopped with hastily poured milk. With a sigh, he picked up a dishcloth and started to wipe it up.

Ella bounded over and her little round face appeared through the serving hatch, her hair, as always, sticking up at odd angles, unmatched earrings dangling from her tiny lobes. 'So? How did it go? Were you top banana?'

She was always doing this. Just when he'd managed to convince himself she was the most selfish, unthinking little brute in the universe, she'd suddenly show she actually had been listening all along. He put the cloth down. 'Well, they did my bit second, after the passion fruit. He was quite good actually, although I thought his accent was a little bit off. They only did twenty takes for him. By the time I'd finished, all the others had arrived. Honestly, Ells, the director was—'

'Bet you're glad you didn't wear that awful surf shirt, aren't you?' She interrupted. 'Anyway, listen. Dougie phoned and asked if you were going to be at five-a-side later and your Secret Agent rang.'

Frankie winced. 'Oh, you didn't say anything stupid this time did you? You know Marina has no sense of humour.'

'That's what makes it so irresistible!' Ella put on the smoky drawl of Frankie's theatrical agent. 'Daarling, she's got you lightly pencilled in for another voice-over next week.'

Frankie's face fell. 'I don't know. I've had enough of that

stuff. She hasn't put me up for a decent part in ages. It's so limiting, working like that.'

'Not as limiting as having no money, though. Anyway, that's enough about you. Let's talk about me for a while. My interview, for example. You haven't even asked me about it yet.'

'Give me a chance! I've only just got in – and I've got all the shopping to put away.' Frankie turned from her, pretending to busy himself in the fridge. He'd completely forgotten about Ella's interview and racked his brains for details – nothing. Knowing Ella and her constantly changing enthusiasms, it could have been for anything from neurosurgeon to jazz pianist – and her complete lack of qualification for either would not have been any deterrent. 'So, how did it go?' he called vaguely over his shoulder from the chilly depths of the fridge.

Luckily, Ella's usual verve saved him and she plunged into an account of her morning at a local radio station. So *that* was it. 'The control desk was really complicated – far harder than the one at uni. I'd have quite liked a go but they wouldn't let me. Anyway, everyone seemed *really* nice. I made the station manager laugh and they said they'd be in touch, so I expect I'll be starting in the next couple of weeks. Isn't it brilliant? I'll be making loads of money. And it's what I've always wanted to do. *And* I'll be able to help you with the bills at last.'

Oh God. She was so happy, he couldn't bear to crush her. And yet he couldn't leave her in her fool's paradise. This would call for all his acting ability. Frankie stood up and turned to face her, carefully masking his features. 'Well,' he laughed lightly. 'If by "always wanted to do", you mean the last two weeks then, yes, I'm sure it'll be great. But it is an incredibly competitive field, you know – lots of people probably chasing the same jobs, so … well, just wait and see, eh? I mean, were there other people there today? At the interview?'

Ella waved her hand airily. 'Oh yes, one or two. Real stiffs, though. Shirt and tie types, y'know? Boring. Anyway, listen. I picked up a local paper while the station manager was out of the room. They have piles and piles of papers there – isn't it weird? You'd think they'd have all the news they wanted without having to get in extra.'

Frankie handed a bowl of humous through the hatch, with sticks of carrot and celery he'd just cut up and set about spreading goat's cheese onto rye bread. Watching Ella tuck in immediately, without even bothering to clear the table, he rolled his eyes. 'Well, maybe they have the papers there so they can read bits out on air. Or find out what's going on locally.'

Ella paled and put down the dishes, then rummaged in her rucksack over by the sofa and pulled out a wodge of newsprint. 'I hope not, cos I've got most of them here. Oh dear! Hope they don't realise it was me.'

Well that was another job she wouldn't be getting. Frankie sighed. Sharing a flat with his kid sister had never been part of his life plan, much less a penniless kid sister who was scraping by on the odd hour at the local cinema. Even having her contribute to the bills seemed like a wild fantasy these days. 'Well, of course they're going to realise it was you. Think about it, Ella.' Frankie could hear the exasperation in his voice, but couldn't be bothered to suppress it this time. 'Papers on desk, you in room. Manager leaves room, you in room, papers disappear. It's not rocket science, y'know.'

As soon as the words left his lips, Frankie knew it was a mistake. Spiky, arrogant and selfish as she could be, his sister could still bring out his protective side and, as she stood there, that stricken look on her pale face with her huge eyes ringed with black kohl, he felt the familiar pang. She blinked fast and spun away suddenly to cover up the hurt. 'Well, I took them for you, as it happens. Wish I hadn't bothered now if that's what you think. I saw an advert. That's all. I was only thinking of you.'

'I'm sorry,' Frankie apologised uncomfortably. 'I didn't mean it. I'm sure it won't matter about the papers. I'm just feeling shitty, cos this banana thing was so – so humiliating, if you must know.'

Ella spun round, a gleam in her eye. 'Well, then you've *got* to look at this!' She brandished a page of small ads in his face, fired up with enthusiasm once more. 'Look. Right here. "Busy Woman Seeks Wife". It's perfect for you.'

'What? I'm not interested in a lonely hearts ad. You're not starting all that again, are you?'

'Noooo. This isn't lonely hearts at all. It's job ads.' Frankie tried to grab the paper but she whisked it away and hopped over towards the window. 'Listen. I'll read it out to you.' Frankie was aghast as his sister read the details. '"Occasional weekends. Good rate of pay for right applicant. Wandsworth area." There are two phone numbers. What do you think?'

'I think you've taken leave of your senses! Are you really suggesting that for me? I'm not a cleaner! I'm not a cook. Most of all, I'm not a woman!'

Ella went through a pantomime of searching the ad. 'It doesn't say anything about them wanting a woman. And you may not be a cleaner or a cook, but you're better at either than anyone I've ever met. Probably better than you are at ...'

'Acting! You were going to say acting, weren't you? Honestly, Ella! I take you in out of the kindness of my heart ...' Frankie tugged the paper from her. 'Let me have a look. Yes, see? "Busy Woman Seeks *Wife*". Wife? Like, female-type person? I may be a brilliant actor, but I just don't have the tits for it.'

'Sexist pig.' Shaking her head in exasperation, Ella pulled

him down to sit beside her on the sofa. 'Think outside the box for once, Frankie. It's not specifically a woman she's after – anyway, that would be against the law. She needs someone who's expert at keeping things shipshape and you're good at that. You know you are.'

Frankie could almost hear that familiar rush of water; that sense he always got with Ella of being swept along. All the reasons he could come up with would be answered and argued away – as usual. He tried another tack. 'OK, so I'm good at cooking and stuff. But I couldn't do this job – I just couldn't logistically. I've got to be free for auditions and castings and stuff.'

Ella shook her head impatiently and flicked him sharply on the ear – something she'd done with tiresome regularity ever since that first time he hid her Brownie sash. 'What? Auditions for being the biggest, stupidest banana in town? Come off it, Frankie. What you need is a sensible job for a bit. We need the dosh, me old darling. Did you *see* that last phone bill?'

'Phone bill? What phone bill?'

Chapter 4

'Thanks, a coffee would be lovely. But only if you're having one.'

Frankie took off his best jacket and hung it on the back of the metal and leather director's chair, then looked around cautiously as the short, cute woman who'd introduced herself as Saff went through to the kitchen. They were waiting for someone else to arrive – her husband presumably – but two calls from a mobile had told of solid traffic. He checked his watch. He'd turned up at six on the dot, and was due to meet Dougie and the boys at the pub in Tooting at eight. If the other interviewer didn't get a move on, he'd have to leave anyway. He walked over to the window. The flat wasn't big and was sparsely decorated. The small table was bare except for the papers the woman had left there.

What the hell was he doing here anyway? Bloody Ella and her interminable phone calls. Where the hell had she been calling for the phone bill to be so huge? Bolivia? If she'd been a bit more sensible for once in her life, he wouldn't have to be here, interviewing for this ridiculous job.

He jumped as Saff came back into the room. 'Couldn't find any biscuits, I'm afraid.' She shrugged apologetically, handing him a chipped mug bearing a sportswear logo. 'And it's instant too. That was all I could find. I hope it's all right?'

With a smile like hers to look at, Frankie thought, he'd happily drink dishwater. He took a sip and flinched. Yep, it wasn't far off dishwater. He quickly put the cup down on the table and took the seat she indicated.

She looked at her watch and shook her head. 'I know we talked briefly on the phone, but I'll need to know a bit more. Shall we make a start? I mean, I'm sure you've got better things to do than wait here with me. This way, I can make some notes at least.' She sat down opposite him, shuffling through the papers. 'Now, where did I put that list of questions …?'

Frankie took the opportunity to study her. In her flowered linen skirt and pink V-necked cardigan, she looked completely out of place in the rather clinical surroundings, and far more appealing. Her round face was generously sprinkled with freckles and she had eyes that looked used to laughing. She hunted round futilely for a little while then shook her head sadly.

'Perhaps I could just make something up?' she suggested.

'Fire away.' He leant forward in the chair and looked at her expectantly. He could definitely work for her.

'Right, well. I've got your full name and address. How old are you?'

'Thirty-two.' He watched as she scrawled on the page with a sequinned biro she produced from her bag.

'Your last job?'

He was damned if he was going to tell her about the banana fiasco, or the list of restaurants he'd appearanced at in the past couple of years. 'Well, that would be *The Bill*. I had quite a few lines but it was heavily cut.'

She nodded sympathetically. 'Always the way, isn't it? Is that what you're really interested in, then, telly? Because this would be a bit of a change for you, wouldn't it?'

Looking across the table at her, Frankie had the sudden feeling that he should be completely honest with this woman – that it would be quite wrong to be anything else, even if it

27

scuppered his chances of getting the job. 'Well, theatre's my first love, of course, but I do mostly fringe stuff, you know.'

'Hmmm. Theatre for flash, telly for cash, eh? Usual story.'

Frankie was a little taken aback by her directness. 'Er, yes.' She wasn't quite as fluffy as she looked.

She glanced at her watch again. 'So, what makes you think you'd be right for this job? It's an odd choice for an actor.'

He'd been anticipating this question and he'd rehearsed a reply on the way over here. He coughed. 'Well, yes, I can see it would seem that way but I'm used to working with people and I'm very flexible too, but what I feel I could really bring to this are my organisational skills. I've done quite a bit of touring, you know, taking small shows on the road. And I always do the logistics and help with the stage managing, so I'm quite used to sorting out problems and, actually, anticipating them before they arise.'

She smiled knowingly, clearly unconvinced, and made a few more notes, tucking fair curls behind her ear with her left hand, momentarily dazzling him with the ruddy great rock on her fourth finger. He wondered what she did for a living that kept her so busy that she needed a 'wife'. There was no evidence of children in the flat so she either had some flashy career or was the type who spent her life playing tennis and having coffee with the girls. She looked up. 'There will be cooking involved. Could you deal with that?'

'Oh yes, cooking is one of my passions. I think Nigel Slater should be knighted for services to chicken. And I can knock up a mean seafood chowder if pushed.'

Saff smiled and relaxed. 'Oh, I love that. Do you use clams?'

'If I can get them, otherwise I settle for mussels.'

Saff scribbled again on her pad, enthusiastically this time.

'Good, good.' She checked her watch again and sighed dramatically. 'Honestly, I'm running out of questions. Er – where do you see yourself in five years' time?'

He looked at her in puzzlement. She returned his look challengingly, a slow smile curving her small mouth into an infectious grin. They both burst out laughing. At that moment, the door opened and a cold draught swept into the room. A tall, dark-haired woman in jeans and a parka strode in, taking them both in at a glance. Then she stopped, her eyes resting on Frankie, her look bewildered.

'Oh, I thought you said the interviewee was here.' She sounded a little irritated and she turned to Saff. 'What's going on?' she asked abruptly, unhooking the bulging messenger bag from across her chest and shrugging off her jacket. Frankie noticed that, unlike most women he knew, she made no effort to smooth her hair and titivate. He was no expert, but even he could see her hair needed a cut or at the very least a comb pulling through it. It seemed of a piece with her tanned, make-up free face. Even her hands were sensible – short nails and no jewellery to be seen.

The rapport he had started to build up with Saff died away with their laughter. So *this* was the Busy Woman. This changed everything and he wasn't sure what tack to take with this forth-right athletic-looking woman. His usual line in light charm wasn't going to work here. He stood up and held out his hand. 'Hello. Frankie Ward. I *am* the interviewee.'

She looked astonished but automatically put her hand out anyway. Her grip was more hesitant than he would have expected, although he could feel strength in her long, thin fingers. 'Alex Hill.' She dropped his hand quickly. 'I don't quite understand. We advertised for a woman, didn't we?'

Saff smiled. 'I didn't specify actually.'

'But it said wife, didn't it?'

'Well *technically* yes, but in fact you're not allowed to exclude anyone no matter what the advert says. That's what the man at the local paper told me.'

'Yes, I know all that, Saff. But that's ridiculous in this instance!' Alex snorted. 'Obviously I can't have a man doing this job. I'm surprised you even asked him to come for an interview.'

Saff put her hands on her hips and raised her chin. 'Why not? Why should a woman be a better wife just by virtue of her sex? You of all people should know that, in your world. What sex you are shouldn't be a barrier to a job. That's what you're always banging on about.'

Frankie looked between the two women who seemed to have forgotten he was there, so different in their manner but obviously very close.

'Max couldn't do what you do!' Alex continued. 'You're always saying how useless he is around the house.'

'Yeah, but that's only because he pretends to be. What I do is easy and he could do it if he had to. If he can run a company, he could probably get his head around making a cake.'

There was an awkward pause and Frankie interjected cautiously, 'I make great brownies.'

Alex's shoulders dropped. 'OK,' she sighed. 'Let's carry on with the interview but only for legal reasons. I'm not comfortable with this. A man I don't know in my house every day? I don't think so. And what would Mum make of it?' She scanned the table. 'Er, Saff, have you got the list of questions? How far did you get?'

With a completely unrepentant smile on her face, Saffron took her seat. 'Sorry – couldn't find it. I might have left it at home. I made some notes, though.'

Alex rubbed her temples and closed her eyes for a moment. She had surprisingly long dark lashes and, although her mouth was quite wide, her lips were pressed tightly together as though she had a headache. She looked exhausted and for a moment Frankie felt quite sorry for her. It must be a tough life being a professional ball breaker, and he wondered what 'her world' was.

'Right.' Alex opened her eyes smartly.

'You look like you could murder a drink.' Saff patted her shoulder. 'Is there a bottle open?'

For the first time Alex smiled and the transformation was astonishing. Her eyes softened and her cheeks dimpled. Now that was something she ought to do more often. 'Would you like one?' She turned to look at him and he flicked his eyes guiltily away.

'No thanks. I haven't finished my coffee.'

She didn't ask twice, reached for her bag, branded, with the famous Zencorp logo and took out a leather folder with the same branding. Either she was a big fan or *this* was her world. That would explain the sporty image. 'Let's get on with it, then. Can you cook? Have you had a recent police check? Do you have references?'

The questions rattled at him like machine-gun fire, each one designed to leave him in no doubt as to the nature of what would be expected of him. Alex glanced up at him occasionally as he tried to formulate his answers. He started to feel uncomfortable, but soldiered on, the size of the phone bill at the front of his mind. Yes, he could cook – he'd worked in restaurants for several years and had even got a basic food hygiene certificate after doing a stint in a sandwich shop in the City. Yes, he'd had a recent police check because he'd done theatre for schools. Yes, he had references – he handed them over.

'Do you have experience of looking after an elderly person?' she asked suddenly. Frankie looked round, surprised. What had this got to do with it?

'Not exactly,' he faltered. 'But I was a porter at St Thomas's Hospital before college.'

Saffron brought a glass of wine for Alex and for herself, and gave him a sympathetic wink as she set them on the table. On and on the interview went and he knew his answers were good but he couldn't help thinking she was just going through the motions.

'I might as well explain the situation,' she said eventually. 'I work very long hours. I'm often away. And now my mother has had a fall and can't look after herself for a while. She's broken her elbow, apparently, and it's in plaster. She can get around, but she needs someone to keep an eye on her. I need someone to – well, to do the things for me that a wife would do for her husband.' Saffron giggled and took a sip of her wine, and Frankie was astonished to see Alex blush a little, but she talked on quickly. 'I have a very demanding job and I can't give her the time she needs ... she deserves at the moment.' There was a pause and Alex looked down. 'I don't even have time to shop for food. That doesn't really matter when it's just me, but my mother will need three meals a day. I'm not sure she's been eating properly.' She paused, 'and she's very demanding.'

'Oh.' This explained it all.

Saffron laughed again, her cheeks a little flushed. 'Don't worry, she's lovely. You'll absolutely love her. She was an actress herself once.'

Alex shot her a sharp look. This wasn't the done-deal Saffron seemed to think it should be. 'Apart from that, it would be a question of keeping the place clean and tidy. Putting the odd load of washing on. Being in for deliveries. Picking up my dry cleaning. That kind of thing. It would only be temporary, of course. Just until my mother is well enough to go home. Could you manage all that?'

Frankie nodded, trying to appear more confident than he felt. He had to make some ground here. 'Absolutely. Sounds right up my street. And I could start as soon as you like. I don't have anything pencilled in for the next few weeks at all.'

Alex nodded and smiled cynically. 'Yes, of course. You're an actor, after all.' There was a long pause and she tapped her pen on the table. 'You are quite well qualified, I suppose.' She shrugged eventually. Had he won her over? She stood up abruptly. 'Well, thanks for coming.' She extended her hand. 'I'll be in touch.'

Chapter 5

Ella woke up. She rubbed her eyes with her fists and quickly wiped the drool from her chin, blinking rapidly. The lights were on and everyone seemed to have left. Everyone, that is, apart from Chris, the cinema manager, who was standing right in front of her, arms folded. Oh bloody hell.

'Oh! Erm, I was just ... my contact lens. I was trying to – it's gone funny again. You have to close your eyes to make it ... erm ... all right again.'

Chris sighed deeply and shook his head. 'Nice try, Ella. Nice try. But the film ended ... let me see ...' he consulted his watch theatrically, 'thirteen minutes ago. I've been standing here for the last five, and both you and I know you don't wear contact lenses. Don't you remember telling me that time how genetically inferior people with bad eyesight were, and about how Marie Stopes wouldn't let her son marry a short-sighted girl? And since you told me you were descended from Marie Stopes, you couldn't betray your family traditions?'

She struggled to her feet from the upholstered comfort of the back row and laughed quickly. 'Oh, I didn't mean any of that. You know I didn't. It was just a joke.'

'Hmmm. I seem to remember you were in deadly earnest at the time. It was the excuse you gave for not going out with me, after all.'

Ella coughed piteously to try and cover up her laugh. 'Oh that! I'd forgotten that. Oh, Chris, I don't know what's wrong

34

with me. I think I'm coming down with something. My head's just splitting. Would you mind if I went home for a bit and maybe came back later if I feel a bit better?'

The tall, bespectacled man went through a pantomime of considering her suggestion, then replied in tones dripping with irony. 'Let's see now. Would I mind if you went home? No, I don't have a problem with that bit at all. The sooner the better, I think. Would I mind if you maybe came back later? Mmm, well that's the bit I'm not totally happy with.'

'What?!' Ella's symptoms were pushed aside by her outrage and she pulled herself up to her full five foot three. 'Are you trying to tell me that you're giving me the sack? Who do you think you are?'

Chris stepped back, looking faintly bored, and started to usher Ella out in front of him. 'I think I'm the manager of this cinema, and running it is quite hard enough without you falling asleep in eight out of the last ten screenings you were supposed to be supervising, eating popcorn like it's going out of style, and telling that Japanese student that *Citizen Kane* was Michael Caine's first movie. I want you out of here now. And don't bother coming back.'

They were halfway down the stairs now, squeezing past the queue of families waiting for the next showing. Chris addressed the punters. 'Sorry everyone,' he announced smoothly. 'There's going to be a bit of a delay before the next showing. This young lady, an ex-employee, thought catching up on her beauty sleep was more important than hoovering up before you, our patrons, came in for the next film.'

At first Ella cringed before the disapproving stares and tuts that followed her down to the foyer, then she came round and rallied. 'Hang on a minute.' She turned and prodded Chris in the chest. 'You can't speak to me like that. I'm not having this.'

Chris stopped in his tracks, taken aback by her sudden recovery. She cleared her throat and addressed the crowd. 'I'd like to make an announcement, too. All right, so I *was* asleep in the film. So what? Lots of people sleep during films. I know, because I've seen you at it. Yes, and snoring too. Once you've got your kids penned in, you all have a nap, don't you?' Shamefaced nodding and agreement from the adults. 'And why do you fall asleep? Same reason I do. Because the films are rubbish! And this one you're about to see is no exception.'

Chris stared about wildly and flapped his hands at Ella, trying to make her stop, but she had her audience now, some of them were laughing in agreement.

'And another thing. The popcorn. Have you ever wondered why the popcorn is so expensive? Have you?'

She had everyone's attention now. 'Go on – why?' a voice came from the queue. Chris clapped his hands to his face in dismay.

'Because they think of a price and then quadruple it. Really, they do. I heard them discussing it one day. Y'know, ounce for ounce, the popcorn here is more expensive than Beluga caviar. And that's very expensive.'

'It's not true,' Chris wailed ineffectually. 'Really, it's not …'

She turned to face Chris and went on in crystal clear tones. 'And while I'm in the mood for exposing the truth, I may not wear contact lenses, but I've got nothing against people who do – or glasses, come to that. Nothing at all. In fact, my brother wears lenses and he's one of my favourite people in the whole world. That stuff about Marie Stopes was just made up. I was trying not to hurt your feelings. I wish I hadn't bothered now. You see, everyone … Chris tried to man-handle Ella down to the foyer but she kept on – and on. 'You see, Chris here asked me out and I really didn't want to go. Well, can you blame me? I mean, look at the way he's behaving now. That's hardly likely to win a girl's heart, is it? But I didn't want to hurt his feelings, so I made up an excuse and ...' They were almost out of the door now, but the queue were laughing, jockeying for a view of the tiny, still-shouting girl and the tall, furiously blushing man whose glasses were now halfway down his face.

Out on the pavement, at last, Chris scowled at her. 'Don't you ever even think of coming here again. Not even to see a film. You're banned, understand? You can do your sleeping somewhere else. And don't come crawling to me for a reference because it'll give me the greatest pleasure to make sure everyone in the world knows what a lazy, lying, conniving little good-for-nothing you are. Now sling your hook – go on!'

Ella brushed herself down and squared her shoulders, a little cheered to hear the boos that greeted Chris on his return to the cinema, before setting off through the afternoon sunshine back to the flat. What did she care? It was a crap job anyway.

By the time she got back home, Ella's mood had dropped. She let herself in cautiously, wondering if Frankie was there. She didn't fancy having to explain that she'd lost yet another job, and he'd be bound to guess if she turned up at this time of the day. Fortunately, there was no sign of him although he'd not been gone long, to judge from the evidence. Ella cut herself a large slice of the still-warm fruit loaf and, scorning a plate, cupped her spare hand beneath to catch the crumbs before ambling over to have a lie-down on the sofa.

She sighed. It wasn't even as if Frankie would be cross when she told him. He'd just look sort of disappointed, the way he did when he didn't get a part he'd auditioned for. And worried too. That was what she really hated – when Frankie looked worried. She knew they were short of cash. She knew she shouldn't have run up such a big phone bill. She knew she should really get a sensible job, but she hadn't heard back from the radio station and there just wasn't anything else out there that seemed even vaguely bearable, let alone interesting.

Maybe she'd call one of her old college friends – although most of them had jobs that kept them busy during the day. She noticed the message light blinking on the phone. She balanced the cake carefully on the arm of the sofa, brushed at the crumbs she'd managed to sprinkle over the seat and stabbed at the 'Play' button. Just one message for Frankie. Ella listened carefully to the husky, well-modulated voice and the rather curt, detached message. She pressed the button and listened again. And again.

A smile began to form on her pale little face, and she paced round the room, thinking fast. She stopped to scribble a few notes to herself, then licked her lips, picked up the phone, and dialled 1471 to find out the caller's number.

Chapter 6

Yeuch, yeuch, yeuch. Alex dodged another puddle and wiped the rain from her eyes. She'd already missed her run yesterday and she wasn't going to miss today's. The noise of the rain splattering on her window when she woke up had almost driven her back under the duvet, but even the prospect of getting soaked was preferable to the appalling discomfort of the single bed. As she ran, she could still feel the twinges in her back from the few nights she'd spent in it but if the delivery people meant what they had promised, she'd have a brand new mattress delivered tomorrow. She'd bolted out at lunchtime yesterday and, like a demented child, had bounced on several in the bedding department of the nearest store, before finally settling on a double for herself and a more comfortable single for her mother.

As she rounded the corner of the road, her trainers soaked and squelchy, she noted with relief that the builder's skip was still there. She'd have another mattress to add to it later. Meanwhile, she tried to avoid looking at her beloved old one which, soaked and stained with rain now, peeped out from beneath even more plasterboard and empty bags of cement.

Fresh from the shower, hair wild and beyond hope, she finished the orange juice in the fridge, then, wrinkling her nose at the sour taste and not daring to look at the Best Before date, she picked up her laptop and bag, and headed out of the door. A bowl of cereal would have been nice but the cupboard was bare. Saff was right. A wife was the answer but there was no one faintly suitable from the batch that had answered the ad. The actor had been eye-candy but was out of the question. She pushed buttons on her phone as she walked.

Four hours later, Alex had the phone tucked under her chin as she mouthed to Camilla to please grab her a sandwich too while she was out getting her own lunch. 'Yes, it's Alex Hill again, about my mother. Yes, that's it. How is she today?' Alex glanced at the spreadsheet on her laptop, trying to work out why her schedule didn't add up, but listened more attentively as the nurse outlined her mother's night.

'She was certainly a bit more comfortable than when you came to visit but the thing is,' she went on, 'we need the bed now so, subject to the consultant's early afternoon rounds, you should be able to take her home well, as soon as you like, really.'

Alex nearly dropped the phone. 'Oh gosh. Are you sure?' She scanned her brain and her desk frantically to see what she had lined up and what was moveable.

'Yes dear. She's been here for five days and her condition is improving. We shall certainly miss her. She's kept us all enter-tained, but she'll be better off in your care.'

'Right. Are you sure she is fit to come out now?' Alex stalled. 'I mean, wouldn't another night or two be a good idea, just to be certain?' There was a disapproving silence at the end of the line. 'No probs. I'll be there as soon as I can then.' She put down the phone. 'Camilla, help!' Her assistant's blonde little head popped up. 'My mother has to be collected this afternoon, I've no beds, a diary full of stuff to do.' She riffled through some papers trying to find the notes she'd written for Toronto. 'And basically, I'm stuffed.'

Camilla came over to the desk and put her hand on Alex's shoulder. 'Now calm down.' She pulled out the sheet of scrawled notes from under Alex's laptop. 'Is this what you're looking for? Leave them for me – I'll put them on the laptop for you while you go and get your mum.' Alex looked into her calm, blue eyes. 'It will all be done by tomorrow. In fact,' she turned the laptop towards her and moved the mouse to close it down, 'I'll do it at home because, as luck would have it, Garth has blown me out this evening – he's got a softball game – so I'll be at home on my ownio. A perfect evening – your notes to type up, a glass of wine and *East Enders*!'

'Oh, come on, you don't want to—'

Camilla held her hand up to stall her boss. 'No really, I mean it. It'll be bliss not to have to listen to his constant whinging about his job. Give your mum my love and I hope she's OK.'

Alex cast about for her stuff, a bit bereft suddenly without her computer and, stuffing a file of notes into her oversized bag, made for the door. 'Camilla, if you aren't a saint already, you soon will be.' She blew her a kiss. 'See you in the morning, that is if Mum and I haven't murdered each other by then.'

Three hours later, as she poured yet another glass of chilled French mineral water into her mother's glass (only Evian would do apparently), she wasn't sure she was that far off the mark. The Bean, resplendent in a bright turquoise, silk kimono and turban to hide what she called her 'hospital hair' was lying, like Joan Crawford, on Alex's sofa and complaining. Nothing appeared to be right, nor had it been since the moment Alex had collected her from hospital, late, as it happened, thanks to failed traffic lights on the journey over. The Bean had been waiting for her impatiently, her bag of things packed neatly by her chair in the waiting area.

'Goodbye, my dears, you have been marvellous! God bless you all.' She'd waved a heavily ringed hand imperiously at the staff on the nurses' station as she was wheeled off, playing it for all she was worth. 'Now, come on, Alex dear, I've been sat there for ages and you know how I *hate* sitting doing nothing.'

Well, she seems quite happy to do so now, thought Alex, as she put the cold glass of water down on the table close to her mother's side so she wouldn't have to 'reach too far'. The TV remote was there too so she wouldn't miss her favourite shows – so that's what she spent her time doing. Feasting on an afternoon menu of *Countdown*, adverts and property programmes. This was quite an eye-opener to her mother's normal home routine and it explained why she considered herself an authority on everything.

'All all right now, Mother? Only I need to make some calls ...'

'Oh dear.' The Bean turned her head weakly from the telly and looked at her daughter as if she'd only just noticed she was there. 'Must you? I was just enjoying your company. Alexandra, dear, that top does nothing for you, you know.' Alex looked down at her chest and the company-branded grey T-shirt she'd found at the bottom of the ironing pile and slung on hastily when she'd come to collect her car on the way to the hospital. 'You really should try and be more feminine, dear. Grey never suited your skin. Very few women can carry it off – you should know that, I've told you often enough. Celia Johnson could of course, but then she looked elegant in anything.'

'Oh Mum, it's only a T-shirt. Now, if you don't mind ...'

'Oh, I don't suppose you have a little biscuit, do you?' She took her eyes off the TV again. 'Just a little shortbread or something? That hospital food is frankly a disgrace – not a trace of luxury and the way they hand it out off the food trolley! No manners.'

Alex sighed and grabbed her keys. 'I'll go and see what Rajesh can offer,' she said, going out of the door. 'For the third time this afternoon,' she muttered under her breath as she careered down the stairs. How soon could she find someone to help?

With her mother finally settled now, a plate of digestives by her side (a compromise and the nearest thing to shortbread Rajesh had to offer), Alex settled herself cross-legged on her bedroom floor and made her calls, several about budgets for the new launch and a couple to Camilla about her PowerPoint presentation for the Toronto trip. Camilla, obviously sensing the panic in her voice, responded reassuringly to Alex's requests that she add things to the Excel spreadsheet and promised they'd be there in the morning when she brought the laptop back. Halfway through trying to learn her presentation from a printout by heart, and trying to ignore the dust and old tissues she could see under the divan – just how often had Manuela turned tricks in her flat? she wondered. Had she done it on her sofa? – Todd rang.

'Hi there, my lovely.' His voice was pure Bournville chocolate. It was for this reason that she'd been intrigued by him long before she'd actually met him, just from the conference calls they'd shared. And as he was Head of Press for Zencorp in the US, there had been a few of those. Over discussions about plans for the launch of the new range, she'd fallen under some sort of spell. The reality when she'd finally met him during one of his now frequent visits to London had been even better.

'Hiya babe.' She dropped her clipped business tone and slipped into something she hoped sounded sultry. 'How was your flight? You must be tired. How's your day going so far?'

'Not so bad, not so bad. It will be all the better when I see you tonight, of course.' Bugger. In all the rush to pick up her mother, she'd forgotten the arrangement to meet tonight.

'Ah. Problem.' And she went on to explain.

By the time he rang her doorbell, at around 8.30, Alex hoped he'd cheered up a bit about the idea of having to spend the evening with her mother there too. The enmity between Todd and her mother had been palpable from the moment they'd first met a few months ago, though masked behind a veneer of feigned bonhomie. Until now Alex had kept contact to the bare minimum – the requisite meet-the-boyfriend visit at The Bean's insistence, once Alex had let slip that she was seeing someone, and a couple of other brief encounters. But supper together would be a first.

They stole a deep kiss in the hallway. Three weeks apart and Alex let herself be pulled towards him into his embrace. She could feel his taught body beneath his shirt and smell his sharp cologne. A little too much of it actually, but it was expensive so perhaps that made it OK. He looked at her intensely with his brown eyes, and she took in his beautifully aligned face. By any criteria he was perfect. 'Well,' he drawled, taking her hand. 'Let battle commence.'

'Mother, it's Todd, do you remember?' Stupid question, and as she bolted for the kitchen and put on the water to boil for the pasta, she could just about make out a stilted conversation with long silences in between.

'Quite vile, dear.' The Bean put down her fork a bit later, not even pretending any more to move the fusilli around the plate. 'Is this the best you could come up with?' Alex looked quickly at Todd who was making a better fist of his food, though only just. Did her mother really have to show her up?

'I'm so sorry, but I didn't have much time.'

'Clearly not.' Her mother pushed her plate away. 'I do hope things will get better while I'm here, though of course I won't be able to do a thing.' She nodded at the cast on her arm, resting in a sling made from an old Hermès scarf. 'Perhaps the lovely Saffron can help. She's a wonderful cook. The most divine sole *Bonne Femme* I've ever tasted. What's her husband called again?'

'Max, Mother. How could you forget that? You've known him for years.'

'Yes, of course. He's a lucky man, having a wife like that. Now your father, he loved the way I cooked ...' And off she went, dominating the conversation for the rest of the evening, luckily not noticing the very mediocre bought apple pie.

'Christ, Alex, you're going to need some help,' said Todd later, wincing as he tried to get comfortable on her bedroom floor, the duvet and blanket she put underneath as a makeshift mattress clearly woefully inadequate. Much as she wanted him to, she hadn't really meant him to stay the night, the bed situation being what it was. Not to mention being unsure about the proximity of her mother in the single room next door, but she'd changed her mind when, as they watched the news side by side on the other sofa, he'd run his hand up her thigh.

'I know,' she groaned. 'God knows what I'm going to do. I can't find anyone suitable. Saff even invited a bloke to come along!'

'Well, my darling.' He turned his naked chest towards her and she could make out the sharp plains of his face in the orangey light thrown by the street lamp outside. 'Much as I think you are delicious, your mother isn't, so let's hope she makes a full recovery real soon.' And she giggled as he slipped down between her legs.

The following day was frantic, meetings and conference calls interspersed with phone calls to her mother – when she wasn't engaged on the phone to her old actress friend, Beryl. Alex had even contemplated asking Beryl to look after The Bean, but she must be knocking seventy herself and it would be too much. When Alex did finally get though, The Bean complained about having to get things from the kitchen herself and wanted to talk in great detail about the phone calls from the neighbour downstairs about the leak and the woman from the curtain makers about the blind for the bathroom. Then there were the bed delivery people who'd made such a fuss about the stairs apparently. Alex had managed to cut her short just in time to take a far more promising call.

'Oh God, you were right,' she howled to Saff later as she finally got time to call her.

'What about?'

'The wife thing. Mother is going to be a full-time job – she's so demanding, it's like running a hotel but without the tips. You know, this morning she wondered why I didn't have Dundee marmalade, for God's sake! And there's such a stack of stuff to do here and at home, frankly, but, guess what? I think I've got the perfect person.'

'Oh, have you? Not that woman who looked like a psychopath with the suspicious references? I do hope you mean that gorgeous bloke Frankie – he seemed ideal!'

'The actor? No way. I couldn't cope with having a man in my flat. I know what you said,' she went on quickly before Saff could interrupt, 'but it would never work. No, it's someone who called today actually. Bit of a last-minute call and she only just caught me between meetings.'

'What!' Saff squeaked. 'You haven't met her?'

'Well, yes, as it happens. She was close to the office so I met her briefly and she was great.' Alex realised she was taking a bit of a risk and hadn't even followed up references – quite unlike her usual style – before asking her to stay at the flat while she was in Canada. 'Sometimes you just get an instinct don't you? She's young but ideal, really. Enthusiastic, fully qualified in caring for the elderly from what she says, and her cooking credentials sound marvellous. Apparently she was involved in film catering or something, and she said she's very reliable. She's almost made to measure. And even better, she's just finished a contract and can start straight away! I can't believe my luck actually, and she only lives around the corner apparently.'

'Mmm.'

Alex ignored the circumspect tone in Saff's voice. 'Come on, Saff, I interview people all the time. I ought to know. I've been on enough boring courses about it.'

'Maybe. What's she called anyway?'

'Her name's Ella. Sweet, isn't it?'

Chapter 7

Salopettes, gloves, sun block, ear muffs for Millie – Saff ticked off the list as she put everyone's ski kit in the bag, and eased herself carefully off her knees. She had pins and needles in her feet now, but at least she had most things packed, except the last-minute bits of course. They would have to go in at dawn tomorrow. The house was quiet after the morning's excitement, the children in a spin at the prospect of leaving for Courchevel first thing tomorrow, and all she could hear was the hum of the dishwasher and the rustle of Millie's hamster in its cage in the corner of the kitchen.

'For goodness' sake, Oscar, calm down!' she'd shrieked at her son as she tried to manoeuvre round a bin lorry on the way to school, traffic hurtling towards her. 'You'll burst if you keep this up all day and there's all the end of term business to get through too.' It was pointless. The dark-haired eleven-year-old had ignored her and, relentlessly hyper, had continued poking his sister throughout the morning rush until they had pulled up outside the school. 'Leave Millie alone,' she'd said through gritted teeth, getting their bags from the boot. 'Now.' She'd turned down the collar of his shirt. 'Don't forget to bring back anything that needs washing. Millie, here's your ballet stuff, and Oscar. Oscar, hang on. Here's some home-made Easter biscuits for Mrs Jackson … careful. I'll see you both later and …' She watched as they both ran off through the gates. 'And have a good day,' she said quietly to herself, realising she hadn't had a chance to kiss them goodbye.

As she fished the passports out of the drawer in Max's study, she thought about how she hated that. Kissing them goodbye was like punctuating the end of a sentence, and not doing so made it all feel unfinished. Of course, they weren't bothered, so why should she be? She glanced briefly at the papers on Max's desk. There was another hefty script, a TV drama it looked like, with *Grass Roots* on the title page and the name of the writer, Greta Dunant – a name Saff recognised from somewhere. It must be good if it had been given to Max to read – only the scripts likely to be made reached him. In the past he'd show them to her for her opinion, but since every evening was now taken up with homework, music practice and some activity or other, there was no time. She closed the door behind her. Shame really. She'd quite enjoyed being involved.

Twenty minutes later she had lugged all the plants up into the bath to sit on wet newspaper. She buried her nose into the sweet fragrance of the tête à tête daffodils that had just unfurled, sad she would miss them at their best when they were away. Max had insisted they go skiing in March, which fitted in better with work. The beginning of the year saw the launch of new shows and schedules, and April was the international TV sales conference in France. As she arranged the colourful pots of spring bulbs, though, she knew she'd rather have gone in January before the snowdrops had even managed to push through, so she didn't have to miss this feast of spring.

'Het? It's Saffron.' Saff pulled the washing out of the machine as she talked to her neighbour, phone to her ear. 'Yup, all packed, thanks. Yes, yes can't wait to go and get a bit of snow. Now be honest, is it still OK about popping in to feed the hamster? Are you sure? I've left some food and bedding beside the cage … Wonderful. I'll bring you back some Swiss chocolate … sorry? No! I'll stick to the gluwein or I'll never squeeze in to my salopettes. Bye. Thanks, bye.'

Unloading the dryer and folding warm pants and vests, she refilled it with the wet laundry and turned on the kettle and picked up the phone again.

'Hi, Bean, it's Saffron. How are you?'

'Daaarling.' Alex's mother's theatrical drawl strung the word out. 'How lovely to hear from you! When are you coming to see me?'

Saff smiled to herself, imagining The Bean holding court to visitors. 'Oh, I'll come very soon I promise, but we're off to Courcheval in the morning for the annual ski fest so I'll pop in when we get back.'

'Well, don't make it too long, dear.'

'Are you being well looked after?'

Saff heard her snort with derision. 'Simply frightful,' she whispered loudly.

'But I thought … I thought Alex had sorted out someone marvellous. She said she was perfect.'

'My dear, you've known the girl for years.' She sounded as if she was talking without moving her lips. 'You know as well as I do how poor a judge of character she can be. Except for you, of course, darling. But the boyfriends! And this last one! Have you met him? He looks like Action Man without the charisma. All white teeth and rippling pectorals and about as much culture as a lamp-post.'

Saff couldn't help giggling. 'Oh, you are cruel. He's not that bad.'

'Hmm – a mild improvement on the last one, but the only way was up.' She lowered her voice again to a deep sultry muttering. 'But this Ella. She's only been here a few hours but I can already tell she's useless. *Useless*. Couldn't make a decent cup of

Lapsang if her life depended on it, and when she's not on her blasted mobile talking to her friends, she's reading the paper in the kitchen. You should see her now – jeans round her hips and radio blaring. She's even singing – listen to this for God's sake!' She held the phone away and Saff could hear a tinny noise and a high pitched voice.

'Have you told Alex?'

'How can I when she's off doing something terribly important in Canada.' Her voice sounded sulky.

'Oh, of course. I've had my head in a suitcase and forgot.' Saff search her brain to think how she could help. 'I could fly over this afternoon.' Knowing full well she couldn't but she'd find a way somehow. 'Make you a decent cup of tea and have a chat?'

'Oh, you are sweet but I'm sure you're far too busy. If only they were all like you.'

'Now you take care,' Saff laughed. 'I bet you'll have her whipped into shape in no time. I'll come over as soon as I get back.'

'Have fun dear. So glamorous. I remember going to St Moritz with Alex's father. We could wear fur in those days. Nothing flatters a woman more ...' And she was off on one of her enchanting and wildly exaggerated stories in which she was always the heroine. Saff smiled and laughed in the right places. The Bean never failed to entertain her, and she had seen her charm a whole room in the past, but she did thank the lord she wasn't *her* mother. On those sorts of occasions, when The Bean was centre stage, she'd seen Alex cringing in the corner, especially when the laughter in the room was at Alex's expense – her clothes, her boyfriends, her total lack of interest in her looks. Alex was one of the most private people Saff knew and so completely straightforward – something The Bean saw as dull – that it must have been very painful for her. Perhaps she hoped Alex would flourish with the light of attention turned on her. There was no doubt she loved her daughter, but she clearly didn't understand her. It was as if they were speaking different languages.

Saff had eaten another three biscuits before she finally extracted herself from The Bean's descriptions of a past on the piste that made everyone sound like James Bond, and, by the time she had attached the table lamps in the hall and landing to timers – though who would that fool? – telephoned Het again to remind her about the code for the alarm, made biscuits for the journey, prepared a chicken casserole for supper – something easy, they'd be rushed – and taken the car to have the bald back wheel replaced, it was time to scoop up the children.

She practically had to peel them off the walls. 'We're going skiing, we're going skiing,' sang Millie at the top of her voice.

'Sssh.' Saff shepherded them towards the car.

'Why Mum?'

'Because not everyone is as lucky as we are. They might not have something so exciting lined up for their holiday.' She made sure they were strapped in and pulled out into the road. 'I've just got to fly into the supermarket on the way back to get some blister plasters.'

'Harry's going to his nan's cos his mum works.'

'Exactly, so it's not nice to crow about what you're lucky enough to be doing.'

'Isn't nan a common word?'

Saff winced. Oh, the melting pots that were London state schools, no matter how sought after. 'Well, people call their grandparents lots of different things. Now, how was your day?'

She had them fed, bathed and quietened down by the time Max came through the door, inevitably late.

'Hello, my darling.' He kissed her on the mouth. 'You smell delicious. Sorry it's later than I said. The inevitable got-to-get-it-done-cos-I'm-off-on-holiday stuff.' He dropped the paper on the table. 'Got a couple more calls to make. Did you sort the tyre by the way?'

Saff turned back to the sink. 'Er, yes. How was your day?'

'Crazy. How much did you pay for it?' he persisted. Cautiously she told him. 'What! Oh Saff. I bet they told you the more expensive ones were better, didn't they?'

She knew this would be his response and she knew too she should have held out for the cheaper ones, but the way they had looked at her at the tyre place as if she'd be an idiot to settle for anything but the most expensive had made her cave in. 'I know. I know, but maybe they'll last longer?'

'Mmm.' He opened the fridge and picked at some olives. 'You are a ninny. It's not like we bomb up motorways all day long. The most that car does is school and back. Is everything ready?'

Saff laughed, relieved at the change of subject. 'Cheeky bugger. I've packed your bag and supper will be ready in about half an hour. Can you tell me where you put the travel insurance documents? I can't find them.'

'I'll dig them out.' Max walked out of the room towards his study.

'And Max ...' But the study door was closed behind him.

With the children finally asleep, their clothes ready for the morning laid out neatly on the chair in their bedrooms, she went back down to the kitchen and put on the vegetables to steam, emptied another load of uniform and school art overalls from the machine and ticked off 'wash bags' on her list. Pouring a glass of wine for herself and Max, she made her way down to the study and, balancing the glasses in one hand, opened the door.

'Sure, that would be great.' He was ending a call. 'I'll see you when I get back, Greta. Have fun.' He dropped the phone and turned to her. 'Thanks love. You OK? Now, what time are we off?'

The 4.30 alarm dragged them all from their beds. Millie refused to eat any breakfast and cried that the hamster would be lonely without her. Oscar wouldn't wear the trousers she'd put out and threw a tantrum when he wasn't allowed to turn on the computer to download more songs onto his MP3 player for the journey, and Max, having forgotten to dig out the health policy, dumped the contents of the filing cabinet on the floor of the study before he found it in the 'car insurance' section. The plane was delayed and Millie was beyond fatigue by the time they reached the hotel.

It was when she'd unpacked the suitcases as Max and the children went to get a pacifying hot chocolate in a favourite café, that Saff realised that she'd been so focused on putting together everyone else's skiwear, her own salopettes were still in the airing cupboard at home.

Chapter 8

'How could you?'

Ella clapped her hands together on a bag of salt'n' vinegar crisps, bursting it open with a pop and a puff of tangy shards, and offered them to Frankie, who shook his head in anger. 'I don't know why you're being so puggy about this. It's not like you'd got the job anyway.'

'That's not the point – you were underhand. You also have the most disgusting eating habits in the world.' Frankie glared at Ella as she continued with her eclectic breakfast. So far, she'd had a chocolate mousse, a slice of cold pizza, toast and peanut butter and several glasses of milk. The crisps were, Frankie fervently hoped, the dessert.

'But why do you care? You didn't want the job in the first place, you know you didn't. You moaned like crazy when I set you up for the interview. You said you didn't even like Alex anyway. What's the problem? At least I'm earning some decent money for a change. Which is more than you are, I might add!' Ella gesticulated at Frankie with her crisp packet, sending a shower of salty crumbs onto the tablecloth. 'I think you're *jealous*!'

Frankie winced. She might be right. He felt incensed that she'd landed the job as 'wife' for Alex, looking after her and her mother, and he couldn't even conceal the fact. With her usual ability to cut through the crap, Ella had got right to the heart of the matter. 'All right, so maybe I am a bit jealous.'

T040238

He knew his voice was raised. 'But look at it from my point of view. OK, so I *didn't* want the job but I would have been perfect for it – we both know that. Much better than you, no offence.'

Ella looked superior. 'Yeah, but I *got* the job, brother dear. You didn't! Anyway, I gave a great interview.'

'Only because you shamelessly picked my brains about what they asked me – without admitting why. I should have smelt a rat there and then. It's not like you to be that interested in what I do.'

'Sticks and stones, sticks and stones!' Ella jumped up and brushed her hands together purposefully, leaving her sticky plate and cup behind her. 'Right, what's the time? I told the old bat I'd be back once I'd grabbed some clean clothes, and I'll have to get some shopping in on my way – my way to *work* – you remember that Frankie, don't you? Work? It's a thing people do to get money. So basically that means I can take it easy for a bit. The old bag'll be so grateful for her cup of Lapsang doo dah by the time I get back, she won't complain like she did yesterday. Alex's bed is fantastically comfy. Now, where's the remote? Oh good, *Pingu* hasn't started yet.' She flung herself down on the sofa.

Frankie stared at her incredulously as he cleared the table. 'What are you doing? You're supposed to be looking after Alex's mother. You can't waste time watching cartoons! Alex is paying you good money to do this job. Don't you think you might at least make an effort?'

'La la la! I'm not listening!' Ella sang loudly, jamming her fingers in her ears, until Frankie walked over to the TV and switched it off. 'Oh, you slimy toad! That's the one when Pingu and Robbie play fish tennis.'

'Come on. What's going on? Really?' Frankie positioned

himself in front of the sofa, arms crossed in what he hoped was an authoritative way. 'You don't want to go, do you?'

Ella crumbled at once. 'Aaw, it's so boring,' she groaned. 'I had to do *ironing* yesterday. Can you imagine? What's the point of ironing, anyway? The stuff just gets wrinkled again when you put it on. And the old lady is sooooo bad tempered. Nothing I did was right! She has this really loud voice, and I couldn't even pretend I couldn't hear her. She wants tea all the time. And she hated my sandwiches. And Alex must be a super-efficient robot woman, she left me with a huge list of things to do, printed out from her computer, if you please ...'

So that was it! The typical Ella reaction to having to actually do something. Frankie had seen this countless times before. But this time his exasperation was tinged with something else. Curiosity? Triumph? He wanted to hear more. 'Go on. What did she ask you to do?'

Ella sat up with her elbows on her knees and sank her head theatrically onto her hands. 'Well,' she sighed. 'Any chance of a cup of tea?'

Frankie smiled ruefully as he put the kettle on and the tale of woe continued. 'Madam was in a big rush, of course, cos she's just off to Toronto, as she was very careful to tell me. God, how do you get a job like hers? I could do that, I'll bet. I'd be like, "Oh yes, sportswear is terribly crucial and right on and important, and don't forget to pick my jacket up from the dry cleaners."' Ella imitated Alex's slighty rushed, earnest way of speaking, dropping her voice lower. 'I mean, who does she think she is?'

Frankie shook his head sternly. 'C'mon, Ells. She's paying you. She trusts you. You shouldn't be taking the mick, even if she is a bit of a ball-breaker. And you can't leave the old lady on her own. That's just wrong.'

Ella rolled her eyes. 'She's a piece of work, I'll tell you that for nothing. Completely different to Alex, too. She must be a changeling or something. The old lady's ever so poised, like one of those old ballet dancers or something. And full slap all the time, you know. As if anyone's going to see her!' Frankie smiled to himself as he warmed the pot and listened to the pitch of her voice gradually change from piteous to indignant. 'But she's on my case the whole time. She treats me like a servant!'

With some effort, Frankie resisted the obvious retort and composed his face sympathetically, bringing her favourite mug right to her and setting it down carefully on the table in front of the sofa. He clasped his own cup of tea and sat down opposite her, readying himself to pep-talk her into going to work again. What line to take this time? Encouragement with just a twist of guilt, perhaps? 'Y'know, Ella, I think it's amazing you taking this on, especially when we're so short of cash and I haven't got anything in the pipeline. I will admit I'm a bit miffed that you got the job and I didn't, but it was really clever of you to get in there, knowing just exactly what Alex wanted. Fair play to you – you beat me, fair and square.'

'Yeah, I did, didn't I?' Ella sat up and reached for her tea. 'Mind you, I did exaggerate just a tiny bit about my experience. Well, you have to, don't you?'

'Er, well. Best not to, really. It can turn around and bite you on the bum sometimes, so I try to stick to the facts. Much easier, don't you think? You didn't ... you pretty much told it like it was, didn't you?'

Ella took a long slurp of tea and wiped her mouth with the back of her hand. 'Mostly, yeah. Just bigged it up a bit. D'you know, she's asked me to drive the old bag to the hospital this afternoon. Bor-ing!'

'No!' Frankie sat bolt upright. The idea of Ella in a car in central London was so horrific, it eradicated any other thought. 'Wouldn't it be easier to take a cab? Y'know, parking and everything? I'm sure Alex would pay you back.'

'You must be kidding!' Ella retorted, then her face lit up. 'I suppose I could just drop her at the clinic – it's bound to take hours – then I can nip up the Fulham Road. Great shops. I can pick her up when I'm all shopped out.'

Frankie felt as though there was a large egg stuck in his throat that wouldn't go down. 'Really, Ella, you can't just—'

The phone rang. 'That'll probably be the old bag now. Get it, would you, Frankie? Say I'm on my way, and I'll bring you tea in bed for a week.'

Frankie held up his hand to silence her. 'Who? Sorry? Ella Ward. Can I ask what it's in connection with? Oh, yes. I'll just see if she's available. Hold the line, please.' He covered the receiver and ignored her frantic gesticulation. 'It's someone called Mike from the radio station. Do you want to—'

Ella ripped the receiver from his hand and plastered a perky smile on her face. 'Hello, Ella here!' Frankie watched in interest as the expression on her face transformed, from cautious to excited to delighted to incredulous. 'Yes, absolutely. I certainly do ... Well, I'd love to. No problem.' She shot a quick look at Frankie. 'Let me just check my diary.' She covered the mouthpiece and turned to him, her face bright and pleading. 'They want me!' she whispered loudly. 'You see, they said they'd call. But the thing is, Frankie, they need me straight away – today. Someone's had to go into hospital suddenly and ...'

'You're dead right someone has to go to hospital. Your old lady! You can't bottle out like this You just can't.'

'But you're not doing anything at the moment. You said so yourself. Oh please, Frankie. She's quite sweet really. And you'd do it so much better than me. I'm a crap driver, too.

I'd probably scrape the car or get it towed away. Oh please, please, PLEASE! It's just for a little while, because they're short. I promise I'll be back on duty by bedtime. And I'll never ask you anything again. And I'll make you tea for a *year*. Honest!'

Frankie shook his head emphatically, closing his eyes with an air of finality, then snapping them open again as he heard her chirp, 'Yes, amazingly enough, I can move a couple of things around and get to you for – oh – say, 12.30?' She was rummaging in the pile of clothes Frankie had sorted the night before, after his trip to the launderette, pulling out tops and discarding them on the floor. He gesticulated at her, shaking his head and mouthing, 'No, NO, NOOOO!', but she turned her back and rapidly concluded the conversation. 'Yes, that's fine. I'll look forward to seeing you then. Thanks! Bye!'

An awful silence fell as they stared at each other. Frankie spoke first, his voice low and serious. 'You have gone too far this time. Call them back at once. You have a job to do and you're bloody well going to do it. You can't leave that old lady in the lurch, and I'm not bailing you out this time.'

'Oh, come on, Frankie. This is my big break! This would be like the RSC calling you. You can't let me down now.'

'No way, no how. Absolutely, definitely not!'

Chapter 9

Frankie let himself in with the key Ella had pressed into his hand before disappearing off to Croydon, seemingly transported by clouds. At least he'd managed to bring her down to earth for long enough to make a call to Alex's mother, informing her that a 'trusted friend' would be taking her for her appointment and that he'd be there very soon, assuring her that she'd be back later as usual. He'd also extracted all kinds of promises of breakfast in bed, trips to the launderette, taking out of the rubbish. If she stuck to all the vows she'd made, the rest of Frankie's life would be one of luxury and indolence. But the chances of that ...

He called out as he made his way upstairs. 'Helloo? Mrs Hill? Are you there? I'm Ella's friend. I've come to take you to your appointment ...'

'About time too! I'm in here,' an imperious voice from a room to his left, caught him unawares. Granny Applecheek she obviously wasn't. Maybe Ella had been right. He pinned on his warmest smile and tapped on the door, which swung open at his touch. There, silhouetted against the window was a profile that sent shivers down his spine, a profile that had done the same for men both young and old ever since the early sixties. That short straight nose, the full lower lip, the hair, now white, caught back in a velvet bow that nestled in the nape of her neck, just as it had been in that ground-breaking film with Terence Stamp. She turned and stared straight at him, the wide-apart, slightly feline eyes pinning him where he stood.

He realised he'd been holding his breath. 'You're The Bean,' he exclaimed.

She shrugged and a hint of her bewitching smile quirked at the corner of her mouth. 'Of course I am, darling. And you, I assume, are the "trusted friend" sent by that wretched girl. Because if you're here to rape and pillage, sweetie, I'm afraid you'll have to come back tomorrow, once my daughter gets home.'

Frankie knew he was gawping, but couldn't quite seem to close his mouth. So this was Alex's mother. This icon of Swinging London, actress turned beatnik model turned screen goddess, nicknamed for her long, slender figure, was sitting right in front of him. Ella couldn't have had a clue who she was. He'd dreamed of a moment like this, of what he'd say and how he'd be. And all he could do was stand there like a goldfish. The Bean took charge.

'I'm gasping for a cup of tea.' She looked him up and down. 'You do know how to make tea, don't you? Because your friend is useless.'

He found his voice. 'She's my sister actually.'

The Bean looked unabashed. 'Hope it's not genetic,' she sniffed. Frankie smiled.

'Lapsang, isn't it?'

She clapped her hands together and raised her eyes. 'Heavens be praised! Someone with a little culture, at last. And perhaps even a lightly boiled egg?'

Frankie nodded, still bemused. 'Toast with that?'

'Perfect. Not too well done though, darling.'

'Anything on it?'

The Bean shrugged eloquently. 'If you can find any butter

in this hellhole. I'm afraid my daughter's tastes are a little unrefined. The best you'll probably find in the refrigerator is a tub of that utterly unspeakable spreadable stuff.'

He headed for the kitchen, found the list of instructions left by Alex before she'd gone away along with the car keys and details of the out-patient appointment. After putting together the most tempting breakfast tray he could from the almost empty cupboards, he returned to The Bean and watched in pleasure as she picked daintily at the little triangles of toast and sipped her tea, then asked for more. Once she'd finished and had sat back in her chair with a contended sigh, he set about the tasks on the list, tackling a pile of ironing left undone by Ella from the day before, making up The Bean's bed and hoovering, with The Bean watching him closely from her chair by the window whenever he came into view. As the time for the appointment came closer, The Bean closed the bathroom door firmly and Frankie could hear the sounds of running water. She was taking a shower. It seemed odd to think of her as an old lady now when she was most famous for that iconic Terry Donovan photograph of her that, like loads of students, Frankie had had on his wall.

When she re-emerged, she was fragrant, chic and beneath her immaculately applied make-up, rather nervous looking. She held onto his arm tightly as they walked downstairs together. Driving through London with The Bean beside him, Frankie had to pinch himself hard. Although he was concentrating on the unfamiliar car, as he drove toward the Chelsea and Westminster, he was intrigued by the running commentary she was keeping up in her throaty, patrician tones.

'Went to the most fantastic party in that house there.' She pointed a varnished nail at an imposing front door. 'Everyone was there. Alan, Julie, Glenda, Vanessa, dear Terence – remind me to tell you all about Terence one day, darling. Oh, it was the most tremendous fun …'

At the hospital, Frankie found a space as close by as he could, then helped her out of the seat. She held tightly to his arm as she unfolded, then immediately pushed him away, brushing irritably at her clothes. As they sat side by side in the waiting area, Frankie found a newspaper and read little snippets out to her – he noticed she wouldn't put on the glasses hanging around her neck, just held them in front of her eyes briefly when she absolutely had to – but far from being interested in the arts reviews, she asked him in detail about the racing results. When she was eventually called in to see her consultant, Frankie watched her sail across the room, looking confident and poised. He shook his head in amazement. That this elegant beauty should have given birth to the tall, slightly gawky woman who had questioned him so seriously at his failed interview seemed incredible. He sat staring at the consulting-room door, still unable to believe what was happening to him, until his mobile rang, earning him a stern look from the receptionist. Since the call was from Ella, he darted outside and took it. From the first wheedling word, it was obvious what she wanted.

'You see, it's gone brilliantly. They all really like me and this other woman's going to be off for a fortnight – her back or something. So could you …?'

'Oh, I don't know.' Frankie shook his head. 'It's really not on. You took this job. You can't just drop it like that. Why don't you tell them you've got to work out your notice first and then you can start, in a few days, so Alex has a chance to find someone else? What do you mean, me take over? What's Alex going to say? She didn't want me in the first place. It was you she wanted. We can't just substitute me for you and hope

64

she doesn't notice. It's dishonest. Look, she's coming out. We'll talk about this later. Yep, yep. You owe me big!'

The Bean had emerged from the consulting room and was looking round vaguely, almost unsteadily, clasping her injured arm. 'Oh, there you are.' The imperious tone couldn't hide her relief as she spotted him. 'Well, that consultant doesn't know a thing. He maintains that I have to stay with Alex for a few weeks at least, and then I have to come back for another X-ray.' She took hold of his arm and leaned close. 'You know what, darling, there's a little bookie's not far from here, perhaps we could pop in on the way back. And then perhaps we could go and get some decent marmalade. If I'm condemned to staying at Alex's, at least I might be comfortable. That idiot sister of yours has no idea about anything. I shall just phone her and tell her I can manage on my own.'

As the afternoon progressed it became increasingly clear she couldn't. When they returned to the flat, bets laid, he watched her struggle to try and take off her jacket, unsure whether she would be insulted by his offer of help – she was so proud. But when a teacup slipped from her hand and shattered on the kitchen floor, he knew he would have to step in.

'Listen,' he said, getting out the dustpan. 'I think I can persuade Ella to give up her job here, and what if I come and help you for a couple of days?' 'Oh, what a relief,' The Bean sighed dramatically. 'You're quite delightful! And I do so love having a man about the house!'

'OK, but your daughter won't be very pleased. There's something I'm going to have to tell you. You see, we've met before ...'

Chapter 10

'Bloody disaster!'

Camilla sat down heavily in the seat opposite Alex. 'What do you mean?'

'I don't think I've ever been so embarrassed in my life,' Alex continued, easing her bag off her shoulder and dumping it under her desk. She gingerly moved her head to try to relieve the strain from carrying the bag from Heathrow on the hot and packed tube. There hadn't been a hope of a taxi. 'Can you get on to tech support? They can take that bloody laptop and sort it out.'

'What went wrong?'

'What didn't, more like!' Alex turned on her desktop and pulled some files out of her briefcase. Everything hurt, her neck, her head but most of all her pride. 'There I was – two hundred sales people staring at me expectantly – this super-duper woman from London to tell them all they needed to know and what happens? The ruddy presentation fails!'

Camilla put her hand to her mouth in horror. 'Oh Alex, what did you do?'

Alex pulled off her sweatshirt, quickly looked round to see if anyone was looking, and whipped off her T-shirt too, ducking behind the desk and pulling on a new one from a box left over from a promo event. She would dearly have liked a shower and a few hours' sleep, but a clean top would have to suffice until she had sorted a few things and could get home later.

She glanced at her watch. Even though it was nearly nine she knew her mother would still be in bed so she wouldn't call yet. Owing to the hectic conference itinerary, she'd only managed two calls home in the short time she'd been away and The Bean had sounded very irritable in the first. 'This girl is simply dreadful,' she'd shrieked and Alex had had to pacify her and promise that she'd sort the problem out as soon as she got back – as soon as she'd sorted out her own, more pressing disaster, that is. During the second call she'd sounded a bit distracted and it took Alex a while to twig that *Countdown* must be on TV.

'Well,' she said, bobbing up from behind her desk, furtively trying to sniff her armpits to check she wasn't too smelly. 'I just had to wing it – and boy, if they were handing out Oscars for bullshit I'd be right up there. God, it still makes me feel sick when I think about it.' She sat down, a vision coming into her head of the awful moment when, after her florid introduction, she had clicked to run the presentation. '*Nada. Rien.* Bugger all. So I sort of launched into a "well this is what it looks like and this is what the fabric feels like and these are the colours". Thank God I decided to take the bigger box of samples instead. Good thing I ignored you!'

'Well, I just thought …'

'No, you were right, it was heavier, but Lord knows what I'd have done without it. In the end I threw a whole load of those crop tops into the audience so they could have a fondle and "feel it like it is".'

'Oh dear,' Camilla laughed. 'That sounds a bit haphazard.'

At that moment Peter, Alex's opposite number in the running-shoe department, loomed into view and tossed a large report onto her desk. 'A little light reading for you,' he said dismissively. 'Interim sales report.'

'Thanks.' Alex moved it out of the way, annoyed at his interruption.

'How did the trip go? Hear there was a royal fuck-up. That was bad luck.' He smiled coldly. 'I always double-check my tech stuff before I go.' And he walked away.

'That'll scupper my plot to electrocute him then,' whispered Camilla. 'Smug tosser. Why's he always got it in for you?'

Alex pulled a face at his departing back and shrugged. 'I don't know but he always manages to make me feel stupid.'

'I'd watch him if I were you.' Camilla leant forward. 'I don't trust him. Anyway, go on. So what happened?'

'Well, do you know, I think they quite enjoyed it? It kept them all awake anyway. Quite a few of them came up to me afterwards and said how much fun it had been and how positive they felt about the product. Easy to entertain, those Canadians.'

'You're a genius! Looks like you saved the day.' Camilla gathered up the papers from her knee and stood up. 'I know you'll have caught up with most of your emails, but Gavin asked me to tell you to look at the updated spreadsheets and he wants a debrief later about the trip.'

Alex turned to her PC and papers. 'I'll go and see him in a minute. I think he'll be proud of my cunning improvisation!' she laughed. 'Better call Mum first, though.'

The phone rang for longer than she'd expected. Where could she be? Ella might have taken her out, I suppose, she thought idly. This was the end of the girl's first week there so she might have started to do things with her mother, but it was odd when she was housekeeper first and nurse second. Alex's eyes and attention wandered to her screen and she forgot she still had the phone under her chin until it was answered abruptly.

'Hill residence. Can I help you?' Her mother's voice sounded breathless.

'It's the Hill Residence chatelaine here. You sound as though you've been running, Mum. What on earth's the matter?'

'Oh, it's you, darling. Just hang on a moment while I sit down. It's those blasted stairs. An abomination. You should have bought a ground floor flat.'

'Where have you been? It's very early for you. Has Ella been out with you?'

'Ella? Good God no … yes! That's it. Ella. Ella. Very much so Ella. We've been out for a coffee on the common. Delightful little place by the deli.'

'Oh, that sounds like a change of heart. When I called you the other day you were ready to murder her.'

'Was I? I don't think I was. What *are* you talking about? She's perfectly marvellous and looking after me beautifully. Aren't you Ella?' Alex could hear a sort of squeak in the background. 'Yes, we've done a bit of shopping and went to that little gallery run by the woman with the unfortunate complexion. Terrible shame, but nice pictures. I've reserved a charming little oil.'

'Mother,' Alex said slowly. 'You can't go buying more pictures.'

'Oh, don't be so bossy, dear. One more won't hurt. Frankie says it's lovely …'

'Frankie?'

'Frankie? What dear? No, no. I said, *frankly* it's lovely.'

'Oh Mum.'

'Never mind "oh Mum".'

Alex felt concerned. 'Is Ella doing all the stuff at home she should be before taking off for little shopping trips? I mean, that's what she's paid to do, you know.'

'Oh yes, wonderfully domesticated. Sheer genius with the

iron. But enough of that, how was your trip? Did you persuade those Canadians about that ghastly nylon PE kit?'

Alex laughed. Wherever she had inherited her interest in sport from it certainly wasn't her mother, whose idea of exercise was stirring a Singapore sling. No, her love of sport had been courtesy of her father who'd been a Cambridge rowing Blue and latterly had a passion for skiing. Together the two of them had tackled black runs while her mother, swathed in furs, got to grips with the glühwein in the mountain bars. She also could have done without inheriting his height and the broad-shouldered physique that came with it though, and had always thought how unfair it was that the gene pool hadn't handed out her mother's petite frame. She could also have done without what he left behind when he died ten years ago just as she was graduating from business school; a demanding mother whom Alex wasn't inclined to indulge like he had, and a financial mess that she was still unravelling.

What made it all the more painful was how much Alex had adored and trusted him. He'd always made her feel protected and she had been carried along with his live-for-today generosity believing it was funded by the investments he mentioned, airily waving away any questions she had. As she had got older and begun to understand these things, she had just assumed he had a nest egg because his occasional business deals with classic vintage cars had to be funded from somewhere, didn't they? They didn't. The school fees, the shiny red E-type, the holidays in Gstaad had all been courtesy of the bank.

'That ghastly PE kit pays the mortgage thanks, and yes, I think they were suitably impressed. Look, I've got a few urgent things to sort out here, then I should be home by three. I'm looking forward to seeing Ella again. She sounds even better than I thought.' She must have the patience of Job too, she reflected as she said goodbye and went to find Gavin, who was sitting, feet up on his desk, a pair of prototype trainers on his feet.

'Phew, you need sunglasses for those!' Alex pretended to protect her eyes from the glare. 'Will it be legal to wear such lurid colours in public?'

Athletically – everyone in the office was athletic – he swung his legs off the desk and stood up, bouncing on his toes, then running on the spot. 'These, dear girl, are where it's at. They are so advanced we won't so much overtake the opposition as lap them. They are so cushioned they will make running on air seem an uncomfortable alternative.' He gesticulated wildly. 'So performance orientated are they, they will make a Jessie Owen of the most sluggish.' He looked down at his feet. 'Isn't this colour awesome though? Fluorescent orange and lime is the new black, which of course was never really explored with trainers. Though come to think of it …' And he sat down quickly and wrote something down on a pad.

Alex waited. She knew better than to interrupt genius when it struck. Or at least genius was how Gavin perceived it. His thought patterns were at best delirious and everyone in the department knew to indulge his random, flighty nature because one idea in ten was pure gold. The rest of the time they simply structured their own lives and ignored his haphazard leadership. While he jotted down some new spec for trainers – an idea Alex had a suspicion would be one of his better ones – she looked out of the huge plate glass windows and over the Thames. A pleasure boat was heading upriver, its wash lapping the banks as it passed, and the passengers, Japanese tourists all no doubt, squinted at the tall city panorama, lit up by spring sunshine.

Alex would rather have been asleep.

'So,' said Gavin, looking back at her now. 'Sorry I couldn't make it to Toronto in the end. Bit of a cock-up I hear. Shouldn't have left you on your own after all, should I?'

'Er . . .' She was a bit suspicious of the smile in his eyes. Was she really being ticked off? 'It was just one of those things. A technical fault, you know?'

'Mmm.' He leant down to undo the trainers. 'Feedback seems to have been OK, but time is too short for fuck-ups, Alex. You know that. We're only a few weeks away from the launch now and I can't afford for this not to go right. I'll be lynched by the top brass if we mess up this range. They want it to be the blast of the decade. Now bugger off.' She turned to go. 'Oh and Alex?' She turned back. 'Next time, take a back-up PC, OK?'

Her mood by the time she got home was so low – fuelled by fatigue, the fact that Todd was back in New York, resentment at the short time-scale Gavin had given her to organise the launch and the prospect of her mother's litany of complaint – that she did what she had never done before and stopped for a half of lager at the pub at the end of her road. God help me, she thought as she tucked herself into the corner, avoiding the intrigued gazes of the three blokes propping up the bar. It's teatime and I'm turning into a lush. Put on a beer belly and I'll be out of a job quicker than you can say 'On Your Marks'. Lardiness was something the company would not tolerate. It wasn't actually in the contract, but as good as. Muffin top overhang on your Lycra shorts was a short cut to a P45. She cupped the lager between her hands and thought about the Toronto mess-up. Had she saved the day with her inspirational tactile tactics, or had Gavin been serious with his warning? Was she a marketing executive who couldn't market? It didn't look great. She slid even further down into her chair as she spotted one of the men from the bar picking up his pint and strolling towards her, a smirk on his face.

'Got a light, love?'

'Er no. No, I don't smoke. Sorry.' He started to move away but turned back.

'Can I get you a pint?'

A pint? OK the T-shirt was bad, but did she really look so butch today that she looked like a pint-woman?

'No, no thanks.'

He looked back at his mates, who were listening with interest and his smirk broadened. He leant over the table towards her. 'Or are you waiting for your girlfriend?'

Alex shot up from her chair and, picking up her bag, marched out of the pub. 'Bet those shoes are comfortable!' was shouted at her receding back.

She slammed the front door of the flat in her anger. Fucking tossers. 'That you daaarling?' her mother called from the sitting room. Alex pushed open the door and dropped her bag abruptly on the carpet. She stopped in her tracks when she saw the tableaux in front of her. The room was immaculate, every surface clean and ordered. It smelt of a mixture of polish and baking. Through the kitchen door she could see a neat pile of ironing, and her mother was lying down on the sofa, a vision in cream silk, surrounded by plumped up cushions, hair immaculate and beside her a tray of tea.

'Oh dear, you look simply awful. Get a cup and I'll pour you some tea. Ella had to leave early to go to the dentist. Would you like one of these?' She held up a china plate of biscuits that could only have been home-made.

Alex smiled. 'Don't mind if I do.'

Chapter 11

Ella softly knocked on Frankie's door, a mug of steaming tea and a plate piled with wholemeal toast and honey balanced on a tray. She listened for the low groan and cautiously opened the door. 'Frankie!' she called gently. 'Frankie, I've got your breakfast. Just like you said.'

From under the quilt, a long pale arm emerged, pushing back the snowy folds of fabric to reveal her brother's tousled hair and unshaven face. For someone who was so tragically neat in waking hours, he started each day looking as though he'd spent the night wrestling with a tiger. He pushed his dark hair back from his face and squinted at her. 'Oh God, is it that time already?'

Ella smiled sympathetically. 'I'm afraid so. Here – have some tea. It might help.'

Frankie levered himself upright and shook his head. 'It'll take more than tea to help. Urgh! Another day to face. I still can't believe I let you talk me into this.'

'I know, I know. And I'm soooo sorry. Really I am. You are absolutely the best brother ever.' She quickly placed the tray on his bedside table and plumped the mangled pillow so he could sit up for breakfast in comfort. 'And I'm so grateful. Now, is there anything I can get you today? Have you done a list for the groceries? I'll pop out at lunchtime. Oh, and I've ironed your shirt. Shall I bring it in for you?' She hoped she wasn't laying it on too thick. She didn't want to sound insincere.

'Mmmm, please.' Frankie extended his hand and Ella quickly fitted the mug of tea into it. It was the very least she could do when he had such an awful day ahead of him. She left him in peace for a while to brace himself and bustled around getting herself ready, then washed up her own breakfast things as quietly as she could, so as not to disturb Frankie. When he eventually emerged, the sitting room and kitchen were spick and span once more, and she darted into his room to retrieve the tray. Wrapped in his Tootal-wash-as-silk paisley dressing gown, a bargain from the Oxfam shop, he watched in silence as she finished the washing-up.

'So,' he sighed eventually. 'What have you got on today?'

'Oh, I'm going on an outside broadcast this morning. We're doing interviews in the park all about what makes people feel like spring is really here, so I'll have to wrap up. Erm – you?' She looked at Frankie cautiously. She hadn't really wanted to ask, but it seemed rude not to, and she braced herself for another catalogue of misery.

'Same old thing again.' Frankie shook his head and pulled a face. 'It's the same every day, really. Ironing, hoovering, making endless cups of tea for The Bea – for the beastly old lady.' He turned away and shrugged sadly. 'At least it's regular money – although …'

Ella carefully wiped over the kitchen surfaces and hung the cloth over the taps to dry, folding it carefully first, just the way Frankie always did. God, domesticity was hard work. 'Have you managed to avoid Alex all right?'

Frankie rolled his eyes. 'Oh, that's another thing. I thought I was going to have to jump out of the window the other day. I was sure I heard her key in the door. Now she's been back from her trip a day or so I'm much more nervous.' He shuddered eloquently. 'And I'm sure the old lady's going to say something one of these days. I just don't know how long I can keep this going. It's really doing my head in.'

Ella shot out of the kitchen and led Frankie to the sofa, sitting him down with care. 'Oh, please Frankie! Just for a bit longer. I couldn't bear to give this job up and I don't know how long they're going to need me. It's the only thing I've ever really enjoyed. Tell you what – if it's really that awful, I can phone Alex at work and give her notice. Or tell her I've fallen over and hurt myself so I can't come in any more.'

'No, no. Er – I think we owe it to the old lady to see it through. And besides, there is that phone bill. Until we've made enough to pay that off, I really feel I have to keep this awful job on.'

What a wonderful brother he was! Ella hugged him impulsively. 'Frankie, you're the best. I really do appreciate you being so supportive. Especially when you're having such a hard time. I'm sorry to have dropped you in it like this. Tell you what, I'll get you one of those strawberry tarts on my way home. Deal?'

His watery smile tugged at Ella's conscience as she hefted her bag onto her shoulder and blew him a goodbye kiss and gently closed the door behind her. She was a very lucky girl.

Chapter 12

Frankie got up from the sofa, stretched luxuriously and strolled to the shower. The Bean wouldn't be up for hours yet, but if he got there early he could get the chores done before she emerged. He shaved with care, surveying his face in the steamy mirror he'd swiped clear with his hand. The Bean had said yesterday that he had a look of David Hemmings in *Blowup*, and he pulled his hair forward and half closed his eyes, trying to capture the likeness. No good. But if The Bean thought so, he certainly wasn't going to argue.

Towelled dry now, he slipped on the pale blue shirt Ella had ironed for him. Hmmmm, Ella. He smiled to himself. Boy, it was fun watching her squirm. He almost felt like letting her off the hook occasionally, but his common sense had thankfully overruled his better nature. This was good for her, having to make an effort and actually considering someone else's feelings for a change. He looked round at the unusually tidy sitting room – Ella's knitting was all bundled in its bag for once and she'd changed the water in the vases. Yes, altogether things at home had definitely changed for the better.

The Bean, as he had anticipated, was still in her 'boudoir', as she liked to call it, so Frankie made straight for the kitchen. His list awaited him, but handwritten this time. Perhaps Alex had been in too much of a rush to programme her commands into her database, or whatever. He peered closely at the paper, hastily torn from a pad adorned with her company logo. She'd used a gel pen, her writing was smaller than he'd expected, with regular curving letters and long loops for the 'g's and 'y's. It was firm but surprisingly girlish:

Hi Ella, Thanks for stepping in so brilliantly. The place looks great and the biscuits were delicious – have to admit I polished them off last night. I'm blaming jet lag! Mum seems delighted with everything you've done for her. I'm sorry if she was a bit tricky at first – but you seem to have bonded fantastically now, so thanks very much for that too. Just a quick list of things I'd like you to do today:

– My washing from Toronto is still in my case – could you do it for me? The running gear is probably a bit yucky and sweaty, so slam some fabric conditioner in with it please. I usually do my running bras by hand (gotta keep that support going!) and there's some handwash stuff under the sink, but sling the knickers in the machine.

– Could you get me a tube of Canesten (sorry to ask)?

– Could you get whatever Mum wants to eat? Her appetite is hopeless so anything tempting will do.

I'll be working late most of this week so I'll do sarnie @ desk. She says you've offered to take her out again today – great. Just don't tire her out too much. Hope I've left enough cash. Let me know if you need any more.

Thanks again,

Alex

Frankie read the note through several times. It was so unlike the abrupt, rather formal Alex he'd met he could hardly reconcile the two versions. Of course, she thought she was leaving her instructions for another woman so she was off her guard. Working in the theatre, Frankie was used to having close

78

female friends with a level of intimacy that perhaps didn't occur in other professions. By force of circumstance, he'd shared dressing rooms, tour vans, bathrooms, even bedrooms (well, it was Edinburgh) with actresses, friends who had stripped off in front of him without any qualms. They'd even shared their tales of woe about their love lives in excruciating detail. It was all par for the course. But they'd known they were sharing with a man. Alex didn't. Reading her note was slightly uncomfortable for Frankie, a bit like reading a secret diary and he felt a sudden pang of remorse about the whole deception issue.

Glancing at the note again, he put his reservations to one side. He had laundry to do, groceries to fetch and Canesten to buy (whatever that was). He made a first cup of tea for The Bean, whom he could now hear moving around in her boudoir, and took in the tray.

'Darling!' she greeted him rapturously from her position by the window. He'd noticed she had an instinct for placing herself in decorative poses, always with her best side forwards and with the most flattering lighting she could find. 'You're a sight for sore eyes.'

He grinned delightedly – he seemed to have trouble doing anything else around The Bean. 'Morning Bean!' He planted a kiss on her cheek. 'Sleep well?'

'Oh ever so much better, thank you. It was lovely to have Alex back. She was exhausted, poor girl, though she wouldn't admit it, of course, so there didn't seem much point staying up. Started that book about Tennessee Williams you lent me. Fascinating life, just fascinating. Oh, one thing, darling. I came perilously close to letting the cat out of the bag about you. She asked me how it was going, if you were working hard – cos I must admit, I did have a little moan the other day about that useless sister of yours – and I think I might have said something about you being awfully handsome. I covered it up, but one will have to be terribly careful.'

Frankie looked at her in horror. The last thing they needed was for Alex to catch them all out, especially when it seemed to suit everyone else so perfectly. The Bean wanted him to stay, Ella was begging him to stay in place so that she could continue with her new job, and he was certain that he would, indeed, make a far better fist of it. Plus, he had to admit, spending time with The Bean was sheer delight. If anything, he felt he should be paying *her* for the privilege.

She returned his look guiltily. 'Yes, I know, sweetheart. It was very silly of me. Very silly indeed. But I think you must take some responsibility. If you weren't so handsome, I shouldn't have said anything. So it's your fault really.' She came close and cupped his cheek with her good hand. 'Couldn't you try to be just a little bit plainer?'

He laughed, charmed as always. 'You will take more care, won't you?'

She crossed her heart with a slender finger, looking up at him coquettishly. 'Promise on my honour!' Then broke into an earthy laugh. 'For what it's worth. Now, darling – are we still on for today?'

Frankie rubbed his hands together, his disquiet put aside. 'You bet! I haven't been to Brighton for ages. I've just got some laundry to do first, I'll get it in the dryer and we'll be off. All right? Shall I make some sandwiches so we can eat on the way?'

The Bean hugged herself. 'Ooh, yummy. Egg mayonnaise for me, please. Plenty of black pepper too, if it's not too much trouble.'

'For you, Bean, nothing is too much!'

Frankie left her to her breakfast and opened the door to

Alex's room. She'd left in a hurry this morning, by the look of it, and her suitcase lay unopened on the floor. The bed was turned back. He hesitated for a moment then lifted the pillow to plump it up. Something grey and cottony slipped to the floor and he stooped to retrieve it. An oversized T-shirt with her company logo. Was that what she wore to sleep? Frankie shook his head. She didn't look the négligé type, but still! He pushed it quickly under the pillow then, smoothing the sheet, he shook the enormous quilt vigorously. He turned to survey the rest of the room. Tidy-ish but with no concession to comfort, aside from the enormous bed and seemingly new bed linen. With a shrug, he picked up her case and carried it into the kitchen.

Later that day, driving home from Brighton with The Bean beside him nodding off gently, Frankie had a feeling he almost didn't recognise and had trouble pinning down. Well-being? Contentment? It was certainly something like that. With the housework done, despite constant interruptions from The Bean asking if it was time to go, they'd squeezed into Alex's little car and set off. The Bean's constant stream of outrageous anecdotes kept Frankie in stitches all the way there and he had to force himself to concentrate on the route and to keep to the speed limits despite The Bean urging him to drive faster. Once there, she took charge, spurning the sandwiches and insisting on lunch at English's, which she paid for after a brief skirmish. Their stroll around The Lanes was punctuated by The Bean darting into antique shops and jewellers. She tucked another neatly wrapped package into her large leather handbag and took his arm again.

'This place has gone to the dogs! It was really something in the sixties. I remember being dragged by a boyfriend to hear The Who at the Starlight Rooms. Such energy. That lovely boy, Daltry. And his trousers! I really thought they were going to split right there and then. Of course, he's quite the country gentleman now. Well, they all are, aren't they? Tragic, with their OBEs and their country estates.' She shuddered. 'Of course, I gave it all up when I had Alex or who knows, I might have been a Dame!' She shrieked with laughter. 'Luckily, darling, I've never been rich enough to be dragged into bourgeois mediocrity. Genteel poverty is more my thing, much more integrity, don't you agree?'

Frankie laughed, but was thoughtful as they strolled down towards the Prom, only half listening to The Bean's tales of mods and rockers and skinny dipping in the early hours between Saturday night and Sunday morning. Who was she kidding? With all those films behind her, she must be rolling in it. And she certainly didn't stint herself in the shops she visited – or at the bookies. He smiled wryly. It must be another one of the many poses she loved to strike.

At the very end of the Palace Pier, they stood leaning against the railing gazing back towards the town, or rather, The Bean gazed at the town, Frankie gazed at The Bean, her hair whipping across her perfect, lined face by the breeze.

She sighed deeply. 'From here it still looks lovely, but it's not what it was. It's so dirty now. So commercial.' She nibbled at the ice cream he'd bought her. 'Or perhaps it's just me. Nothing seems as good as it was.' She turned away to look out to sea. 'It's bloody, being old. I hate it.'

'You? Never! Come off it, Beanie. Not only do you look fantastic, you're a total legend. How could you be old? You're The Bean.'

She turned back, smiling tightly, and squeezed his hand. 'Thank you, darling. Much appreciated, but I'm an *old* bean now. Now you, you have so much in front of you. Don't waste your life wondering if you can succeed – make it happen. I've seen careers thrown away on wishes. Think how you'd feel at my age if all you had to remember were "if onlys". I can just see you in a romantic lead somewhere.'

Frankie snorted, thinking about his disastrous love life. 'Yeah right. I can't even manage that in real life, it seems.'

'Oh darling, women must be falling at your feet!'

'Well, I haven't tripped over any recently.'

She touched his arm reassuringly. 'Just you wait. The right girl will come along when you least expect it. I met my darling Johnny on the Promenade des Anglais at three in the morning. He was drunk as a lord and asked me to marry him on the spot.' She roared with laughter. 'Just don't marry an actress. Two artistic temperaments will never work. Here,' she handed the ice cream to him, 'finish this for me, would you? I think I'm starting to feel a little bit tired. Shall we go?'

Her mood had soon lifted as they walked back to the car. She'd spotted a beautifully preserved Lambretta and was off with another anecdote, describing what sounded like a hair-raising ride down from London, freezing in her miniskirt. Several people had stopped them and asked for her autograph, and she was as charming and gracious as he'd ever seen her. The fans left in an ecstatic daze, while he proudly took her arm and strolled away with her in the opposite direction. Fortunately, she hadn't heard the whispered comment, speculating on whether he was her son or her toyboy.

At Frankie's urging, The Bean called home to check that Alex wasn't back. 'The coast's clear, darling.' She smiled. 'Alex need never even know what fun we've had today. Or how much I've spent. I certainly won't tell her. And you *can't*!' She pinched his cheek roguishly but Frankie clapped his hand to his head. 'I forgot to get … er … something. What was it again?' He fished in his pocket for the list, then pulled in on a double yellow line and dashed into a pharmacy, leaving The Bean with instructions to exert her charm on any traffic wardens.

'Can I have some Canesten, please?'

The young girl gestured to the wall of products behind her. 'Certainly. Which kind?'

'Err ....'

'Pessary? Cream?'

Frankie's face must have shown total bewilderment. The girl leaned forward slightly. 'Thrush? Athlete's foot? Nappy rash?'

'Not nappy rash, certainly. Erm ....'

'There's a preparation for cystitis too. Is it for you or your partner?'

'She's not my ... erm.'

'Are *you* experiencing itching or redness? Because it's very important to treat both partners.'

'It's not for me!' Frankie said, far louder than he intended. Everyone turned to look. 'I'll come back.'

He slammed the car door shut and did up his seatbelt as fast as possible. The Bean looked at his flaming face with mild curiosity but said nothing. It wasn't until they got back and he'd supplied her with tea, then had written and torn up at least three notes to Alex, asking exactly what type of Canesten she required, that The Bean leaned forward confidingly and said, 'No need to be embarrassed, dear. Were you buying some of those French letters?' Frankie could feel himself going even redder, startled by her directness. 'They're so much better than they were in my day,' she chortled. 'I gather now you can get them ribbed and fruit flavoured, like tea!' She nudged him in a matey way. 'What do you young things call it? Are you going on the pull?' And she rocked back in her chair in hysterical laughter.

84

Chapter 13

'Mummy! He's not moving!' Millie had had the car door open almost before they pulled up outside the front door and was inside and into the kitchen before Max had the engine off. Struggling to the top of the stairs, Saff dropped the suitcases on the landing and flexed her hands to get the feeling back. They were heavier than she'd thought. She could hear Max storing the skis back in the shed.

'What Mills? Hang on, I'm coming down.' The house felt airless even after just a week and she couldn't wait to throw open the windows and let in the spring air.

'Aaaah! He's dead. Widget's dead!' Millie's face was contorted in a howl of grief when Saff joined her by the hamster's cage. Her daughter threw her arms around her and clung on desperately. 'She's killed him!'

'Now now, love, let me see. He's probably asleep or hibernating.'

'But it's spring, Mummy! They don't hibernate now!' Millie sniffed dramatically.

Saff, not exactly relishing the prospect of what she might find, carefully opened the cage and put her hand inside. This was maternal sacrifice indeed. She wasn't mad about furry things alive, but definitely not dead. Through a pile of sawdust and cotton wool she could see the creature's nose peeping out and she cupped her hand around its body. Stiff as a board.

'Oh, Millie love, I think you may be right.' The wail crescendoed as Millie wiped her snotty face on Saff's T-shirt. 'Well darling, they don't live for ever you know. I did warn you at the pet shop.'

'She killed him!'

'I'm sure she didn't.' Saff looked around the kitchen. The sink was dry, the dishcloth stiff over the tap. It looked suspiciously as if their neighbour had forgotten to come over after all.

Half an hour later, the limp plants retrieved from the bath and having a long drink, and the brown tête à tête daffodils put out by the back door to die back to their bulbs, Saff was scrabbling through the recycling trying to find an old shoe box to double as a coffin. She pulled out one from a pair of trainers Max had bought in one of his must-lose-weight phases, but discarded it – the poor hamster would rattle and slide about in that. Lodged at the bottom of the recycling, however, was an oatcake box, so she packed the stiff little corpse into it, holding it in place with screwed up bits of the *Telegraph* – at least it was going out in a broadsheet – and taped the lid down firmly.

'Can I write a prayer?'

'That's a lovely idea, darling, then we could have a little funeral.'

'Make sure you dig it deep enough,' said Max wandering into the kitchen to make a cup of coffee before going back to his study to sort through post and emails.

'Why, Daddy?'

'Well, if you don't, some buggery dog will dig it—'

'Thank you, Max.' Saff scowled at her husband. 'Daddy means that we need to make sure he is cosy and warm so he can go up to heaven. Perhaps we might put a big stone on top of his grave – a bit like a gravestone.' She led Millie outside hoping she'd distracted her from Max's tactless remark. He hated the hamster – 'vermin, just vermin' he'd snorted the day it arrived – and had studiously ignored it, though not without commenting that Saff shouldn't have given in to Millie's pestering. Usually Saff would have found his remark about the buggery dog funny, but today it annoyed her. In fact, she'd felt pretty narked with him throughout the holiday and had turned her back and pretended to be asleep the one night he'd made a play for some action. It had all started with the discovery of the missing salopettes. His response had been less than sympathetic, but then, she'd thought as she scoured the shops at the resort to try and find some that didn't cost the earth, he was all right Jack, wasn't he? Because *she'd* remembered to pack all *his* stuff. He hadn't even had to think about his toothbrush, had he? And she'd been so busy thinking about everyone else, guess who she'd forgotten? Wasn't that just the story of life these days?

She'd snarled as she trawled the shop rails. Max had been even more off when, out of spite, she'd come back to the hotel with a very flash (and satisfyingly expensive) pair, paid for with his credit card. 'What on earth do you need them for?' he'd shouted. 'They won't make you go any faster.' And she'd done her best to out-ski him just to serve him right. Of course, he'd beaten her every time and headed off with Oscar to much more challenging pistes. Leaving her to look after Millie.

'Muuum,' Millie sobbed now as Saff dug a hole with the spade under the lilac tree at the end of the garden. Even Oscar had joined them and, after a stern look from Saff, was trying to appear suitably serious. 'I can't help thinking,' she sniffed. 'I can't help thinking how the sunlight used to shine though his ears ...'

Better than your father, thought Saff, putting all her weight behind her foot on the shovel, who thinks the sun shines out of his arse.

'Dear God, keep Widget safe in heaven. Amen.' And with that, Millie ran, howling, up to her bedroom.

After lunch Saff stuck her head around Max's study door. 'Right, the children are upstairs playing. I'm going to nip over and see The Bean. Please don't just carry on with your work and ignore them?'

Max was dialling a number on the phone. 'Sure. See you later. Are you sure she'll be there?'

'She's incapacitated, isn't she? I can't imagine she can go anywhere.'

'Hi there. How are you?' Ignoring her, Max began speaking into the phone.

Saffron manoeuvred through the traffic, listening to something classical on Radio Three, enjoying a moment's peace, something she hadn't really had all week. She had no idea who the composer was but it helped ease the tension out of her shoulders which she'd hadn't even been aware was there. She took her time, driving around the common three times before heading off for Alex's road. She was looking forward to seeing The Bean – it was always a tonic. At school she would always turn up late for speech days and sports days (pissing off Alex who naturally excelled at everything and picked up all the medals), but her arrival would always cause a stir, especially in the early days when she was still something of an icon.

The Bean would always have a little sports car and dispense champagne and Pimms from the back of it in paper cups so the teachers wouldn't know the girls were drinking, and she'd throw her fragrant arms around all Alex's friends. Alex, on the other hand, would cower away and Saff would often find her drinking tea with *her* parents in the back of their camper van – a vehicle Saff found acutely embarrassing in a car park full of Mercedes and BMWs. The two of them used to joke that they should do a parent swap. Alex's father, the utterly charming and rakish Johnny, would never grace such events – he was always off on some unspecified business trip – and The Bean, who so hated to be alone, would arrive with an actor she was working with in tow. One year she turned up with a man so breathtakingly beautiful the girls just stood and stared, while he sat impassive in leather jacket and jeans, hidden behind dark glasses.

The cherry trees on Alex's road were in full burst of pink when Saff turrned the corner and she had a relaxed, almost benign sensation when she pulled into a parking space and put the pay and display ticket on her dashboard. She was looking forward to this. How odd to imagine The Bean ensconced in Alex's minimal and unloved flat. Saff rang the doorbell and waited. It took a while before she heard the intercom being picked up.

'Hello, yes?'

'Hellooo! Bean, it's me.'

'Who, dear?' The voice sounded small and nervous.

'It's me. Saff.'

There was a pause. 'I'm quite busy, dear. Can you come another time?'

This didn't sound right at all, and suddenly Saff was worried. The ridiculous thought crossed her mind that perhaps she had a lover there. She might even be being held hostage. She looked about her, not quite sure what she was hoping to find, then pressed the bell again. 'Bean, can you let me in. I've come all this way and I only wanted to say hello.'

There was another long pause. 'All right, dear, but just for a moment. I … I have to wash my hair.' Saff pushed open the door at the click and made her way up the stairs to Alex's flat door, which was opened gingerly by The Bean. Saff noticed her hair looked immaculate and her welcoming hug, though familiarly laced with Arpège, was not as enthusiastic as usual.

'Hello, Saffron dear. Come on through. I'm just in here … as one would be, I suppose.' Saff was led through to the sitting room as if she'd never been here before in her life. Around the sofa The Bean had set up some kind of camp with copies of *Vogue*, her nail polish and a large pile of papers that looked remarkably like one of Max's scripts.

'Are you auditioning for something?' Saff peered down at the papers. 'Is this some long-overdue comeback?'

'Good lord, no.' Confusingly, The Bean picked up the papers and stuffed them under the cushion. 'Can I get you something?' she enquired, her perfectly plucked eyebrows arching questioningly. There was an uncomfortable moment. Being asked to sit down would be a start, thought Saff. Instead The Bean hovered.

'Er, well, tea would be nice, but where's Ella? Can't she get that?'

'Ella?' If anything The Bean's eyebrows rose even further until they were almost at her hairline. 'Ella, yes. She's busy. She's very busy. She's out actually!'

'Right,' said Saff slowly, not quite sure what was going on here. She put her bag down on a chair. 'You sit down and I'll put the kettle on.' Before The Bean could argue, she turned on her heel and walked into the small kitchen. It was tidier than the last time she'd been here and it smelt of bleach. On the side was a bag of groceries, half unpacked, with oranges escaping from it, and beside the kettle laid out on a tray was a teapot, containing two tea bags, a bowl of sugar lumps and two china cups. Was The Bean expecting someone else? Well, Saff could add another cup to the tray if that someone turned up.

Once the tea was made, she carried the tray back through

and put it down on the table between them. Instead of reclining comfortably, Alex's mother was perched on the edge of the seat, a distracted look on her face.

'Are you all right?' Saff asked. 'Is your arm playing up?'

'Fine dear, just fine. Now, how was your glamorous holiday? Do tell.'

So, pouring the tea for them both, Saff began to relay the holiday story, playing up the salopettes issue with a drama she knew The Bean would enjoy.

But instead of a laugh, The Bean gulped down the scalding tea, muttered something about 'gosh, poor you' then stood up. 'Now, I have to go out shopping, so if you don't mind ...'

Saff put down her barely touched cup. She'd been going to wash her hair, hadn't she? 'Oh. Right. Fine. Only, it looks as though Ella's already done the shopping from the bag in the kitchen—'

At that moment, from behind the closed bedroom door, came an enormous sneeze. Saff froze. So did The Bean. Christ, she'd been right about the lover! How embarrassing. But now what? Should she just disappear? She looked from the bedroom door back to The Bean, but instead of seeing embarrassment as she had expected, the woman's eyes were full of glee.

'Oh Saff, dear, I'm so sorry. Can you keep a secret?'

Chapter 14

Ella searched through the pile of papers yet again, as if willing the list to be there would somehow make it appear. In the next door office, she could hear the staccato rattle of Mike's fingers on the computer keyboard. Her new boss typed in spurts, furiously active for a couple of minutes, then pausing for thought or inspiration, or something. Ah, inspiration. If only Ella could dredge up some of that!

She'd had the crucial sheet of paper only that morning, after typing it out laboriously on Frankie's laptop at home the previous evening. At the time, he'd done a comedy double-take, as if the sight of her working was so incredible he had to look again in case his eyes were deceiving him. She'd pushed her hair irritably out of her eyes and paused in her hunt-and-peck two-finger attempt at word processing to stick her tongue out at him, then had continued doggedly.

'This looks serious,' he'd mocked. 'Homework? Last time I saw you do anything this close to hard work must have been – well, let's see now – never?'

Ella had simply gritted her teeth and continued, determined not to let him get her riled. The old Ella would have jumped up and started a cushion fight. The new Ella was too busy for such nonsense – although she was still sorely tempted. Frankie had knocked off teasing almost straight away and had come to peer over her shoulder. Predictably, though, his first comment was a criticism.

'You need to give that a bit of a spell check. See those wavy red lines? Right click and choose the right spelling.'

Count to ten, Ella. 'If I *knew* the right spelling, I'd have *put* the right spelling,' she'd said with icy disdain. 'I'm a bit dyslexic, not stupid.'

That had shut him up. But Ella had looked anxiously at the screen. She didn't want Mike or anyone else at the radio station laughing at her ideas, just because they weren't spelt right. Frankie was still hovering.

'"New hospital wing delay," he'd read. "Mobile phone mast. Brown-field development. Environmental survey." What's all this, Ells?'

'Oh nothing really,' she'd evaded. 'Just some ideas for a programme I thought of. A sort of investigation thing, you know.'

He obviously didn't from the look on his face. He'd stared at her as if she'd grown another head.

'What?' She'd shaken her head irritably. 'Get lost, you goof ball. I'm trying to concentrate.'

He'd raised his eyebrows in that annoying, supercilious way of his. 'Nothing, nothing. Shall I bring you a cup of tea?'

Ella had snorted and carried on typing. 'That would make a nice change. I thought I had to make you tea for eternity to make up for you having to put up with the old bag.'

'Er, yes. Well, just this once, eh? Since you're obviously busy.'

She'd waved him away, lost again in the ideas she was gradually formulating. Yes, something on sweatshops as well. That would be a challenge.

And now, here she was in the office, five minutes to go until the ideas meeting and no trace of her ideas. She couldn't write out another list, even if she could remember any of the subjects she'd come up with, because then everyone would see her spelling. Oh God, when would she learn to be more organised? She had a GCSE in excuses for homework not completed, and now for once she'd worked hard and the bloody thing had disappeared.

The other two researchers walked confidently into the room so Ella gave up the frantic search, leaning back against the table with studied cool. Both of them seemed to have pages and pages of notes, tucked into efficient-looking notebooks. She grabbed up a clipboard from a pile on the filing cabinet in the corner and held it against her chest. Mike threw open the door to his lair. His wild, badly cut hair and monobrow gave him a dark, lupine look. He was rangy too, his top button was never done up and his shirt always hanging out at the back. It had clearly never come into close contact with an iron. In the month or so Ella had been there, she'd heard him chew out an average of four staff members each week. So far she'd avoided the worst of his temper, but maybe today was her day. She took a seat by the window and pretended to check over her non-existent list. He started with Kerry.

Her ideas for drive-time games were dissected minutely, and most dismissed before her grilling was over. Ella could feel sweat breaking out on the palms of her hands. Luke's scheduling ideas were well presented, with printed out copies not only for Mike, but for Ella and Kerry too. She tried not to glare at him as he returned smugly to his seat. Creep.

Mike read through the notes carefully, before throwing them in the bin. 'Sell me your ideas,' he barked. 'I don't want to read about them. This is radio. I want to hear, I want to be persuaded. I want to be *seduced*.'

Gross thought, winced Ella. He must be at least thirty-five, though for an old man he did have a Clive Owenish appeal, and his dismissal of Luke's ideas did offer a chink of hope for Ella. Luke stammered his way through an utterly unseductive pitch before trailing off as Mike shook his head. 'I'm not feeling it,' was all he said before turning to Ella. 'OK, new girl. Let's see what you've got.'

Ella cleared her throat. 'Well, I sent you a copy of my ideas by email this morning,' she lied, casually tapping the empty clipboard. 'But it's probably better if I talk you through them. I see an undercover investigation series into local issues that are bothering everyone in the area. This is a local station after all. People can listen to national radio for world events. We need to bring people in and get some community spirit going. Really find out what people are thinking, what worries them, what they want ...' She ploughed on and, miraculously, under pressure last night's ideas started to flood back. She hardly dared look up but she instinctively knew she had them. She had them in the palm of her hand. Frankie might be the actor but she was the improv queen today. Kerry and Luke were both glaring at her – an excellent sign – while Mike nodded thoughtfully, throwing the odd question her way and making notes.

When she got to the end of her spiel, he sat back in his chair and steepled his fingers together. 'You and you.' He nodded at Kerry and Luke. 'Bugger off. I'd like a moment with Lois Lane here. Sit down there.' He indicated the chair in front of him that Kerry had just vacated, as the other two shuffled resentfully through the door, then extended his hand. 'And let's have a look at those notes.'

'Erm, they're in shorthand. My own special shorthand only I can read,' Ella bluffed frantically.

Mike extended his hand again and she slowly handed over the empty clipboard. He looked briefly down, as if to confirm what he already knew, and handed it back to her. Ella felt a sinking sensation in her stomach. This must be what it felt like to be a lion's lunch.

He smiled slowly. 'There's no email either, is there?' She shook her head wordlessly. 'And the dog ate your print-out, did it?'

Ella jumped to her own defence. 'No, there was one. Honest. I had it earlier. I put it down. I just couldn't find it, so I just said what I could remember.'

Mike swivelled round in his chair. 'Coffee?' He fiddled with the drip filter permanently steaming by his desk. 'You forgot to mention the sweatshops though, didn't you?'

'What?' Ella jerked forward. 'How did you ...?'

Mike turned back towards her and handed over a murky cup of coffee, then opened his desk drawer and handed her the list she'd made. 'You can't kid a kidder, Ella. Didn't anyone teach you that? I'm the biggest bullshitter I've ever met.' The smile on his face was very broad by now. 'I just thought I'd see how well you could think on your feet. You've got to think fast in this business. You passed. You'll go far.'

'You ... you ... You ...!' For once, words failed her.

Mike grinned in satisfaction. 'Now, bugger off, kid.'

Chapter 15

'I'm thinking bagels.' Maurice, head honcho of Gorgeous Gourmet, put down his papers as if he'd announced a cure for the common cold and waited expectantly.

'Bagels?'

'For the launch. Teensy weensy little ones, mind, ever so sweet, full of smoked salmon or chocolate. Even foie gras ...'

Alex's tummy rumbled. She'd been so rushed this morning that breakfast had been a slab of Ella's deliciously moist fruit loaf that she'd found in a tin in the kitchen. Her usual bolt into Starbucks on the way to work had been stalled by a call from Todd, who was en route to Munich and wanting to kill time at the airport. They hadn't seen each other now for two weeks and he was clearly feeling frustrated.

Maurice was now waxing lyrical about itsy-bitsy croissants, his striped shirt – so tight it appeared almost painted onto his skinny frame – was rippling with excitement. Alex had never actually met him before, but she had tasted some delicious muffins at a marketing conference a few months ago and, when the food issue for the launch had come up, she'd got Camilla on to the case to find out who'd catered the event and get some recommendations. With his carefully gelled, artistically sculpted blonde hair, and diamond nose-stud, he made an unlikely-looking type to be involved in the catering business. Alex had a moment's disquiet.

'You're absolutely sure you can cope with an event this size aren't you, Maurice? I mean, we're talking three hundred press, VIPs, athletes, and it's very important for us to get it right.' She leant forward to drive home her point. 'I mean, very, very important. Possibly the biggest thing we've ever done, and I need breakfast circulating constantly so no one thinks we've scrimped, athletic-looking waiters … you know the kind of thing.'

Maurice leant back in his seat, an offended expression on his face, and sighed theatrically. 'Alex, you have come to *absolutely* the right person. All my clients say that what I don't know about brunch canapés isn't worth knowing.' He crossed his tightly-trousered legs, his silver thumb-ring catching the light as he feathered the hair forwards around his ears. Alex watched in fascination. 'Of course there are the tricky ones to think about.'

'Sorry?'

Maurice giggled girlishly and brushed something non-existent off his sleeve. 'Those sensitive little souls like myself who have special diets. I blame all the sliced white bread we had as children.' He leant forward again conspiratorially. 'I'm a martyr to my digestion, frankly.' He started to count off on his fingers. 'We need to allow for the gluten intolerant, lactose intolerant, soya intolerant, wheat intolerant …' This was beginning to sound like an allergy conference. Alex stopped him.

'Keep it simple, Maurice.'

He looked crestfallen. 'Oh, so you won't want to know about my fruit sculpture then?'

'Fruit sculpture?'

'Oh yes.' He leant even further forward. 'We must have fruit for all those sporty people. Now, I'm thinking something big, bold and spectacular. I'm thinking fruits to reflect the international audience. I'm thinking a full-size statue of an athlete, maybe even more than full size. Yes! Let's go gigantic. All muscles and pectorals.' His eyes glazed over for a moment in erotic reverie. 'But, wait for it, made *entirely out of fruit*. Watermelon for the head, all carved exquisitely. Paw paw, mangoes, luscious strawberries and blueberries.' He warmed to his theme, his hand gestures going wild. 'Slices of apple and pineapple to make shape and form. Cantaloupe and ripe apricots?'

Alex looked at her watch, feeling very ill at ease. 'Right.'

'And there he would stand in all his glory.' Now Maurice's arms were stretched wide like the Messiah. 'Proud and strong at the end of the runway, the colours on his fruit-created clothing reflecting the colours of your clothing range ...'

'Maurice, how much is this ... this art work going to be?'

Without dropping his arms, Maurice looked down at his notes and mentioned a figure.

'You are joking!' Alex shouted so loud that startled heads bobbed up from behind computers in the open plan office. 'That's outrageous!'

'Well.' Maurice dropped his arms and looked down sulkily at his nails. 'You have to pay for creativity you know. These things take time to do and you did say this was *very, very* important.'

Alex could see her entire launch budget being blown out of the water by a fruit salad. There was a small cough. 'It would look tremendous,' Camilla said quietly from her seat. She'd barely spoken since the meeting had started. 'It might even impress the most hardened hacks, Alex?'

Alex shook her head. 'But it's way too expensive, Cam.'

'Well.' Camilla shrugged. 'I'm sure Maurice could re-look at his quote, but in the end it's up to you, of course.'

What Alex really needed now was her assistant's characteristic decisiveness, but she knew Camilla was right. It was up to her to make the final decision. She glanced across the office at Gavin, deep in conversation with Peter, running-shoe marketing manager and terrier on the heels of Alex's job, and realised that this launch had to be good. Better than good. It had to be great. And she had to produce something that would make a gimmick-weary press sit up and notice. A fruit sculpture, ridiculous as it sounded, might just do it.

'O-K,' she said slowly. 'If you can re-look at the costings, we'll go with the sculpture.' The caterer's face lit up.

'But Maurice.' Alex paused. 'No strategically placed bananas, hey?'

Maurice threw back his head and laughed, a sound that Alex could only describe as a demented cackle. 'Oooh you!' he teased, and once he had shut his baby-blue briefcase with a click, he minced out of the office, with a 'nice to do business with you'.

Alex turned to Camilla. 'Did I dream that?'

Camilla had a small smile on her lips. 'Isn't he a piece of work?'

'Oh God, I hope I've made the right decision. I mean, will he cope? I've only ever seen him do a low-key event. Perhaps we should have used someone bigger?'

'Well.' Camilla uncrossed her legs and crossed them the other way. 'You did say you liked his muffins – if you'll pardon the expression! – and his references sounded good. On the way up in the lift he told me he'd done an ice sculpture of Rodin's *Kiss* for a wedding in Chorleywood.'

'Gosh. Well, let's see shall we? Now, what time is Donatella coming in?'

Camilla looked at her watch. 'She's always fashionably late but she is the best and this is *very*, *very* important ...' Her imitation of Maurice was spot on and they both laughed.

Chapter 16

By the time Alex spotted the hair of Donatella Cappuccio, somewhere between Cruella De Vil's and a skunk's, sashaying across the office, she had managed two calls to Italy and Holland and a large pain au chocolat. The stylist, undoubtedly London's most sought after and over six foot in Vivienne Westwood stacks, leopard print jacket, black tights and tartan shorts, folded herself into the seat Maurice had recently vacated. She was so out of place in the office, a shrine to Lycra and trainers that Alex almost laughed, and looked down at her own clumsy jeans and navy sweatshirt. Donatella hadn't even spoken, just proffered a cool, limp hand, but the expression of distaste on her face said it all, and it turned into frank disbelief when she glanced over at the new range hanging on rails behind Alex.

'Is that the collection?' she asked in bored tones.

'Yes, yes.' Alex jumped to her feet in an attempt to justify the vibrant colours of the Urban Classics Range. 'Yes, this is it. We are very excited by it …' Alex finished lamely. How could she possibly excite this woman whose natural milieu was Galliano and Stella McCartney, and setting runways on fire, sometimes literally, at London Fashion Week with her exotic ideas. Donatella got to her feet and wandered over to Alex. She smelt strongly of something heady and expensive and Alex looked on enviously as she ran long, French-manicured fingers along the rails. Would she just turn round and say: 'There's nothing I can do here'? It had been such a coup to get her even to consider being involved – but if she turned them down, and this late in the day? Well, Alex wasn't sure what she'd do.

The stylist picked the odd thing off the rack, looked at it and put it back without saying a word. 'What's your message here?' she asked eventually, turning around and Alex breathed out.

'Well,' she gushed, looking up at the woman, not something she often had to do at five foot nine herself. 'It's that sportswear need not be butch. It can be elegant and urban and sexy.'

'And chavvy,' Donatella spat.

'Well, yes, obviously some brands have been adopted by the, er … less athletic, but Zencorp Urban Classics are going to change all that. This range will cross over the sports to fashion classics divide stylishly and seamlessly.'

Donatella looked down at Alex and assessed her through heavily mascaraed eyelashes. 'You sound like a press release.'

Alex shrugged and suddenly felt defeated. 'I'm not surprised. I've thought about little else but this for about six months. I even dream in marketing speak.' Donatella went back to the range and took down a lemon-yellow and pink vest, the company logo discreetly hidden on the shoulder. She held it out and assessed it, her eyes narrowed.

'Yup,' she said eventually. 'I think I can work with this.'

'Fantastic. When can you give me your ideas—'

'But,' Donatella interrupted, 'I will need to be given a free reign. Let do it my way, you understand. Trust me. I haven't let anyone down yet. And who's your big name?'

'Big name? Well, we do have the athletes we sponsor who are contracted to make appearances.' Alex trotted out the names.

'Mmm.' Donatella put a long finger thoughtfully to her cheek. 'No, we need a model. We need someone who, by the very fact she's modelling this, will be telling the world this is good enough to wear anywhere, every day. I need a Kate or a Naomi. Better still, Bettina Gordino. Get her and you've got me.'

'I have the feeling I'm being bullied,' Alex sighed when the stylist had left, not before giving Alex an even more alarming estimate of costs. 'She had better be as good as they say.'

Camilla brought over the initial press release Alex had drafted for her to check. 'I think her presentations are a bit over the top to be honest.'

'Oh?'

'Well, it's all a bit too flashy, don't you think? That thing with flares at the V&A, for example. Peter said he'd heard she could be tricky. Bit of a prima donna. But if you've got the budget and you seem sure, so …'

'Camilla, we need the best here. Something monumental. There must be a good reason why she's so expensive and she gets featured in *Vogue*, and people keep asking her back.'

Alex thought about Camilla's reticence during the frantic afternoon that followed. Camilla had always been so behind Alex with campaigns in the past. Always there to encourage, and super-efficient when given a task to do. By the time she escaped the office she was beginning to question her own judgement. Perhaps, she thought as she squeezed onto the packed tube platform, she'd taken too big a risk with Donatella. She glanced at the people around her – many of them wearing trainers and football tops, joggers and baseball hats, many sporting the company's brand. Did she need to spend so much to get the message out there?

'The competition are on to this already, aren't they Peter?' Gavin had said earlier this afternoon, turning to the oleaginous creep beside him. 'Peter tells me some of them have already got a similar urban crossover idea on the drawing board. Someone must have said something out of school, but frankly the idea is not that original, Alex. This launch will have to blow them out of the water.'

Thanks Gavin. Defeated even before she opened the door of the flat, she couldn't bear the idea of an evening with her mother nagging. How much nicer it would be to spend it with Todd – though she wasn't even sure she had the energy for his American enthusiasms tonight. All she wanted was to strip off her clothes, have a long hot shower, wash her hair and flop in front of something inane on the TV. Instead, she was more likely to have an evening of her mother making her sit through an old film and regaling her with reminiscences about how the leading man had once been in love with her. Sometimes it was hard being the daughter of an icon. She pushed open the door.

'Hellooo darling,' The Bean called cheerily from the sitting room. 'I've struggled manfully to put the kettle on.' She opened the door and stood in the doorway, her white hair neat and clean. For once she was out of her lounging peignoir and in navy cotton trousers and a white shirt. Her face, under the ever-present make-up, looked fresh. Alex was taken aback. 'Or would you rather a gin and tonic, my darling? Oh look at you.' She held out her good arm. 'You look knackered in your ghastly sweatshirt. I do wish you'd get a job marketing something glamorous.'

'Thanks, Mum.' Alex dumped her bag on the chair and brushed her hands through her hair. 'I am pretty bushed as it happens and a cup of tea would be fab. Builders' please, none of your fragrant nonsense.'

Her mother tutted and went into the kitchen, chatting as she went. 'Have you had a hassley day, sweetheart? I do wish you could relax.'

Alex sat down to undo her laces. If she could dredge up the energy she'd go for a quick run before her shower. 'Yup, pretty much, and relaxing is definitely not an option until the launch is over. What have you been up to?'

'Oh, this and that,' her mother called over the noise of tea making. 'I went out for a lovely walk in the park actually. It was gorgeous in the spring sunshine. London is so charming at this time of year.' She brought in a china cup and saucer balanced precariously in her good hand and handed it to Alex, who would have preferred a mug. Her mother however had always thought them vulgar.

'Thanks. That must be why you look so good.'

The Bean went to look in the mirror over the fireplace and put her hand to her cheek. 'Oh, do you think so, dear? It must have been the sunshine. Do you know,' she turned round to Alex, 'we saw a heron scoop up a fish out of the pond – just like that!'

'We?'

'We? Did I say we? Well, of course I meant all the other people by the pond. And that Ella girl, of course. Anyway, what shall we eat? I've bought some lovely monkfish and some of that delicious parma ham from that delightful deli. Antonio is becoming quite a friend—'

'God, Mum, it's so expensive there!' Alex spluttered her tea. 'We can't afford to eat like this all the time!' She sighed. 'We've been through this so many times before.'

Her mother brushed away her concerns with her hand. 'Oh, you do fuss so. It will be delicious, we deserve a treat, and you can't expect me to eat that rubbish you call food. Now, you go and freshen up and I'll put the lasagne er ... Ella's left in the oven. Oh! I can't wait to get this bloody cast off.'

Alex stood up wearily. 'Crikey, Mum.' She stretched. 'This

Ella seems to have had a miraculous effect on you. You are almost bearable to live with! You'll be jogging next!'

'Pah!' her mother snorted. 'At my age?'

'Ever so good for your heart, you know. Exercise is also good for your skin, and your bones.' Alex bent down and picked up her trainers. 'Talking of which, I might go for a quick run before supper if you don't mind?'

The Bean had a look of disgust in her face. 'Perfectly masochistic if you ask me. I've always had the figure of a seventeen-year-old, so what do I need with this power walking nonsense? And that awful stuff you wear! Can you imagine most people of my age in one of those ghastly crop tops and the leggings? It would be like stuffing a bag of frozen peas into a balloon.' And with that she flounced into the kitchen.

A swift twenty minutes around the block later and Alex was at last under a hot shower, letting the shampoo run down her back. She rubbed the soap over her stomach and thighs, a body so unlike her mother's who had always embarrassed her enormously by introducing her to people as 'amazonian, like her father'. The Bean had always been thin, hence the name, but that didn't mean she didn't need to do some gentle exercise. Even so, in just a few days she'd begun to look better – Ella had obviously heeded her note about getting out. As Alex rinsed her hair she thought about what her mother had said. She was right. Exercise kit really was aimed at the young, with the grey market turning up at the gym in baggy T-shirts and baggier tracksuit bottoms. A germ of an idea began to form in her head.

Towelled dry and feeling quite relaxed now, she padded into her mother's room to get a fresh bath mat from the airing cupboard. She looked around at her mother's things strewn everywhere – clothes on the chair and hanging over the cupboard doors, flat pumps in every colour tucked under the dressing table, piled high with bottles and scarves, and beside them lay a little pile of shells and grains of sand. Odd. Where had they come from?

Chapter 17

'More tea?' Frankie called through the open doors to where The Bean stood clad in a vest top and jeans, cautiously prodding her newly-freed arm. Without the plaster, sliced off a few days earlier, it looked terrible. Pale, slack, spindly. He looked away quickly. But not quickly enough. She snatched up her habitual silk peignoir, wincing as her arm extended beyond its usual restricted movement.

'For God's sake,' she snapped. 'Can't I even have a moment's privacy? Why do you do that all the time? Creep up on people? It's incredibly annoying.'

Frankie backed out and returned to the kitchen – fast. What did she mean? Creep up? He didn't creep up! He'd never crept anywhere in his life. He put the tray down firmly on to the kitchen counter. It wasn't the first time The Bean had scolded him. In fact, she was always on at him, picking him up on his posture, his diction, even the way his hair was always a mess. But it was usually in an affectionate, patronising, almost motherly tone that served mainly to remind him that he was merely Frankie, whereas she was, and always would be, the iconic Bean. She'd never sounded this cranky before though. This arm business must be getting to her.

She was always hard to shift unless some entertainment was the incentive, but Frankie had noticed how much more reluctant she had been to go out lately. It was as if she was more nervous with her arm exposed than she had been with it rigidly bent and slinged. She had an appointment to see the physio soon, yet she wasn't even attempting to get it moving, as the young orthopaedic houseman had advised. Frankie frowned. He had never seen The Bean at a disadvantage before. No wonder, he hadn't recognised the signs. Slowly, he emptied the cup of cooling tea, then went to the door.

'Bean!' he called gently along the corridor. 'Just give me the word and I'll bring you a fresh pot.'

Her door opened slowly. She had done her make-up and slipped a jacket on but her arm was still bent and held defensively at her side as she walked cautiously towards him. 'Oh, you don't need to do that, you silly boy! I'm here now.'

Frankie concealed a wry smile. Not a word of apology, of course. He cleared his throat. 'I thought it might be fun to go out today, just for a bit.'

She turned to him, alarmed. 'Oh darling, look at the weather.' She gesticulated at the pale blue sky. 'I'm sure it's going to rain later. Anyway, I must catch *Countdown* today. That new chap is really very good. And there's racing from Chepstow.'

He was going to have to be cleverer if he was going to get her moving about. 'Well, there's a new exhibition at Tate Modern. We could drive up, just have a little walk around, grab a bite to eat, you know. Pay homage at the Globe while we're at it.'

She sat down at the kitchen table. 'Ah, dear Sam! What drive! What vision! Of course, it's not really on the site of the original Globe, but it doesn't matter. I was at the opening, did I tell you about it?'

He poured her tea and set her toast in front of her, a little out of reach so she had to stretch for it. She barely noticed. 'Tell you what!' he continued. 'Why don't you show me round it later? I'm almost ashamed to admit, I've never even been there.' He crossed his fingers behind his back. 'I'd love to go.'

Putty in his hands! As long as he got her home in time for *Countdown*, she promised gleefully she'd give him a private tour. He smiled to himself as he tidied her breakfast things away into the dishwasher, then picked up Alex's note to read her list of suggestions for the day. He was rather enjoying now trying to guess what she wanted before she even asked for it – and she had clearly noticed. The tone of her note was warmer than ever.

> *Hey Ella – thanks for turning my washing round so fast. Those trousers are my absolute faves – no VPL, so no need for the dreaded thong! Could you possibly change my sheets today? Todd's in town. And can you get Mum to at least try to move her arm? She's very stroppy with me if I dare to say anything. Any chance of you making some more of that yummy fruit loaf?'*
> *Ta – as ever. Cheque on the side.*
> *Alex*

Todd? Who the hell was Todd? This was the first he'd heard of any Todd! What a ridiculous name. And the more he said it, the more ridiculous it became. He sounded like a cartoon character, lantern-jawed and bulging-biceped. He probably communicated in grunts. How was it that attractive, clever women always fell for complete idiots, especially ones with stupid names? He'd have thought Alex had better taste than that? 'Yuk!' He shook his head decisively and glanced at his watch. He could change the sheets before they went out. Ah – sod it. They could wait until later.

At Tate Modern, a couple of hours later, The Bean was typically and loudly scathing about the latest installation in the Turbine Hall, but Frankie wasn't really in the mood for a bitching session, and only nodded vaguely at her more out-rageous comments. As long as it kept her moving and enter-tained and, more importantly, away from her usual post in front of the television, he didn't really care.

'Just look at it, darling!' she groaned, gesticulating at the piles of carefully arranged *objets trouvés* through which they had to wind. 'Thrown together! It looks likes like Brick Lane on a bad day. It would take a greater talent than this Gottfried character to make sense of a space like this. Mind you, it would be fantastic to stage something like Beckett here, don't you think? Or to do a production of *The Dream* like that fabulous Peter Brooke one. No one's ever bettered that, in my opinion. *You* should do some Shakespeare, sweetie, before it's too late. You're still young enough for Hamlet, but you're no Romeo any more.'

Frankie felt suddenly dispirited. How miserable to have missed the boat on a great role before he'd really started. The Bean made it sound as if it was all up to him to simply decide. Like he could choose between productions and make a con-sidered choice between a cascade of offers to steer his brilliant career in the direction he wanted it to go. She just didn't get it. His brilliant career was currently so far up shit creek, that it had now entered previously unexplored territory. It had been over six weeks now since he'd last heard from his agent, and only then because she wanted the mobile number for a girl he knew from drama school. And it didn't really help that his mates were ribbing him constantly about being a housewife. He sighed deeply. The Bean was on to him straight away.

'What is it?' she coaxed, reaching out – with both arms, he noticed – to smooth imaginary fluff off his shirt. 'Are you bored? Would you like to move on to the Globe?'

He shook his head vehemently. 'No, no! I'm fine here as

long as you are. It's just … well, I haven't been up for any decent parts for ages and I feel as if things are passing me by a bit …' Frankie trailed off and looked over The Bean's shoulder into the distant corners of the huge hall. He couldn't meet her eyes. There he was, a loser in a world where she had been one of the greatest winners of her time.

'But look at you!' she said indignantly, stepping backwards. 'You're young, talented, fabulously good-looking … yes, you are darling. London should be at your feet. I believe in you, Frankie, I do. And I'm never wrong.'

Frankie shook his head almost irritated at the gulf of misunderstanding. She had no idea about his life, or his talent, come to that. 'Bean, it's very sweet of you,' he sighed. 'And I do appreciate the fact that you want to make me feel better, but you don't really know the first thing about my life. You really don't know how spectacularly uneventful my career has been to date. You say I'm talented, but really, what have you seen me do? Make tea? Drive you to the shops and back? Do the sodding washing and change sheets?' He stopped and frowned. Bloody Todd.

The Bean looked at him steadily for a moment. Not one of her flirtatious glances, nor the teasing look she would sometimes throw when she'd said something outrageous and was waiting for a reaction. She caught his eyes and stared at him, weighing him up carefully. It was an unnerving experience and Frankie was struck for the first time by the similarity between The Bean and Alex, who had searched his face in exactly the same way at that disastrous interview. He hoped he was doing better this time. At last she spoke.

'My darling boy.' She reached up to grasp his shoulders, and her voice was low and steady. 'This is exactly the moment your training has prepared you for. The moment when you feel nothing is going right, but when you must act as if you are on top of the world. This is the moment to show what you're made of! You're going to call that agent of yours and demand she pull her finger out. Tell you what. Sod the Globe! It'll be there tomorrow. Let's go home. I'm going to make some calls. If I can't double the number of auditions you've had in the last month, I'll treat you to lunch at the Ivy. Then we're going to get you ready to do battle – and you're going to win!' Without even waiting for a response, she marched off up the long slope towards the main entrance where the sunny South Bank was waiting for them. Trying to quell his unease, Frankie followed in her wake. Double his auditions? What was two times zero?

Back at the flat, The Bean disappeared into her room with her battered address book. She'd been too preoccupied to talk much in the car and Frankie hadn't wanted to ask what she had in mind. Whatever it was, it certainly couldn't make things worse. He just didn't want to look like a prat. And, he had to admit, she hadn't looked this enthusiastic about anything since he'd met her. She hadn't even asked if it was time for *Countdown* or paused to flick through one of the awful gossip magazines she was always buying when they were out. He went to prepare her a snack. If it kept The Bean happy, he'd go along with it.

Later that afternoon, all his other tasks completed, Frankie finally went into Alex's room. She'd given up all pretence of being efficient now and obviously felt quite comfortable with the fact that he would put away her clean laundry. She was like a ghost, everywhere but never there, apart from her little notes and a basket of dirty laundry. How would Alex feel if she knew a man she didn't even know had bought her tampons last week? What would she say if she knew he had ironed her T-shirts and folded her sensible cotton knickers and bras into neat piles?

Frankie shrugged and stripped the bed. No use wasting time thinking about that now. He had work to do. There was no reason on earth why Alex should ever find out how intimately he knew her now. The Bean was almost well enough to go home and soon the whole charade could end. Frankie shook out the pyjamas under the pillow and caught the now familiar scent of Alex's skin – clean, warm and a little bit soapy. He folded them carefully and laid them on the chair while he stripped the bed of its white cotton sheets.

Chapter 18

Saff glanced at the clock as she slammed the pan drawer. Max was late. Usually he'd ring her if he was going to be this late.

'Come on,' she chivvied Oscar who was lying out on the sofa watching *The Simpsons*. 'Clarinet practice then bed.'

The boy groaned. 'Why? Clarinet is pants.'

'Because you need to practise.' She pulled him gently by the legs and puffed up the cushion behind him. He seemed so long now, taking up almost all the sofa. How had that happened without her noticing? Perhaps he grew in the night like Jack's beanstalk. Where was Max?

'But Mum, it's sooo boring, and Mr Tredington is a pillock, and anyway I know my scales.'

'But your pieces are not so great, Oscar,' she bit with an aggression that surprised her. 'And you are going to look like the pillock in the exam if you don't get them right.'

'Who cares?' He unfolded himself and stood up, his body slouched sulkily. 'I wish I played something cool like the drums. Ricky plays the drums and everyone says he's cool.'

'Well you don't and you *should* care. It shouldn't always be me who has to get you to do things.'

'Why not? You don't do anything else all day.'

Saff felt as though she had been slapped, and stood there, tea towel hanging limply in her hand, as Oscar pushed past her, deliberately banging against her arm. She knew she should have pulled him up and explained very clearly how she spent her time caring for his dad and him and Millie, and how she cleaned and cooked for them, and made their rooms nice, and organised their busy lives. But somehow she couldn't get a word out.

Back in the kitchen she cast about for something to busy herself with, half an ear listening out for Oscar's very half-hearted attempts at his grade two pieces. She'd show him. She folded the tea towel and hung it neatly next to the other matching ones on the rail by the oven, and picked up a wind-up snail Millie had left on the table. Then she rearranged the fruit in the fruit bowl. But that was it really. There was nothing else to do. The dishwasher hummed in the corner, cleaning the plates from supper, the little ironing there had been to do was airing upstairs. The school bags for tomorrow were ready, reading diaries signed and snacks prepared, and Millie's school summer skirt was drying on the rack. Saff drummed her fingers on the table, spun around, turned off the light and headed upstairs to talk to Millie in the bath.

The bath, though full of water, was empty now except for some lingering bubbles, a flannel and a bath toy floating about disconsolately. Her towel was folded neatly on the towel rail and the little girl herself was lain out on her bedroom floor, pyjamaed, and plugged in to a Jacqueline Wilson story on a tape as she coloured in a picture. Saff picked up a cardigan that had been left on the floor and hung it over her chair, then wandered into her own bedroom. The warmth of the day had cooled now and she shut the window and ran her hands over the bed spread to smooth out non-existent creases. The room smelt of a mixture of her perfume and polish from when she'd cleaned it earlier.

She sat down on the bed, then lay back staring at the ceiling. She loved this room, with its Colefax pink roses and her little boudoir chair in deep pink linen. She turned her head and she could see her beloved dressing table, a present from her grandmother, and on top pictures of the children as babies, Oscar smiling toothlessly, and next to it, a picture of Max on their wedding day, his face wreathed in smiles looking right at the camera and right at her now. He had more hair then, and looked so young. Odd to have a picture of him on her dressing table when he slept here every night, but the expression on his face had so much hope in it that she'd kept it there. He'd been a producer at the BBC then, and he'd gone on about how he intended to make really important programmes that would win awards, and she'd be beside him. There'd be no question.

The scales had stopped now but she hadn't the energy to go down and crack the whip again. She turned to look back up at the ceiling. She had been there always, ready to listen to Max's ideas, and watching with pride when he and his mate Neil set up Offcut, the strident production company that in six years had managed to achieve a clutch of awards and some considerable clout in the business. 'You don't do anything else all day.' The words stung, but why? Because she knew she didn't. She knew she'd justified everything in terms of being everyone else's support, there to provide the essential elements that kept life ticking over. And everyone else was having the fun.

'All right for some.'

Saff turned her head sharply at his voice and sat up. 'Hello, you're late.'

Max rubbed a hand over his face wearily then sat on the edge of the bed beside her. 'I had lunch with Greta Dunant to go over her script then she came back to the office. It's a great script but a risk for us. I've got my reservations.'

'Why?'

He waved a hand dismissively. 'Oh, it's a bit complicated.

Stuff that's hard to explain.' Clearly 'stuff' was something Saff wouldn't understand. How worthless I am, she thought suddenly. Oscar had made it plain she was pointless, Millie didn't even need her help in the bath and Max thought complications weren't worth explaining. Greta, of course, would understand them.

'Do you fancy her?'

Max turned to look at her profile. '*What*?' he snorted with laughter.

'Greta. Do you find her intelligence attractive, a turn on? Do you?' Saff could feel her throat burn and her eyes filled with tears, and she looked at him beseechingly.

'Saff love, what's this all about?' He put a hand up to her face and rubbed away a tear with his thumb.

Saff looked down at her hands in her lap. 'I just feel a bit insecure that's all.' Max put his hand under her chin and turned her face towards him.

'Saff, my love, no I don't fancy her. She's overweight and hairy, she wears revolting shoes that look like something Millie used to wear in nursery, and she has a live-in partner called Helen.'

'Oh.' Saff smiled sheepishly. 'I see.' Max kissed her on the nose.

'You, my darling, are everything I want, and I'm not going to give you up for some dyke, even if she is an awesome writer. Now get me my dinner woman!' And he patted her on the knee.

Next morning Saff struggled to pull herself out of bed, despite the sunshine and the cacophany of birdsong outside the window. She'd been awake at 3.50 when the first one had started tuning up and she'd lain awake listening to the others join in ever since. As Max had snored gently beside her, she'd plumbed the depths of herself. What am I all about? What am I for? Why am I hurtling towards forty with nothing much to show for it? Eyes staring up at the ceiling, she'd thought about Alex and how people needed her skills. As close as they'd been all through school, when it came to work and career Alex had always been driven. Saff had always wanted to lie in the sunshine and make daisy chains while she should have been revising for O Level biology, but Alex? She'd be in her room swotting.

Saff felt tired even before she'd dropped the children at school, and turned the car round wearily to head back home to a day of – what? Turning out another cupboard that was already immaculate? Mowing the lawn in case the grass had grown half a millimetre in the night? No, today she couldn't face it. What had shocked her most last night and what had kept her awake listening to the dawn chorus was the awful realisation that she was only part of a whole. Of course, the idea of Max having an affair with Greta was ridiculous, but what if he ever did, with someone else, and he left? What would remain? Would there be any point in her? She wouldn't even be someone's wife. She reversed again into a driveway and headed off in the other direction towards Alex's place and the secret duo. It had become a refuge in recent days. From … what? Boredom and that flat feeling she couldn't shake off.

'Oh, you gave me a fright.' The Bean held her hand dramatically to her chest as she opened the door. 'It's quite doing my nerves in all this deception, but it's rather exciting, don't you think, dear?' She gave Saff a 'mwah' kiss on each cheek and shut the door behind her. 'Of course, Alex has no idea. She's too wrapped up in her launch. Come and have a cup of Frankie's delicious coffee. He's quite a find.' She led the way into the sitting room. 'Such a shame you are already married, darling, because I think you two would be perfect for each other. Now, if you'll excuse me, I'll just go and apply my war paint.'

Frankie stuck his head around the kitchen door as Saff walked in. Mmm, wasn't it a shame indeed that she was married, because he was really very attractive, and even more so now that he had a bit of an early summer tan and had lost the woebegone actor look.

'Saff, how you doing?' He leaned forward and gave her a kiss on the cheek.

'You smell of baking.' Saff dumped her bag down. 'Let me put the kettle on.'

'Do I? I'm just doing some brownies. The mistress has demanded them.'

Saff put the kettle under the tap. 'The Bean? I thought she ate like a sparrow. Anything I've ever baked for her she's left to go mouldy in the tin.'

Frankie laughed as he mixed the gooey mixture in the bowl with a wooden spoon. 'No, not that mistress. The Absent One. She Who Must Be Obeyed.'

'Oh, I see – yes, she's very partial to a bit of home baking.' Saff leant back against the worktop, folded her arms and watched him work. This was a novelty. The most Max ever did was make toast.

Frankie scooped the mixture out into a baking tray. 'Well, it must be someone else's baking because judging by the equipment in this place she never does more than make tea. I even had to buy this spoon.'

Saff laughed. 'Sounds like Alex, far too busy to eat.'

'What's she like, this friend of yours? I feel like I'm looking after a ghost sometimes.'

'Alex? She's clever, funny, very loyal. And fiercely independent. Having you help her goes right against the grain. I remember once at school she got the blame for something – I can't remember what it was now. Something stupid anyway. But she emphatically would not let me tell the teacher it wasn't her fault. She just sort of took it on the chin.'

Frankie stopped what he was doing and looked up. 'She seems chalk to her mother's cheese.'

'Good thing too really. If she was like The Bean there would be even worse fireworks. You can't have two egos that size in one family!'

'Yes and no,' Saff thought for a moment. 'The Bean loves the attention – now that's something Alex hates – but neither like to be treated like a fool.'

'And what about Alex's dad? You must have known him.'

'Oh I did. Bit of a dandy. Funny, life and soul of the party, but terribly unreliable. I think Alex must be a genetic throwback to an earlier generation. The Bean's parents come from hard-grafting, middle-class stock – she's not the aristo she pretends to be – and I think Alex must have something of that in her.' Saff paused. 'I love her to bits and sometimes I wish I was like her.'

Frankie looked at her sidelong and continued scraping out the mixture. 'Oh, this damned spoon isn't any good. How do you get the stuff out from around the edges?'

'You need a plastic spatula. I'll get you one – they're brilliant!' Saff enthused. 'One of my kitchen essentials. I noticed you put in a pinch of salt. I've never done that.'

Frankie laughed and slipped the tray into the oven. 'Brings out the flavour. Eat your heart out Jamie Oliver. You see, I'm not merely decorative!'

He was certainly that. Saff filled the cafetière and the coffee fragrance pervaded her nose. With Alex it was a mug of instant with milk if you were lucky. It was fun being around these two.

'You obviously love cooking, Frankie. Alex waxes lyrical about the suppers you leave – well, Ella's cooking actually! I love cooking too. It's so relaxing. I think it's about the only thing I *can* do.' She suddenly had the urge to cry and looked down at her feet.

'Hey Saff? What's up?'

'Right!' The door burst open. 'Time for your lesson, Frankie, my boy.'

Saff rubbed her eyes quickly, glad of the interruption, and watched The Bean sweep out again. 'Lesson? She's not teaching you poker now is she?'

Frankie smiled mischievously. 'She is actually! I'm getting quite good at it – if I could remember what each hand was worth. She keeps telling me about strip poker games they had when she was young and wearing eight pairs of knickers so she never had to take all her clothes off! You probably knew her then or at least soon after.'

Saff thought back to the first time she'd met Alex's mother, as she'd dropped her daughter off at their boarding school. Of course, they had been so young then, perhaps nine or ten. 'I remember she had a Mercedes sports car but I had no idea who this beautiful woman in her floating kaftan and turban was.' She laughed. 'But my father's chin hit the floor and I remember my mum being a bit jealous. "That's The Bean," she whispered in awe and said how they'd all wanted to look like her and fancy her having a daughter in my year. I've known her so long now as Alex's mum – you know, she even came to my wedding – that I forget what an icon she was.'

'It must be tough for Alex.' Frankie fetched down the cups and laid them out. 'I mean, doesn't she ever get jealous?'

Saff hadn't really thought about this but knew that *she* always had been. But the glamorous lifestyle, the invitations to first nights and swanky parties, even after her mother had given up film roles, had gone right over Alex's head whereas Saff had yearned to be a part of it. Someone else's life. Someone else's fun. 'No, she just gets exasperated.'

The kitchen door opened again abruptly. 'Are you two having a meeting about something?' The Bean's eyebrows were arched and she looked quite stern. 'Come along, Frankie. If you want half a chance at this part you need to be prepared, my darling.'

Saff followed him out of the kitchen carrying the coffee. 'Part? What's this?'

'Well, it's all thanks to this lovely woman really.' Frankie put down the tray and put his arm around The Bean's skinny shoulders. She brushed him away laughing like a school girl. 'She's persuaded David Herschmann to let me read for the new production of *The Sentinel* he's putting on at the National.'

'Crikey, Frankie!' Saff spontaneously clapped her hands together with glee. She wasn't familiar with the play but even she knew that Herschmann was the best and anything he touched seemed to turn to box-office gold.

'Perfect.' The Bean clapped her hands together as if calling a class to order. 'Explain to Saff the part you are reading for. It might help you see into the character.'

Saff sat down on the armchair as one-woman audience. 'Right,' began Frankie, smiling a little shyly and looking up to the ceiling as he remembered. 'I'm reading for Joel. Joel is about twenty-five – bit of artistic licence there ...'

'You look beautifully young, you fool. That skin!' gushed The Bean, directing proceedings from her position on the sofa.

'Whatever. And he is angst-ridden. I'm ace at angst as it happens. Anyway, in this bit his lover is about to go back to another man and he is devastated.'

Saff chuckled. 'You can see his point!'

'Quite.' Frankie picked up the script which was a bit curled at the edges. The Bean rehearsals had obviously been pretty intensive. 'Right …' He began to read the part and the Frankie with whom she'd made the coffee left the room and a new person stood in front of her. The grief he displayed and the words of the script, though a good way over the top for Saff, were not a million miles from how she felt this morning. Empty and pointless.

'What can she see in him, his face like a speckled toad.' He paused, script in hand. 'Does it mean nothing to her, after the things we've been through?'

Brrrr. Brrr. Saff's phone burst to life in her pocket.

'I'm so sorry.' She fumbled to find it and pulled it out, about to hit the call-divert button until she saw who was calling her. 'Oh shit, it's Alex.' All three of them stopped dead and The Bean looked towards her bedroom as if she was about to bolt and hide.

'Sssh. Answer it dear. We'll keep dead quiet.' Frankie sat close to her on the sofa and, perched on the edge of their seats, the two of them looked on intently as Saff answered.

'Hiya,' she said airily, trying to sound as normal as possible. 'How's life?'

'Hi.' Alex sounded slightly breathless and rushed as usual. 'What are you up to?' She always asked, bless her.

'Oh, just chores, washing, you know.' Saff could hear the slightly hysterical squeak in her own voice.

'What, at home? But I've just called your landline.'

'Washing powder. I'm on my way out to buy washing powder.' Her face felt hot. She'd always been crap at lying, a trait she thought was admirable until now.

'It sounds very quiet wherever you are. Anyway, short notice

I know but I need to schmooze Gavin a bit – I'll explain why later – and I wondered if you and Max could make it for supper on Friday at my place?'

'Crikey. A dinner party? You?' Saff couldn't hide her incredulity. 'I'm busy during the day so I won't be able to cook for you like I did at the Introduce Todd party.'

'Oh, you were a brick that day. No, don't worry. I've asked Ella. She's going to do it. She sounded a bit unsure when I called her just now, but I buttered her up. Todd will be there too. He flies in that morning. Can't wait. Can you make it?'

'Babysitter permitting, I'm sure we can.'

'Brill. See you about eight? Gotta go. Love ya!'

Saff turned off the phone, looked at the two expectant faces in front on her, and explained the content of the call.

There was a pause, then Frankie smiled slowly. 'Are you thinking what I'm thinking?' At that his mobile began to ring. He flipped it open without even looking to see who was calling. 'OK sis, what's it worth?'

Chapter 19

Ella wiped her hands down the front of the striped apron she'd found hanging on the back of the kitchen door. When she'd slipped it over her head, she'd detected a trace of Frankie's shower gel and it had made her feel safe, as though he were there with her instead of pacing up and down the pavement outside. They'd gone through it again and again that afternoon and the list was in her pocket. Frankie was at the end of the phone if she needed him. What could go wrong? Yet Ella felt like she was having to land a jumbo jet full of screaming passengers after the pilot's passed out, having never flown a plane before.

When she'd arrived earlier, Alex had hugged her warmly, which was a weird feeling in itself, because Ella hadn't done a single one of the amazing things Alex was thanking her for. They hadn't even met since that first day. Still, she'd been dead modest and said how much she'd enjoyed being with The Bean. That had stuck in her throat a bit, but even the old bag had seemed pleased to see her this time. She'd have to remember to pass the hug on to Frankie later. And now here she was, mixing up Pimms for a roomful of people who were expecting a three course dinner! Talk about flying by the seat of your pants. The most elaborate meal Ella had ever made was macaroni cheese from a tin with sausages that she'd grilled herself (and managed to burn). She looked around the immaculate kitchen – of course, Frankie had left everything nice and organised. She loaded the jug and glasses on to the tray and shoved her way out through the door. Saff and her tall husband, Max, were there already, along with a rather twitchy bloke called Gavin, Alex's boss apparently, who hadn't stopped talking since he arrived. The Bean had emerged from her room looking really pretty good for someone so old. She'd given Ella a little wink before sitting down next to Saff and kept going on about how 'brilliantly' Ella had been looking after her. Alex hadn't sat down and was hovering in a kind of awkward way with a bowl of Bombay Mix Ella had found in the cupboard and had been eating in the kitchen until Alex had pounced.

'Here we are, everybody. Get stuck in!' Max looked up and stared. Was that the wrong thing to say? Gavin had stopped in full flow while Saff seemed to be choking on something. Ella quickly dumped the tray on the floor and thumped her on the back until Saff waved her away. At the same moment, the doorbell rang and Alex rushed to answer it, Bombay Mix still clutched to her chest. It was probably the Yank boyfriend.

After standing looking round at everyone for a moment, Ella returned to the kitchen to tick off the next item on Frankie's neat list. 'Put green tray (cheese gougères) in oven for eight minutes. Take off foil first.' Easy enough, as Frankie had marked the different temperatures on the oven controls with coloured sticky labels that keyed into different instructions on his list, and she'd already set the oven to green. She looked round the covered trays and plates lined up along the kitchen surfaces for a matching green label and peeled back the foil to reveal little round blobby things. Yuk! In they went and Ella sat down for a moment to carry on with the Sudoku she'd started earlier. She really wanted to go in and get a look at this Todd, to whom Frankie seemed to have taken a violent dislike – although she wasn't sure why, or even when they'd met. It was most unlike Frankie to be so spiteful, so she was longing to see the cause of it.

The timer she'd set went off before she'd finished the puzzle, but she diligently laid it aside and opened the oven. Wow! The yukky blobs had turned into little brown puffs that smelt deliciously cheesy. She remembered what Frankie had said about using oven gloves and transferred them, without too much trouble, to the serving dish with the green label and helped herself to a couple before taking them out to the waiting company. Alex was sitting now, next to a beefcake of a man with unfeasibly neat hair that actually looked as if it had been coloured in with felt pen. He was holding forth, even giving Gavin a run for his money, saying something about 'global strategies'. The Bean was looking pointedly the other way.

'Can you clear some space, please?' Ella interrupted, slightly irritated to see the table cluttered up with glasses. Saff and Max obliged, moving them on to side tables and, although Saff seemed to be having that choking problem again, she'd have to sort it out for herself this time. The next thing on the list had been: 'PHONE ME', so Ella hurried back to the kitchen and picked up her mobile. Frankie answered on the first ring.

'Well?'

'Well what? I just served up the green things. They're yummy.'

Frankie sounded suspicious. 'How many did you eat?'

'Oh, only a couple. There were plenty left for everyone else.' She opened the kitchen door a crack and peeped through, then shut it quickly. 'They're eating them now. That Todd's a real gannet. He's taken a handful!'

'What's he like?' Frankie's voice sounded urgent.

'What do you mean? What's he like? You know what he's like. You're the one who told me he was appalling, remember?

You're absolutely right, of course. He looks like Gaston from Disney's *Beauty and the Beast*, don't you think? All kind of pumped up and clean cut with a really corny cleft chin. Bet he irons his underpants. Bet he's hopeless in bed.'

Frankie roared. 'Ella Ward! What a disgusting thing to say!' He paused. 'Do you really think so? What makes you say that?'

Ella shrugged and sipped the glass of Pimms she'd poured herself earlier. 'Women's intuition? Dunno really, you can just tell. I bet he keeps trying to catch a glimpse of himself in the mirror. Poor Alex! She wants her head looking at.' She glanced idly at the list. 'Oh shit! I haven't turned the oven up to red yet.'

At the end of the phone she could hear Frankie moan softly. 'Hurry up then. Do it now. You did put those chicken parcely things in earlier, didn't you? Don't take the foil off them yet though.'

'Oh shit, wasn't I supposed to take it off?' Ella smiled as Frankie started to yell frantic instructions, and held the phone away from her ear, peeping in the oven at the foil-wrapped parcels. She could never resist winding him up!

Twenty minutes later, red-faced and sweating, her good mood had evaporated. With the phone tucked under her chin, she was trying to shake carrots free from the bottom of a saucepan without any of the burnt bits coming away. The carefully reduced glaze of sugar, lemon juice, butter and stock had frazzled to a bubbling, tar-coloured sludge, which was so unfair because she'd only been distracted for a few minutes whilst trying to break the frozen peas into small enough chunks to fit in a little saucepan. The medium-sized saucepan was already being occupied by her personal supply of Pimms in the absence of another jug. Now the carrots looked and smelled rank. And

Frankie was barking instructions down her ear so she could hardly think!

'Well, how brown are they? Twenty per cent? Thirty? Are some of the carrots still stuck? I suppose you could make a salad ...'

'Frankie, shut up! Stop wittering. This is me you're talking to. Of course I can't make a salad. I'd probably burn that as well.'

'Look, there's some cucumber in the fridge. Get that out. Let's see. Avocados and tomatoes too. Just cut them into rough chunks, like dice, and stick them in a bowl. There's an earthenware one in a cupboard in the corner. And I left some dressing in the fridge in a jam jar with a screw-top lid. But make sure it is really dressing you use, not the jam.'

Ella threw open the fridge door. She'd seen that jam jar when she first arrived and Frankie had talked her through all the stages of preparing the meal. If only he could have stayed there, hidden in the broom cupboard as she'd suggested! She pulled out packages and containers careful not to dislodge the Tiramisu he'd proudly shown her. She'd have to remember to put tiny servings of that out, so she could polish it off herself later. It was hungry work, feeding other people. Ah! There it was.

'How are you doing?' The Bean stuck her head around the door and whispered theatrically. 'All fine out here. Terribly boring conversation though. How lucky to have that clever brother of yours down the phone!' And she disappeared.

With the bowl, the dressing and the ingredients, she was set. She turned off the oven and left the chicken to 'rest' as Frankie instructed. 'Bloody hell, it's me that needs the rest not the chicken.' And got stuck in.

Saff leaned close as Ella filled up her wine glass. 'Delicious starter, Ella.' She smiled broadly and winked. 'You must give me the recipe!'

'Any time!' Then, with the final two bowls, Ella shouldered her way through the door into the dining room. The conversation was about work – again. Max and Todd were talking, literally, over Saff's head about sacking people.

'Well, absolutely,' Todd was droning on in his East Coast drawl. 'You've gotta keep every single email and piece of correspondence, so you can make sure you have a watertight case for getting rid of personnel who aren't pulling their weight in the team. You've gotta be able to get rid of the dead wood. It's like surgery. You identify them, you isolate them, you discard them. Simple as that.'

Saff's face was going red, and her hair was starting to escape from the pretty clips Ella had noticed when she'd first arrived. She'd hardly spoken for most of the evening, except to The Bean and to thank Ella for things, but she sat up straighter now and cleared her throat. 'Todd, I can't believe the way you speak about people as if they're a disease. Did it never occur to you that the "dead wood" have families, bills to pay, problems of their own? You can't just "discard" people. It's inhumane. It's callous.' She turned to her husband. 'Max, tell me you wouldn't do that. Just toss people aside as if they were rubbish?'

Max was about to reply but Todd spoke over him, leaning back in his chair now with an amused look on his perfectly chiselled face. 'Let me guess, Sally, you don't work. Or if you do, it's some kind of caring role – volunteering or maybe working with kids or old people. Am I right?'

Saff nodded, looking so furious Ella thought she might explode or worse, burst into tears. She hovered by the kitchen door.

'I knew it.' Todd was nodding complacently. 'See, I can

always tell. It's fine for you to have all your liberal principles intact. And I totally respect that. I do. But they have no place in a competitive environment like ours. Back me up on this, Alex, Gavin, Max, am I right or am I right? The organisation is what matters, Sarah. Not the individual. If people don't fit right in – they're out. Simple as that.'

'Todd, her name's Saffron,' hissed Alex. 'And she does work – she's the greatest mum ever.'

But despite this, Saff's face looked all the more crestfallen. Ella moved forwards to the table, the dishes still clutched in her hands. She placed the chicken down carefully, and slammed the salad next to Todd then leant down next to Saff and whispered in her ear, 'He's a dickhead. Just ignore him. I'm going to spit in his tiramisu. And if you make an excuse to come out to the kitchen, you can as well.' This time, when Saff appeared to be choking, Ella just withdrew quietly to the kitchen and left her to it.

Chapter 20

From her position outside the café, Alex could watch the world go by and still see the doorway of the agent's office. She'd never been to Milan before, despite her increasingly encyclopaedic knowledge of Europe since starting this job, and it excited her. Well, Lord knows she'd had enough opportunity to explore it. Keen to get Bettina Gordino, the supermodel, on board to secure Donatella she'd spent what felt like hours on the phone to Bettina's intractable Milanese agent, Matteo Corniani. He had finally shown a chink of optimism that his adored client might just deign to do the launch, and she'd pushed harder. That was why she'd spent three hours so far this morning walking around the Italian city, killing time until the agent decided finally when he might honour their appointment to discuss 'dee possibiliteee'.

She sipped the scalding coffee, and wished she'd brought lighter clothes. London had been unseasonably cold for June and she'd been in such a hurry that she'd thrown in the first thing that came to hand – her 'important meeting' fail-safe navy blue skirt, a bit of a standing joke at the office. Now she felt sticky and bulky. She sighed, reflecting on how she could have done without this unscheduled trip. The last thing she needed, with only a few weeks until the launch, was to be away from the office but when Corniani had given her the amber light, she'd barked at Camilla to book her an early plane ticket, asking that she make the trip as brief as possible – twelve hours at the most

– so she could be back in London for the critical late afternoon press pre-briefing. She then checked with her mother that she'd be all right on her own.

'Oh Alex, this stress isn't good for you,' Camilla had said soothingly. 'You look all wrung out.'

'My, thanks,' Alex had snorted, though she knew she was right. Her mother had been telling her almost every evening when she got home that her hair was lank and her skin was pale, begging her to follow her example and take things easy. Over the last few weeks The Bean had certainly benefited from her diet of fresh air and day trips, but for Alex the opportunity to relax was laughable. Nor did it help that, despite giving Ella money to take her mother out – a ruse she hoped would keep her mother's spending in check – she had found a credit card bill stuffed in her mother's dressing-gown pocket. She knew from what she had been wearing at the dinner party that she'd obviously been shopping, but Christ! Did it have to be Sloane Street? It would have to wait until she was paid before Alex could settle up that one.

'I hope you've got yourself a holiday booked for when it's all over,' Camilla had asked during two minutes between meetings. 'You need a break.'

'Haven't even had time to think about it,' Alex sighed. 'Though Todd's mentioned going over to the States to stay with him, but frankly I've been on so many bloody planes recently I'd just like a week in Clacton. Actually Clapham would do.'

So, a morning in searingly hot Milan was a bit unexpected, and she felt displaced from where she ought to be, guilty that she hadn't managed to persuade the agent on the phone and concerned that when she did finally get to see him, he'd say no and it would all have been for nothing.

Two lattes and some expensive peanuts later, her mobile

finally rang with the summons across the road to Corniani's office, which had leather doors, was blissfully air conditioned and full of exquisitely beautiful women. They sat behind black desks and were preserved, like precious flowers, from wilting in the sun by venetian-blinded windows. All over the taupe-painted walls were moody fashion photographs of equally moody models, many of them Bettina herself. Five quid *her* hair never went lank, thought Alex sulkily.

Corniani, in shirtsleeves, perfectly cut trousers and shiny loafers, greeted her in a waft of cologne, and with as much warmth as he probably showed his cleaner. 'OK, she says she'll do it,' he barked at her in impeccable English once he was back behind his giant desk. He barely looked at her and certainly didn't ask her to sit down. 'She will arrive the night before from Rome and you will fly her first class. She can only give you an hour. A few things, she will only ever drink mineral water from Switzerland, and she also bathes in it. Make sure the hotel knows. She only stays at Claridges, of course, and only the Brook Penthouse suite. It goes without saying. And Irish linen sheets. My people will give your people the itinerary, including what she eats for breakfast.' He then mentioned the fee.

Bastard. Alex stepped out again into the sunshine. Bloody bastard. He could have told me all that over the sodding telephone, including the extortionate fee that would see a small African country out of debt. Alex hailed a taxi for the airport, so angry that she stared resolutely out of the window all the way there ignoring the driver's attempts to practise his English.

'Alex Hill,' she almost shouted at the check-in desk, and handed over her passport and tapped her fingers on the desk. The BA girl's eyes scanned the screen in front of her. 'No, there's no one of that name.'

'Flight for London? There must be!' Alex leaned round to

look at the screen and the girl put her hand over it protectively and frowned. 'I'm very sorry, madam, I have no one of that name booked on to the flight.'

When someone finally answered the phone on Camilla's desk it was Peter. 'She's gone out for her lunch break and her mobile is here on her desk. She said she was off to the dentist. Not another problem surely?' he drawled smugly. 'Anything I can do?' God he was irritating, with his constant desire to catch her out. She wouldn't ask for his help if she was on fire.

'Well, you could get me out of bloody Italy.'

'Oh dear. Are you stuck?'

Camilla wasn't back at her desk until after three by which point Alex was apoplectic. 'I did tell you, Alex, but maybe you weren't listening. I couldn't get you on the Heathrow flight from Milan Linate, so I booked you on one from Turin. It's only about ninety miles away. There was an airport transfer at eleven.' She paused. 'Oh dear, you must have missed that. I did explain that it was difficult getting the right flights at such short notice.' She paused again. 'You could try Milan Malpensa?'

Alex could feel the panic rising. 'Camilla, you'll have to cancel the PR briefing.'

'It's awfully short notice.'

It was and also very unprofessional. But someone had to be there. 'Can you handle it?'

'Oh, I'm sure I can,' said Camilla warmly and Alex, frantically scanning the departures board for some way out, outlined where her notes were and what she had been going to say.

'Cam, you need to stress the USP and of course the Bettina Gordino scoop. Big it up, Camilla.'

'Of course I will,' said Camilla. 'Trust me, Alex.'

Alex smiled and let her shoulders drop. 'Of course I do. You'll be great – better than I would be probably. Oh and Cam, call

Claridges and book the Brook Penthouse for the night before the launch. Call me later if you need anything else explaining. With a bit of luck I might just make it in time.'

She didn't. The woman at the Linate information desk had been so slow scanning flights that, when she eventually tracked one leaving soon from Malpensa, Alex had to leg it out of the terminal to squeeze on to a roasting shuttle bus. Couldn't these stupid idiots sense her haste? Just her luck to get the only un-aggressive driver in Italy. Seventy-five sweaty minutes later, she pulled up her skirt over her knees and dashed across the con-course to the check-in desk. To be told the flight had closed. She could try the information desk? *Ciao*.

Over there things were even slower and the queue slumped in defeat. Completely despondent now, Alex left a message on her answering machine at home to tell her mother she'd either be very late or would have to stay overnight. By the time the man in front of her in the information queue had settled his diatribe about his flight delays, the man behind the counter had lost interest and suggested she fly to Dublin, until finally tracing a flight which left shortly to Gatwick. Via Geneva.

Alex handed over her credit card and winced.

'Now concentrate, Saff dear. I've explained it twice already. That's called the Ante. It's the minimum bet that each of us has to put in before we can start a new hand.'

Saff shook her head and put two more matchsticks into the middle of the table. It had taken some persuasion to talk The Bean out of using real money – Frankie had looked panic stricken when she'd opened her purse – and The Bean had sniffed dismissively. To her this was clearly a Mickey Mouse poker school.

'Now, dears. How do we stand?' She peered at her tally

sheet over her glasses. 'Frankie, you have won two hundred thousand.'

Frankie groaned. 'God, I wish.'

'Saff? Good grief! You're up half a million. Must be beginners luck. Now I'll deal.'

The three of them studied their hands in silence. Saff's wasn't brilliant. 'What time is Alex back?' she asked as she sorted the pairs. These Poker sessions were so much fun, but there was a slight feel of unease in Saff's stomach.

'Oh till very late. Maybe not even until tomorrow. Some hold-up in Italy I gather. She left a message.' The Bean was peering intently at her cards. 'What a life that girl has. I do love Milan, though it's not a patch on Rome of course. I had the most divine Italian lover once ...

'Oi!' Frankie admonished. 'That's underhand tactics designed to put us off. For that you can make some more tea. Regard it as physio. And he added his matchsticks to the pile.

It had been a long time since Alex had folded herself into an Economy seat – business class being one perk of frequent travel – and by the time they'd landed, twice, she felt she'd gone long haul. She'd certainly gone the distance with the man beside her who was keen she know all about his battle with his weight – a losing one from where she sat – his Jack Russell called Madonna, and the problems he had in establishing relationships with women. It was early evening by the time she landed at Gatwick and, looking at her watch, she knew the meeting would be long over. She'd go straight home. She jumped on the Gatwick Express and, ignoring the request on the window sticker not to use her mobile and the filthy looks from the woman beside her, she tried Camilla, whose phone went straight to voicemail. Oh hell. Alex rubbed her eyes. She was so tired. This launch was really taking it out of her. Why did it all have to be so last minute? There seemed to be no time for anything. Ever. She felt guilty about her friends – thank God Saff was such a brick. She felt guilty about her love life, which was so sporadic as to be virtually pointless, despite Todd's demands. She felt guilty about work, because she hadn't been there when she should have been thanks to that precious agent, and she felt guilty that her relationship with her mother was reduced to a brief chat between coming home late from work and leaving early in the morning. It must be how some men felt towards their wives.

Alex looked out of the window. She had to tackle the money issue with her mother soon, but she knew that bailing her out was partly driven by guilt. If she was able to spend more time with her, not only could she keep tabs on her spending, she'd have a right to be tougher with her. By being so busy and employing someone else to care for The Bean, she had abrogated that right and was literally paying the price.

'You bastard!' screeched Saff, tossing another handful of peanuts into her mouth. 'I was sure you were bluffing!'

Frankie scooped up his matchstick winnings in triumph. 'It's the actor in me. I always thought I'd make a great James Bond. Now, who'd like a drink?'

Saff looked at her watch. 'I ought to go in a minute. The children will need picking up.'

'Surely you've time for a quick one? Oh, wouldn't a dry martini be heavenly! The most elegant drink, don't you think?' The Bean put her hand to her chest dreamily. 'I remember I had ...'

'Don't tell me!' protested Frankie, opening another bottle of white. 'You first drank one in Monte Carlo with Omar Sharif as he declared his undying love for you?'

'How did you guess?' she twinkled, and the three of them dissolved with laughter again.

By the time she turned the corner into her road, Alex could smell her own armpits and her feet hurt. She heaved against the flat door, glad she'd got back sooner than her worst estimate, the prospect of a glass of the coolish bottle of Sauvignon Blanc she had in the carrier bag from Rajesh's shop making her mouth water. She kicked open her bedroom door to dump her bag.

'Hi Mum,' she called over her shoulder, easing off her shoes and wiggling her toes. 'Sorry I didn't call again – nightmare of a day, total nightmare.' She padded over to the sitting-room door and pushed it open. 'I've been halfway round ...'

The tableau in front of her was like something from a Spaghetti Western: her mother in a white T-shirt and one of Alex's running visors keeping her hair from her eyes. Next to her, Saff, her hair tied up in a loose ponytail. And beside Saff, the man from the job interview, the one with the very distinctive face. They were all sitting on the floor around her coffee table which was strewn with playing cards, the contents of a box of matches and three full wine glasses. On each face was a whole gamut of expressions from disbelief to utter horror.

'This looks like fun!' Alex was wracking her brains, and couldn't work out what the guy was doing here – what was his name again? – and what was he doing with her mother? 'Are you leading everyone astray, Mum, teaching them to gamble?' she asked uncertainly, playing for time.

'Hello dear.' The Bean jumped to her feet now. 'We weren't really expecting you. Er ... there's no supper though I'm sure Frankie can get you some.' There was a pause, filled only by Saff's gasp.

Frankie, yes that was his name. But why would he get her supper? 'Has Ella gone home?' she asked the faces in front of her. All three were standing now and in complete silence, looking at Alex somehow expectantly. It was a look she hadn't seen since she was sixteen and had walked without knocking into her boyfriend's study at college to find him sitting very close to Lydia Adams. Something was deeply wrong.

'Ella doesn't come here, does she?' She had phrased the question before it had been fully formed in her mind.

There was no response, except Saff coughing quietly and shuffling her feet. Frankie was the first to speak. 'No,' he said, looking directly at Alex. 'No, Ella doesn't come here. She couldn't. She got another job. I'm her brother and I've been looking after your mother, and I have to say it's been a delight.'

Alex looked at her mother. Perhaps he'd lied to protect her for some reason. 'Is this true?'

'Well, yes, darling.' The Bean pulled off her visor and put it down next to the poker chips. 'But he's been lovely. We've had such fun, haven't we, Frankie? But Alex, we didn't want you to worry – you've got so much on darling.' She came forward and put her hand on Alex's arm.

Alex suddenly felt filled with utter fury. 'Don't touch me,' she said in as controlled a voice as she could manage.

The Bean snatched her hand away. Alex dragged her eyes over to Saff. 'And you? How long have you known about this?'

'Um.' Saff looked down at the floor. 'A while, but,' she looked up, 'not that long, and we didn't want to upset you—'

'Get out. All of you.'

Her mother put her hand out again.

'Get all you need and get out. I'll drop the rest round another time. Perhaps your new friend,' she spat, 'can drive you home. Now get out.' Alex had to get away and she walked into the kitchen, spying the remains of some sort of salad in a bowl on the side, covered in cling film, and the corkscrew lying with the cork still in it. Her corkscrew.

She braced herself against the worktop and breathed deeply, her head flooding with thoughts. They'd all known about it. The dinner party. They'd all known then. He'd changed her sheets, he'd ironed her underwear. He'd bought her tampons. She'd thought he was a woman.

Behind her she heard the kitchen door open. 'Al?'

'Go away, Saff.'

'But Alex listen ...'

Alex felt the bile rise and she turned. 'You've lied to me, Saff. You knew he was here – you knew I didn't want him here – Christ, you were here when I interviewed him and you still didn't tell me. What the hell do you expect? That I'd be pleased? Now get out of my flat.' She put her hands against Saff's shoulders and pushed her out of the door. '*My* flat – do you hear? It's mine.'

Scuttling like rabbits, they gathered their things – Saff her bag, Frankie his rucksack and her mother came out of her room with a hastily packed overnight bag. It would serve her bloody well right if she hadn't had time to get her precious make-up together. Then they stood by the front door, like children waiting to be dismissed from class.

Alex turned on her heels and stalked back into the kitchen, slamming the door behind her and waited, her heart pounding, until she heard the flat door close behind them. Then she picked up a wine glass from the side and hurled it at the wall. Damn them. Damn them all. She picked up the salad and ramming her foot on to the pedal of the bin, she lobbed the whole thing in, bowl and all. She looked around the room – the bag of peanuts half empty, the bottle of wine, plates that she hadn't eaten off stacked in the drainer. A life that had gone on without her. In her flat.

She felt violated. It had been a totally shit day, with everything going wrong at work that could go wrong, and what did she come back to find? Her best friend cosied up with her mother and a bloke she specifically hadn't given a job to. They'd lied. All of them. And there was her mother, a constant bloody drain on everything Alex worked her backside off to earn and who was now being looked after at Alex's expense, holding court as always and looking like someone from a speakeasy.

Alex realised she was trembling with anger. It was always the same. 'Alex won't mind. Good old reliable Alex. I'll take over her friends and laugh at her behind her back, and carry on buying sodding knick-knacks and backing useless horses as if I was loaded.' And all the time they had been making themselves at home in *her* flat, her poky little flat that was all she could afford after her mother had creamed everything to pay off her debts. But still, at least it was *hers*, and a place where she could be herself, as opposed to some ball-breaking exec or some has-been's daughter. Or the sad single friend of a yummy-mummy who has enough time to play poker all afternoon.

Picking up her bag she headed for her room and, as she passed, she caught sight of herself in the mirror. There she was, hollow-eyed and grey with fatigue, her hair lank, a crease of stress between her eyebrows. Who was this woman? Is this what she was working her arse off for? Too busy to live a life, with a second-division relationship and no one she could trust? She could see her lips start to tremble and she turned away in disgust.

Chapter 21

Frankie picked up the phone again, just to check it was working. He checked his emails again: a few offers for viagra or rather vi*a*gra, a cunning spam ploy his computer seemed powerless to repel. He sighed and looked round at the flat to distract himself. There was nothing left to clean or to tidy. Frankie tugged at his normally neat hair as he paced around the room, leaving it in spikes and tufts. Today's audition had been his big chance – maybe his one and only big chance. And he had blown it. He couldn't face anyone – not even Ella at the moment. Her perkiness just made it worse. And she certainly didn't understand how the whole Alex thing had thrown him. Apart from the obvious loss of income his dismissal caused, Ella didn't even see it was a problem. At breakfast that morning, she had been positively breezy.

'You could work in that cinema, like I did. You'd be perfect for it – you never fall asleep in films, do you? Always staying on to see the last boring credit, that's you! Just change your surname, perhaps, if you do apply. Anyway, look on the bright side. You've got more free time. You don't have to do that woman's ironing any more. And you don't have to hang out with that weird old lady. Yes, I know you liked her. That's cos you're weird too. But in a good way. See you later. Off to work, tra la la!'

Frankie sat down and tried to read the paper. He'd gone out to get it earlier as a way of trying to get the phone to ring but not even that had worked. Unemployment figures up! Great, even more people to compete with. Frankie thought again about the other actors who had been at the rehearsal rooms in St John's Wood going up for the part of the angst-ridden Joel. They'd clearly all had more experience, even after applying the bullshit formula. Frankie knew, because he'd done it himself, you could discount around thirty per cent of what anyone said, rising to forty per cent before an audition, and as much as sixty per cent if it was film or telly. He should just have left there and then, and not bothered to have humiliated himself. But after such an awful confrontation with Alex, everything The Bean had taught him had gone out of the window when it came to reading for the part.

Frankie pushed Alex out of his mind. He had his own problems and it wasn't as if he hadn't tried to apologise. He'd left three answerphone messages and had even written a letter. If she was too pigheaded to see that everyone had just been trying to help her and her precious career, that was certainly not his problem. But The Bean. Frankie stood up and started to pace again. He really had to go and see her, but he'd let her down too, and after she'd pulled so many strings to get the producer to see him. He caught sight of himself in the mirror. He looked bloody awful. Like a wanted man. If only he were! That decided him. He couldn't hide out here anymore like a housework obsessed desperado, cleaning and polishing while the world passed him by. He'd go out, take the bike and go to see The Bean. Perhaps she could cheer him up. Maybe, if he came clean and told her just how badly he'd messed up at the audition, they could go over it together. It would be painful, of course, but he might at least learn something.

Chapter 22

Ella sipped her coffee and resumed typing. She was definitely getting faster, although it would probably be physically impossible for her to type any slower. Was it possible to type backwards? She still couldn't do it, however, without her tongue sticking out, ever so slightly – a fact which Mike, the boss, had teased her about mercilessly. She heard him stirring in his lair. He had seemed grumpier than ever this morning and she didn't want to draw any more of his fire than she absolutely had to. Although she had learned by now that he was largely benign, at least to her. Even so, if he thought she looked in need of something to do, he might pull her off to go and do some photocopying or filing – both of which she hated. She quickly tucked her tongue back in and returned to the keyboard.

Of course, it really wasn't difficult for Ella to stay occupied in this job. She was loving it. She had always had a good memory for things people had told her, and now she found she could fit seemingly random facts together and turn them into a story – or at least the germ of a story – that she could chase up. And the fact that she was so small and young-looking made it easy for her to get talking to people, to hang around unnoticed and watch what was going on. People weren't careful about what they said when she was around. Like yesterday, when she'd stood watching that big four-wheel drive with the tinted windows parked on the pavement, engine running, a handwritten note on the dash saying 'We'll unlock your mobile phone while-u-wait'.

And now here she was, writing it up as part of her story about the increase in street crime in the area, and the irony of how criminals are providing a stolen mobile phone un-locking service for street thieves. Ella sat back and stretched, glancing around at the other desks in the room. Kerry had just arrived and treated Ella to a glare before sitting at her computer and checking through her emails. 'Oh! Now that's interesting!' Kerry did this a lot – making statements in the hope someone would ask her to expand. Ella gave her a scornful glance and shuffled through her sketchy handwritten notes to make sure she hadn't missed anything.

Luke came in, checking his watch against the one on the wall as he did every morning. God, he was tedious. Kerry spun round in her chair and greeted Luke with surprising warmth. 'Hi! Good morning and how are you today?'

'Er, all right thanks,' he stammered, his Adam's apple wobbling up and down as he swallowed nervously.

'Check your email. I've just had one from Lindsay. Bet she's copied it to you.'

Luke switched on his screen. 'Oh, do you think so? Let's have a look.'

Ella kept her eyes squarely on the screen, but was now listening to the conversation going on behind her. Lindsay was the woman she'd been called in to replace, all that time ago, when she'd just started that stupid job looking after The Bean. It seemed a lifetime ago now. She shook her head wryly. How long would she have been able to stick that out? God bless Lindsay and her bad back!

She jumped when her phone buzzed. 'Hello Mike! And what can I do for you?'

'Ella? In here now. We need to have a talk.'

Ella scowled as she replaced the phone. That didn't sound

good. He hadn't called her Lois, his usual nickname for her. This could only mean one thing. She sighed, picked up her notes and went through to his cave. 'Please God, no more photocopying. I'm better than that!' she groaned, as she perched on the chair in front of his desk. 'By the way, when I said God just then, I didn't mean you. Whatever it is, can we be quick, cos I want to get back out on this story. Any chance I could borrow your mobile?'

Mike hadn't looked up from the papers he was shuffling on his desk. When, at last, she trailed off he raised his eyes and stared at her for a moment. 'Sorry, kid. I'm going to have to let you go. I've just heard from Lindsay. She's been given the all-clear to come back.' Ella felt a sudden sharp pain in her stomach. He shrugged. 'Well, you knew it was only going to be for a while, eh?'

Her notes slipped from her hands and she dropped to the floor to gather them up. 'Oh well. Yes of course,' she jabbered. 'I'll be off then. I wanted to go, er, shopping anyway and I've got loads of things to do.' Her mind was racing. She stood up without looking at him, concentrating so hard on the pages crumpled in her hands that she didn't even hear him call her name as she rushed headlong from the room to gather up her jacket and rucksack.

Chapter 23

Saff dropped the clothes in the washing basket and opened the bathroom window. The heat today was stifling, with a humidity that wasn't even relieved by opening all the windows. Lucky Max would be sitting in an air conditioned office. He'd been so busy these last couple of weeks they'd barely had time to speak, and when he was home he was holed up in his study on some new investigative documentary project about benefit fraud. Or something.

Saff wiped some storm bugs off the window sill and looked out at the dry patch of garden. How lovely it would be to have a view of fields and to keep chickens, and to have a dog to walk in the woods. At least that would give her something interesting to do. Some friends had mentioned meeting for coffee at Starbuck's, but she couldn't face the inane chatter about holidays and children and men.

Slowly she walked into Oscar's room, the remnants of the morning discarded all over the floor, his pyjama bottoms lying in a pool on top of his slippers where they'd dropped as if he'd been propelled out of them. She sighed and leant down to pick them up. So dull, so boring to do this every morning. So stultifyingly tedious that each day was a landscape of the same tasks, broken only by the occasional highlight, and the other night playing poker had been one of them. They had laughed so much the three of them, and The Bean had been in her element teaching them both how to bluff. Then Alex had walked in.

Saff slumped on Oscar's unmade bed, her stomach clenching again as it had almost constantly since she'd seen Alex standing there in her flat doorway, her face so drawn and her eyes so questioning. They had done a terrible thing. They may have convinced themselves the Frankie deception was to 'help Alex out' but it had gone too far – she winced as she remembered the dinner party. She realised now they should have let on that Ella couldn't do the job and given Alex the chance to replace her. Frankie stepping in was only meant to be temporary, but instead he had stayed and it had become a sort of bonding joke. So much so they had actually forgotten about the feelings of the person they were deceiving. Shame on them.

Saff threw the pyjama bottoms on to the floor again. How could they have done such a thing? Alex was the most honest person she knew. She despised artifice which explained why she found her mother's expansive gestures and exaggeration so irritating. Knowing all that, how could Saff have put her oldest friendship in such jeopardy? She'd tried calling Alex at home but had got the answering machine. She hadn't bothered with the mobile because she knew her number would come up and Alex would ignore it. Even at the office her calls had been diverted to her assistant who kept saying she was 'away from her desk', a phrase Saff loathed.

Turning her back on Oscar's mess Saff made her way downstairs and, making herself a cup of coffee, went out to sit on the garden bench, surrounded by her flowering tubs, an urban apology for a garden. With a surge, she realised how lonely she was. The children were at school, too excited and busy to bother with irrelevancies like being tidy; Max was being important and needed; Alex didn't want to speak to her and she deserved that. Saff could hear her mother's voice in her ear telling her to pull herself together. Do some charity work. Visit the elderly. Join a committee. But Saff knew she couldn't find the energy or the enthusiasm. The phone rang in the kitchen.

'Hi Saff? It's Ella. Frankie got your number from The Bean for me. I hope you don't mind me calling?'

Saff smiled in surprise. She'd liked Ella when they'd met at the famous dinner party and despite everything was pleased to hear from her. 'No, no not at all.'

'Only I heard about the Alex thing and wanted to say … well, I'm sorry. It's probably all my fault.'

'It was all our faults,' Saff sighed. 'Mine most of all. Don't blame yourself.'

There was a pause. 'I wondered, if you're not too busy, are you free for a coffee?'

Saff laughed drily. 'I'm never busy.'

An hour later they were both sitting on the garden bench. 'Oh, this house is so lovely, Saff. It's a real home.'

'Is it?' Saff could hear the bitterness in her own voice. 'It's not much of an achievement just being a housewife.'

Ella nudged her. 'Hey there's nothing wrong with that, you know. People need lovely homes to come back to and people to look after them.'

Saff looked down at the cup in her hands. 'It's not so great when you are stuck in it all the time.' She looked at the girl beside her, envious of her youthful energy and optimism. For all the girl's scattiness, she was surprisingly thoughtful. It was she who'd noticed how condescending Todd had been at the dinner party, and any relation of Frankie's couldn't be all bad. 'I'm bored rigid,' she blurted out, surprising herself. 'What I need is something to do. A job, but one that I can do *and* look after the children cos I'd never earn enough to pay for childcare, not with my lack of skills. Besides …' She looked down again. 'I want to be here for them or what's the point?'

Ella tutted. 'Yeah, jobs. They're not all they are cracked up to be.'

'That sounds heartfelt. Yours not going well? I thought Frankie said you were enjoying it?'

'Yeah, well, it's not so much going as gone.' Ella too studied the contents of her coffee cup. 'The position I was covering – well, the girl had a bad back and now she's recovered and is coming back. Why couldn't she have had something serious, or at least something lingering?' Saff smiled at Ella's directness. 'For once I was really enjoying myself. Making calls, chasing stories, meeting people. I've had so many lousy jobs – really dead-end stuff like waitressing, flipping burgers, working in the sodding cinema – but I think they really helped. They seemed like preparation for the radio station because they made me able to talk to people. But more than that, I know what it feels like to be at the bottom of the pile, to have to sign on and justify yourself all the time. For the first time it was something I really thought I could do. I thought I could make a difference by covering stories that aired people's grievances.' She paused. 'And now he doesn't want me.'

'Who?'

'Mike. My boss. He's quite cute actually, in an old kind of way. No offence!'

There was silence between them for a while as they listened to a lawnmower in the distance, then Ella said: 'That's the best you can hope for isn't it?'

'What?'

'You know, that you can end up doing something you enjoy doing, even if it doesn't make a fortune. I mean, look at Frankie. All he wants is to act – and he'll put up with all sorts of rejection on the off chance he might find his dream, land the perfect role.'

Saff thought about the passion he put into his audition practice with The Bean. 'He could always cook if all else failed. He's brilliant at that.'

There was a pause, then Ella turned to Saff. 'That's it! That's what *you* should do. For money, I mean. Properly like. You'd love that!'

'What?'

'Cooking. Catering. Whatever they call it.'

Saff smiled at the excitement in the girl's eyes. 'That, Ella, is the crappest idea I've ever heard!'

Chapter 24

Over in Chelsea, things weren't looking much better. If anything, they were worse. The Bean had buzzed Frankie into her little mews house and had greeted him distractedly, but she was still in her peignoir, evidence of a scanty breakfast still at her elbow as she avidly watched on TV the efforts of two over-enthusiastic estate agents to interest a smart Asian couple in a house with three shower rooms and no bath. She barely took her eyes off it as he started to clear up around her. In the three days since Alex had sent them all packing, she seemed to have physically shrunk and was looking tired, rather the way she had that first day he'd met her. Until now, Frankie hadn't realised how much she had come on while she had been staying with Alex. The last time they had been there, she had been wisecracking, cheating wildly at poker, doing ludicrous impersonations of various actors and directors – until Alex walked in.

Frankie felt another wave of guilt. He'd spent the days since then fretting about that stupid audition when all the time The Bean had been at home, sinking back into her old, insular ways, bored out of her skull, missing her daughter, watching mindless daytime television programmes and neglecting herself. What had he been thinking? Suddenly the audition and his own miserable career seemed very insignificant. It wasn't just that he needed The Bean. The Bean needed him. But, independent as a cat, she would rather suffer on her own than admit she needed anyone or anything. An image of Alex came into his mind again, standing there furious, white and trembling. 'Get out, all of you!' He wondered, briefly, if she regretted what she had said. Probably not. And who could blame her?

Frankie shook himself. Alex was not his problem any more, but The Bean … right! Time for some acting. He took the remote from her hand and knelt down in front of her, looking seriously into her still-lovely face. 'Bean, let me be frank, as opposed to Frankie, for a moment.' She smiled sadly and refocused her eyes on his. 'This is not good. I know it's going to be more difficult for us to see each other, now you're back home, but I still need your help. I'm pretty sure I messed up the audition, big time. And, to be honest, I've been too embarrassed to tell you. But do you think we could talk it through, so you can help me work out what went wrong and how I can put it right next time?'

The Bean leaned forward in her chair. 'Messed it up? You can't have. With your talent? You'd better tell me all about it.'

Frankie hid a smile. OK, so it was going to be painful to dredge up his humiliation, but The Bean was hooked. 'Well, I will, but could we go for a walk? I'll find it easier to talk, and maybe we can get a bite to eat? There's that nice café in St James' Park. Or perhaps we could go to the RA. There's that exhibition on you wanted to see.'

The Bean unfolded herself from her chair and stretched. 'Yes,' she purred. 'That would be lovely. Tell you what, I'll have a shower and get dressed and you make me a cup of tea. What do you say?'

Frankie grinned. 'Your wish is my command!'

She disappeared into the bathroom and Frankie tidied the old fashioned little kitchen, which looked no more lived-in than when he'd dropped her back the night Alex found them all. Even though the little flat was crammed with things – every

155

inch of the wall covered in pictures from *Spotlight* and framed cast lists, every table littered with beautiful ornaments, oil paintings in ornate frames leaning up against the walls – none of it seemed used. A museum to a better past. It was obvious to him now; The Bean needed people around her. All that had been wrong with her when she first moved in with Alex was that she had been starved of company, and preferably admiring company. With even a little attention, she had blossomed. Sitting there with no make-up, watching crap TV, she had atrophied again. All his good work over the last few weeks had been for nothing. He could hear her high-pitched warble as she washed and he looked around again at the small, unused pans, the single cup teapot and the mug turned upside down in the drainer. This was too sad, and even if he was the last person she wanted to see, he had to speak to Alex. If that work-obsessed, career-driven woman couldn't see how lonely her mother was, then maybe Frankie would have to tell her.

Chapter 25

Alex deleted Saff's apologetic text without even reading it. It was the fifth one she'd got from her. She'd started to read the first two and then couldn't bear any more. She tossed the phone back into her bag.

Things were wonderfully quiet tonight and she'd been able to have a shower, then eat ice cream out of the tub and have total control of the remote for the first time in ages. Her mother had called, leaving a message on the answering machine asking how she was, but Alex had ignored the interruption. They could all go to hell, she thought defiantly, and poured herself another glass of wine. She channel hopped for a while, but it was all rubbish about D-list celebs making exhibitions of themselves, so she cast an eye over the flat. Her things were everywhere, a pile of this evening's running kit on the floor in front of the machine, washing up on the side from breakfast. There was even a layer of dust she could see on the coffee table. The order of the last few weeks had disappeared, but then so had her mother's presence, which was a relief. In its way. And anyway, things being so tidy all the time had begun to get on her nerves.

She looked at her watch. Only ten o'clock. Bliss. Perhaps she should make the most of having an early night? Lord knew she could do with one. Slooshing water over her face and cleaning her teeth, she slipped into a vest top and knickers and, turning off the hallway light and pulling the door of her mother's now-empty room closed, Alex climbed into bed and picked up her 'to do' list. She still had to settle the order of interviews with the main stars appearing at the launch, and there was the relentlessly pushy woman from *Today*! Magazine to deal with who would not give up until she had secured an exclusive with Bettina Gordino. Alex ticked various things as she scanned down the list. So much still to do. She could do with some rest.

Half an hour later she was still lying on her back and listening to the noise of a barbecue in a distant garden. People shrieking with laughter. How selfish. The bed felt rumpled next to her skin, not smooth and cool as it did when the bed had been made up with fresh sheets by ... by Frankie. Alex turned on to her side and punched the pillows violently to plump them up. Oh well, it was a pain that she'd have to change them herself now but all good things come to an end. She sighed and closed her eyes.

Damn him, damn her mother and damn Saff, she railed fifteen minutes later as she stood in the kitchen, dropping a tea bag into a cup. Most of all, damn Saff. Her mother had always been tricky. So mercurial. Everyone else seemed to find her endlessly entertaining – even Frankie had clearly fallen under her spell – but to Alex it was shallow, done to impress people, done to be adored. And who was left sorting out the chaos she left in her wake? As for Frankie, well she didn't know him. He was good-looking all right, but an actor? God help her! He was probably as precious and difficult as The Bean or the sports stars she spent her time mollycoddling. Alex helped herself to the last flapjack in the tin. OK, so he could cook but what did that prove? So could any fool.

But it was Saff's deception that really hurt. If she couldn't trust her then who the hell could she trust? They'd known each other since they were in pigtails, they'd shared boyfriend pains,

Alex was godmother to Millie (and about eight other people's children, but such was the lot of the unmarried thirty-something – people always imagined being a godmother would somehow compensate for not having your own).

Alex tipped the remains of the cup into the sink, rinsed it out under the tap, and turned it up on the empty drainer. If she couldn't trust anyone she'd just row her bloody boat on her own and, slamming the bedroom door behind her, she slumped into bed.

'Right, Cam, a meeting!' Alex knew she was barking orders but there had been an early text from Gavin the next morning wanting an update, and it had unnerved her. Why was he asking now? He'd never done that before. 'Gavin is on the warpath,' she explained, turning on her computer as Camilla sat down on the chair opposite her desk.

'I know – I was in early and he was hovering around your desk, looking at your papers.' Camilla tapped her pen with her teeth. She looked very fresh and quite tanned in white T-shirt and pink cotton capri pants.

Hovering? That was out of character for Gavin. He was twitchy, yes, but he never *hovered*. Alex felt her stomach clench. What was this all about? 'Did he ... did he say anything?' It didn't seem right to sound so paranoid but she had to ask and Camilla would know what she meant.

'Well, he sort of asked me for an update. I said we had everything under control for the event, of course, but I have to say,' she lowered her voice, 'I've never seen him like this before. It's as if ... well, I don't know how to say this, but it's as if he sort of doesn't trust it to go without a cock-up.'

'Mmm. Well, we've had our glitches but let's just make sure nothing else goes wrong, hey?'

Alex dealt with some pressing emails and was about to call Maurice the caterer for an update when her phone rang. 'Alex, it's Rowena.' Alex's heart sank. The *Today!* journalist was not so much a terrier for a story as a Rottweiler. She came straight to the point without her usual gushing preamble. 'Can you assure me of Bettina Gordano? Only I thought you said we would get an exclusive and now I hear that *Scorch* have secured it ahead of us. You know I asked about this straight after the PR briefing the other day – of course, you couldn't be there which was a shame, but I was assured by Camilla she would be ours.'

'Well.' Alex finally managed to stem her flow. 'I haven't been told about this. I'll get back to you.'

'What do you mean I *was* told?' Alex could feel the panic rising as she asked Camilla a moment later.

'I told you that *Scorch* had made an earlier play for the interview the morning after your Milan hitch. Don't you re-member?' Camilla frowned with concern. 'Oh Alex. I said it the same time as I mentioned the *Express* wanting to talk to Malcolm Sanferino for their American Football special. Have you not done anything about it?' She paused and looked at Alex's aghast face.

'Oh bollocky bollocks.'

'You'd better make some calls before Gavin gets wind of it. I'll call the *Express* for you if that would help?'

'You are an angel,' Alex gulped, and dialled *Scorch*.

She managed to pacify them and was being savaged again by the Rottweiler when Peter dropped a note in front of her that read 'launch running order?' and walked off. Camilla mouthed to her, and pointed to her watch theatrically. Alex raised a questioning eyebrow.

'Meeting. You haven't forgotten have you?'

Holding the phone slightly away from her to protect it from

the Rottweiler's vitriol at her lost exclusive, Alex flicked up her schedule on her PC. There it was: 11.30 at the launch venue in Brixton. Holy shit. But that was supposed to happen tomorrow. Wasn't it?

'What in God's name is going on?' Gavin wasn't even seated and fidgeting – his normal stance. This time he was standing over her desk, hands on hips and voice raised for anyone to hear. There was silence in the open-plan office, and Alex could see out of the corner of her eye that people were hovering, pretending to do things.

'You're missing interview requests, press briefings, and now venue meetings. Great, yeah, you got Gordino but what bloody use is she prancing up and down if we fuck up the publicity for her? And missing the *Express* Sanferino exclusive ... that is just bloody ridiculous.' How had he known about that? Alex wondered fleetingly.

This was torture. Alex looked across the room at anyone who caught her eye and looked away quickly. Could she just resign now, walk away and perhaps join the Foreign Legion so she would never have to see any of them again?

Gavin leant over her desk and said quite quietly now, 'If you screw this up, Alex Hill, I won't so much murder you as skin you alive. My arse is on the line here and I will sacrifice yours to make sure I'm OK – do you understand?' Alex couldn't look at him. 'Now just get out of here and we'll talk about it tomorrow.'

By the time she had got home and slammed the front door, she was ready to punch someone. What in God's name had happened? She was usually punctilious about things – obsessive even – and, when it really mattered, things were going wrong? She didn't need Gavin to tell her how important this launch was. Did he need reminding that this whole thing had been her idea? It had been she who had suggested an apparel line that people could wear as normal clothes, a classics range that would cross cultures and sexes and leisure pursuits – and now not only was it about to go tits up, it suddenly wasn't her idea at all. Gavin had purloined it and made it his own. Alex began to make herself a cup of tea but, when she opened the fridge, there was no milk. Damn. Bloody bloody damn.

She dialled Todd's number. He'd be in the office now. 'Hi, it's me.'

'Hi babe. Everything OK?' His voice, all the way from New York, sounded close by.

'No, not great.' Alex slumped down on the sofa. Through the kitchen door she could see the dirty running kit from yesterday still festering in a pile.

'Mmm I heard.'

Alex sat up. 'What do you mean?'

'Well, I had a call from your right-hand girl. I gather Gavin has asked her to contact all the press to confirm interviews. I asked her what the problem was – well, knowing you has to have some advantages,' he laughed deeply, 'and she just said there had been some glitches.'

'Glitches?'

'That's what she said, babe.' Alex hated the way he called her that. A babe she wasn't. 'You have made sure all the US interviews are lined up, haven't you? I mean I've made some pretty firm promises, Alex and I can't afford to have screw-ups.'

Well, thanks a bunch for asking how I am, thought Alex, reassuring him as convincingly as she could and terminating the call, claiming she had another call to deal with.

And indeed she had. For the next two hours texts and calls came in, including one from Maurice explaining some hold-up with fruit delivery for the statue, one from the factory in

Turkey wanting information about Bettina Gordino's size for her special apparel for the launch, and one from Camilla asking if she'd passed the press-pack copy which had to go to the printer. Alex had and said she would email it over, but half an hour later she was still looking for the file on her laptop. It had been there yesterday. She went through her history. Where was the goddamn file? Camilla called again. 'Give me a minute,' Alex said, trying to hide the panic in her voice.

'Alex, they have been on the phone twice already. They need it now. It's a complicated bit of binding apparently and they say if they don't get it tonight it's going to be touch and go if they can have it proofed and printed in time. Would you like me to try and put something together here?'

'No,' she said, more violently than she meant to. 'I'll sort it out and get back to the printers direct.' Alex had the intense feeling that her life at that moment was like trying to hold on to a slippery fish which was fast escaping her grasp. She could see it swimming away from her and she would be left on the bank with nothing in her hands. She felt sick. If she had lost this document then she would have to rewrite it and pronto. So, without even blinking she sat on the floor in front of the coffee table with her laptop in front of her and set to, trying to remember what on earth she had written in the press pack the first time around.

The doorbell interrupted her thoughts a little while later. Alex looked at her watch – it was a bit earlier than she would normally be home so who on earth would know she was here? 'Hello?' she asked irritably, picking up the intercom handset.

'Alex, it's Frankie.'

Frankie? What did he want? 'What do you want?'

His voice crackled into the flat. 'I think I might have left a sweatshirt of mine on the back of the kitchen door, and I've still got your key which I wanted to drop back. Would you mind if I ... if you're not too busy?' Reluctantly she pressed the buzzer.

'I wasn't expecting you to be home actually.' Frankie ducked his tall frame in through the door.

'So, what were you going to do?' Alex asked sharply. 'Just let yourself in?'

Frankie at least had the decency to look sheepish. 'Well, yes actually. I thought you might never let me in to get it and it is one of my favourites, so I was going to collect it and then drop the key back through your letter box ...' Alex was aware he was some way taller than she was. Standing in the close proximity of the hallway made it feel even smaller. His pale blue T-shirt had a surfing logo on the front. His shorts were beige and, glancing quickly, she could see his legs were strong and lightly hairy. She looked up into his face. She couldn't quite make out the colour of his eyes but she thought they were brown and flecked with gold.

'Bloody cheek. But then you're good at that, aren't you? Just doing things without people knowing. I suppose you'd better come and get it – seeing as how you know my kitchen so well.' She turned into the sitting room and stood with her arms crossed not trusting herself to say anything else. Frankie walked passed her hesitantly into the kitchen and she kept her eyes firmly on the rug in front of her.

'Er.' He came back through, the sweatshirt in his hand. 'You may have noticed that the little control button has come off the toaster. I was going to mention it but ...'

'But what, Frankie?' she said, louder than she meant to. 'You were going to put it in one of ... She almost said 'our' but it sounded too intimate. 'One of your little notes. But I happened to turn up didn't I, and mess up your little ménage à trois? How inconvenient that must have felt, hey Frankie?' She moved closer to him, trying to cover up the urge to howl and rail at him with anger. 'Do you know what it feels like to be fooled Frankie? And by people you trust?'

'Frankie's voice was low. 'No, no I don't. I'm sorry.'

'Sorry? Do you think sorry really covers it Frankie? Am I meant to thank you for getting the washing machine mended? For doing my washing? For ironing my knickers? Can you imagine what a violation that feels like?'

'Alex, Ella couldn't do it – she got the job she'd been dying for, and your mother needed looking after.'

'Oh yes, Ella. She played along beautifully, didn't she? And the dinner party. In my house! People I'd invited and half of them were in on the little joke, weren't they?' Oh God, Max too. She'd forgotten about Max. 'Were you hiding in the broom cupboard? Were you, Frankie?' She hadn't realised but she was holding on to his arms. She dropped her hands quickly.

'No. No. I was outside.'

'Christ.' She turned away.

'Alex,' he said gently after a moment. 'I know what we did was unforgivable but all I can hope is that I helped. It is my fault about Saff. She turned up one day, and we asked her not to mention it because we knew that you'd fire me and she knew your mother needed caring for. I think she still does. I think she needs …'

Alex turned on her heel. She could feel a tear slip down her cheek and brushed it away irritably. 'Yes, Frankie she needed caring for, because –' careful Alex – 'because my mother always needs things. She takes up all the emotional oxygen. You can be stifled if you stay around her too long. You may have had the pleasure of her company for a few weeks, but there are things you don't know about her and I will be the judge of just how much help she … needs. And you don't happen to be the person who I employed to help anyway.' Alex stopped herself before she went too far. 'Now, I don't have time for this. I have a press pack to write, for the second sodding time as it happens, for an event which is probably the most important in my career and which is rapidly turning into a massive disaster.' She sunk down into her previous position in front of her laptop and turned determinedly towards it. 'Now please leave.'

Frankie stood there towering above her for a moment, looking at her very intently, then turned and went quietly out of the front door.

The flat was very still and, she admitted grudgingly, felt strangely emptier than ever.

Chapter 26

Frankie pulled the door of the building closed behind him and turned into the road. Well done, you idiot, that went brilliantly. The perfect and unexpected opportunity to talk to her about how dejected her mother had been looking and he'd blown it. Her mind was clearly made up about The Bean and all he'd done was make her more angry. He shook his head. It was none of his business anyway. Why should he play peacekeeper? He kicked a Coke can violently across the road and headed home.

He could hear the phone ringing as he struggled with the lock. 'Hello?' he gasped, grabbing it from where Ella had left it on the sofa, and listened to the rasping smoker's voice at the other end. 'They want me there when? Yes, St John's Wood again? Yep, no problem. Any particular piece they want prepared? Yep, yep, OK. I'll be there. Yeah! I know. I can't believe it! Thanks, Marina, you're a star!'

'Er, no, Frankie,' his agent replied, but he could hear the smile. 'That'll be you. And Frankie, just do whatever you did last time. They obviously liked it, so stop putting yourself down, OK? And if you could land the part, I'd be most grateful as I could do with a holiday on the commission! But I won't book it just yet, hey? In case I lose my deposit!' And she laughed so much she was reduced to a coughing fit.

Thanks for your vote of confidence, thought Frankie replacing the phone, and then stood staring at it for several seconds before letting out the most jubilant whoop of excitement, and embarking on a frenzied victory dance around the flat. He suddenly had a feeling that anything was possible. He'd have to call Ella. He'd have to call his dad. He'd have to call The Bean. He'd have to call Saff. He even felt like calling Alex, not that she'd want to hear from him. But maybe if he did, she'd realise that things could turn around for her as well. And, really, if it wasn't for her, he'd never have met The Bean in the first place, and he wouldn't be in this situation now! Maybe he'd even send The Bean some flowers. Yes, that's what he'd do. She'd like that.

Chapter 27

'Bloody hell, not another cake, surely?' Max leant over her and kissed Saff's hair. 'Oh God, you're not pregnant are you? Or are you just trying to fatten me up so I lose all my cred as a babe magnet?'

Feeling foolish suddenly, she briskly dropped the wooden spoon into the washing-up bowl and turned over the note pad on which she'd made some jottings. 'No, no – just had a bit of time on my hands so I thought I'd try something out that's all. Some banana cake …' She trailed off when she saw he wasn't listening and was opening the phone bill on the kitchen table. She wiped her hands on her apron and went to the fridge. 'Can of lager, darling?'

'Mmm,' he murmured absent-mindedly. 'Christ, this bill is huge. It's all that gassing to Alex and people you do during the day.'

'I bloody well do not – it's when you're working from home, that's what cranks it up.' Saff slammed the can down in front of him. 'Anyway, Alex is flatly refusing to talk to me.'

Max looked up. 'Is she still pissed off?'

Saff peered through the oven door at the rapidly rising cake. 'She must be. She won't answer texts or voicemails I've left. I've even left a message with Camilla at work, who promised to ask her to call me. I don't know. It's all a bit sad really. She just won't see that we didn't mean to be malicious. We just wanted to keep The Bean happy and help Alex …'

Max took out a stack of Pringles from the tube in the cupboard and put three at once into his mouth, then wiped his hand on his trousers. 'You can't really blame her, Saff love. It was pretty deceitful, and you should know by now, no one gets one over on Alex, which doesn't really explain that tosser of an American she's seeing.'

'No. Her taste in men always has been a bit dodgy – they're all scared witless by her.'

With Max safely upstairs saying goodnight to the children and persuading Oscar that his mother was right and he *was* too young for an air rifle, Saff slipped the cake out of the oven and inserted a skewer. It came out clean so she turned it out on to the cooling rack, and took a sniff to absorb the sweet aroma. Tentatively she cut into it and popped a piece into her mouth. The light brown sponge was warm and moist on her tongue. And bland. Saff frowned. Something was missing. Ten minutes later Max found her poring over a pile of cook books she'd pulled from her shelf to scour other people's recipes. On her pad she'd jotted down a couple of ideas but there was nothing very different. Nothing unusual.

'Crikey. This looks serious.'

Saff pushed her reading glasses up on to her head. 'Yup. Cakes are. The right cake is one of life's treasures.'

Max reached for another can of lager in the back of the fridge. 'Yeah maybe, but why the research all of a sudden?' He pulled back the ring pull.

Saff still wasn't sure she wanted to reveal the tiny idea that was forming in her head, thanks to Ella. It was stupid anyway. 'Oh, just ideas for Millie's birthday.'

'Bloody hell, that's thinking ahead. It's not till October.'

Saff shut her book and sighed. 'Yes. Silly really. Supper won't be long.'

'OK. I'll just have a quick look at this script I was given today. Give me a shout when it's time to lay the table.' And he left the room.

Script. That reminded her. Tomorrow was Frankie's big day. She'd been delighted to hear the excitement in his voice on her answering machine.

'Hi Frankie, it's Saff.'

'Hi there.' He sounded genuinely pleased to hear from her.

'I just wanted to wish you luck tomorrow. Give it your best shot.'

'Oh thanks. Yes. Yes, I will, though I've got a cat in hell's chance.' He sighed deeply. 'It's such a lousy way to make a living.'

'You'll be fine. Have confidence and remember all your lessons from The Bean. Project daarling!'

Frankie laughed deeply. 'That reminds me. I dropped by Alex's yesterday. I was hoping not to see her but she was there. It was a bit difficult really.'

Saff felt her stomach clench. 'Still angry?'

'Yes, still angry. And she seemed very stressed too – something to do with this launch she's organising.'

'She's always stressed. Alex seems to be faced with issues that us mere mortals will never experience.' A thought struck her. 'Why did you go back, if you don't mind me asking?'

'To collect a sweatshirt. I'd left it there in the hurried exodus. Anyway, let's not dwell on that ... what are you up to?'

'Oh, not much really.' Now he might have an idea. 'Frankie, what can I add to banana cake to make it more ... you know, interesting?' There was a long pause and Saff suddenly felt very stupid and very embarrassed. The man had a major audition tomorrow and she was discussing baking ingredients.

'I had a girlfriend once,' he said eventually. 'Strange girl.

Had an unhealthy obsession with animal welfare. She kept terrapins in the bath. But, anyway, her mother was lovely and she was a fantastic baker. Now what was it she added to her banana cake? I know, pistachio nuts. Fabulous!'

Saff thought for a moment. 'Frankie, you are a genius, and the finest actor ever. Knock 'em dead!'

Chapter 28

The following afternoon Frankie was back in the theatre's rehearsal rooms in the same church hall. Considering what starry casts the company usually had, it was a tatty old venue, but maybe the anonymity suited them. It wouldn't do to be mobbed by fans when they were just trying to do a job.

Frankie pushed his way back in through the thickly painted doors into the dim light, such a contrast to the bright sun outside, and was greeted by the casting director he'd met last time. Highlighted hair, too young for her leathery, tanned face, fell from a chignon and, once again, she was dressed in layers of washed-out linen and had a knobbly cardigan slung around her shoulders, in spite of the warmth. She tucked her hair back behind her ears and ticked him off the list. 'David's in today,' she breathed. 'He flew in yesterday but he's still terribly jet lagged.'

Frankie nodded, and tried to look pleased but his stomach cramped up with panic. David Herschmann was known to be enigmatic at the best of times. Perhaps that was the privilege of a successful Hollywood actor turned theatre director. With a case of jet lag, he'd be positively gnomic. Frankie sighed. Herschmann anecdotes were legion on the circuit, and he racked his brains to try and recall some of his weirder pieces of direction. 'More space around it!' was one that had stumped his casts. 'Can you do it all faster, but kind of slow it down?' was another. Well, if Frankie could be a banana, he could be anything! He went to sit down on one of the stacking chairs lined up in the hallway, nodding cautiously to the other two actors there before him. They were both television regulars and he could almost hear them thinking, 'What's HE doing here?'

The minutes ticked past. Frankie closed his eyes and tried to remember everything The Bean had taught him, about drawing people's eyes to him just by being stiller, about imagining himself filling up the space and pushing against it. The character Joel was a complex one and, although he wasn't the lead, it was a fantastic part. He'd seen Daniel Day-Lewis do it once, and his burning intensity when he realised he'd been betrayed by his girlfriend and his best friend had been mesmerising. Yet Frankie didn't just want to produce a copy of that performance. He shifted on the plastic chair. He was starting to feel agitated again and struggled to bring his attention back to what he was about to do. The last few days had been such a roller-coaster of emotion, it had thrown him completely.

The other two actors were called in, one after the other. The first one was only in for just over five minutes, the second one for more like fifteen. Was that better or worse? Frankie braced himself. If they didn't like him enough for Joel, perhaps they would still consider him for a walk-on. They wouldn't have cast those yet. Should he ask? No, no. That would look desperate. Frankie looked at his watch again. It was nearly three minutes since the last bloke had left. Maybe they'd forgotten he was there. Maybe they weren't going to bother seeing him at all and they'd already decided. That second one had been pretty good in *The Bill*. Maybe …

'Frankie? Would you come in now, please?' The head disappeared back through the door and Frankie stood up slowly.

Two hours later, Frankie was back in Chelsea in The Bean's cool sitting room. 'So, I went in and it was quite dark, and

Herschmann was sitting there in a great big armchair, leaning right back as if he was looking at the ceiling with his legs stretched out. He didn't even look at me.'

The Bean tutted. 'Honestly, these power games. I find it all so tiresome. I hope you waited until he sat up properly. That's what I would have done.'

Yeah, right. 'Well, when I'm as famous as you, perhaps I will but just for now, I think I'm better off playing the game, don't you?'

'Never mind all that.' The Bean gestured irritably at the chair opposite her. 'Get on with it. What did they say? Did you read straight away or did they ask you any questions?'

Frankie lifted a pile of unopened envelopes from the chair and put them on the table next to him. 'Bean, don't you ever open your mail? I don't know how you can bear to just leave it.'

'Oh, it's just tiresome stuff. I open anything that looks interesting. Now get on with the story, or I shall burst!'

'Right, where was I? Oh, yes. The casting director did all the talking. Herschmann kind of murmured his instructions to her, just turning his head sideways. It was weird.'

'And was anyone else there? Anyone watching?' Bean helped herself to a slice of the fruitcake Frankie had found in a flowery tin in the kitchen. 'Here,' she commanded. 'You try some, too. Saffron made it. It's very good, I think.'

Frankie broke off a piece and nodded in appreciation. So that pinch of salt had worked! The Bean was almost on the edge of her seat with impatience, so he continued. 'Yes, the producer and there was someone with a digital camera recording it all. They did ask if I minded, but I thought I couldn't really object.'

'And? And?'

'Well, I did it the way we'd rehearsed, you know. It was pretty similar to the way I did it in the last audition, because I thought if they liked it that time, they'd like it again.'

'Yes, yes. And did Herschmann say anything?'

'No, not at first. I thought he might be asleep, because it was quite dark in there. They'd closed some of the curtains. He was just rolling his head from side to side on the back of his chair. And then suddenly, it was so unexpected I nearly laughed, he sat right up and stared at me really hard. And he said, "Listen, you're giving me too much. You've just discovered you've been betrayed by the people you trust most in the world. Your life has no more meaning. It's like they've reached down inside you and ripped out your heart. I want to hear the sound of that emptiness within you." So I stopped for a bit ...' Frankie faltered. How could he tell The Bean that at that moment, he'd seen Alex's devastated face before his eyes. He'd seen how, that moment when she'd realised what was going on in her flat, she'd struggled, not wanting to believe what her eyes – those big, hurt eyes – were seeing.

The Bean thumped him hard on the leg. 'Frankie, if you don't tell me what happened this instant, I shan't be responsible for my actions!'

'Oh, right. I ... I toned it down completely, as if I could make it not true just by refusing to see it. It was quite different to Day-Lewis, but d'ya know? I think it kind of worked.'

There was a moment's silence. The Bean looked sceptical. 'So you didn't do it the way we rehearsed?' She looked slightly miffed and Frankie answered carefully.

'I did – first of all. But when he asked me to try something different, I just adapted it. That was right, wasn't it?' Frankie suddenly felt uncertain.

The Bean brushed invisible lint off her sleeves. 'Well, I

suppose it was good in a way that Herschmann asked you for a different interpretation. At least he's seen your range. Well, let's hope he likes your look. Even if they don't use you in this, they'll remember you. I'm sure they will.'

Frankie felt deflated. He cleared up the tea things and took them to the kitchen, glad to be on his own for a moment. As he dried and put the little china cups away, he opened a cupboard to find more of the brown envelopes he'd seen on the chair. On impulse, he picked one up. Through the address window he could see red print. He picked up another, unopened, but from Barclaycard. And another, and another. Frankie felt himself go cold. The Bean was ignoring her bills. And still spending like the man who broke the bank at Monte Carlo, from what he could tell by the parcels, carrier bags and canvases piled up in the hallway.

Did Alex realise? Should he tell her?

Chapter 29

'Look, Alex, it's me again. I know you don't want to speak to me, but I'm finding this very upsetting and I need to talk to you. To explain.' Saff stumbled on, determined not to cry. She looked hard at the Florentines cooling on the side. She wasn't sure how much recording time Alex had on her machine so she'd have to talk fast.

'Alex, I really thought what we were doing was for the best. You have more than enough stress at the moment without The Bean on your plate.' Saff almost laughed hysterically at her pun. 'I do know what she can be like, Alex. Remember that awful, wet holiday in Prestatyn when we were ten? She was more bored than we were and sulked in her room. God you were a saint that week ... anyway, that's all I wanted to say.' She trailed off, not knowing if she could trust herself now.

'And I miss you.' She put down the phone.

Chapter 30

They met on neutral ground. Going to the flat again to see her didn't seem right, and Frankie didn't even suggest it. Neither, he noted, did she. She'd been surprised to hear from him so soon after their confrontation at her flat, but hadn't hung up on him, as he'd feared. And when he explained that he wanted to talk about The Bean, she'd agreed straight away. And now here they were at Palace Gate in Kensington Gardens, just standing looking at each other after an awkward hello. He realised with a jolt that she was waiting for him to explain why he'd called. The early evening sun was slanting through the trees, but was still warm enough for Alex to have removed her jacket. Frankie steered her into the park and over to a bench and they sat together. She seemed as self-conscious as he felt, so he didn't waste any time.

'Look Alex, you made it clear you don't like me, or trust me, or want anything to do with me, but I think you should know something. The thing is, I went to see your mother yesterday and, well, I found some unopened letters – lots actually and I think they're probably bills. I didn't say anything to her. Well, I didn't know what to think. I mean, I've got no idea what her circumstances are but, well, I just thought you should know, and since you don't really ever go to her place, I thought you might not realise.'

Alex stared at him for a moment, blinking fast. Was she going to slap his face? Shout at him again? Frankie sat back and looked straight ahead at the children and dogs and lovers and old men walking by. He was preparing himself for an explosion, but none came. Instead he felt, rather than saw, Alex slump back as if she'd been punched. 'Oh no!' she breathed. 'We're not in this nightmare again!' Frankie turned to her. She looked quite exhausted. There were violet smudges of exhaustion under her eyes and a crease between the eyebrows that looked as though it might not go away. She shook her head slowly. 'I knew, actually. Or at least I suspected. This isn't the first time, you see.' Alex hesitated and looked down at her hands. 'Well, I don't suppose there's any harm telling you. You know most of it already. She's basically broke. Despite all the money she made and the residuals and everything, she's cleaned out. Has been for years, but she doesn't seem to realise – although, God knows, I thought I'd explained it after last time. Luckily her house is mortgage free, but basically ...' She paused. 'I pay for everything else.'

Frankie sat back again heavily. God, he'd had no idea. The Bean had always acted as though money were no object. And Frankie – in spite of the heat a cold sweat swept over his skin as he remembered – had aided and abetted, driving her to the bookies carrying the parcels and canvases around Brighton, giving his opinion on her choice of party dress in Harvey Nicks on one of her shopping sprees, as if it were all a game. Now he felt sick at the thought. 'You mean, she's done this before?' he asked feebly.

Alex's shoulders sagged and Frankie could hear her draw a slightly unsteady breath. 'Yes. I expect she hasn't really stopped, although she promised last time she'd try to.' She rubbed at her face with her short-nailed hands. 'I haven't even finished paying off the debts she racked up last year. I expect it's my fault, really. She's got no idea about money – never has had. I adored my dad, but after he died I discovered he had bled her dry, investing in one crazy scheme after another, but they always lived it up. Winters in the south of France and handmade shoes. He acted as if he was the heir to a fortune or something. The great playboy.' She waved her hand dismissively. 'He left nothing but debts and I spent the next two years selling the few shares he had left and a couple of nasty flats in Gateshead which he was convinced would be the "next big thing". Mum just carried on as before. I should have taken more time to explain, shown her the figures. But she was never interested, you know?' Alex turned beseeching eyes on Frankie and he hardly dared move in case it broke the spell of this outpouring. 'I couldn't bring myself to tell her the whole truth at first.' She looked down at her hands again. 'She always made me feel dull because I worked out if I could afford something before I bought it. And now,' she laughed shortly. 'Now I can't afford anything because I'm having to pay for what *she* buys.'

Frankie hesitated. If it had been anyone else but Alex, he'd have put a comforting arm around her shoulders but, given her recent hostility towards him, it didn't seem quite right. Sitting hunched forward on the bench, lost in her worries while the rest of London seemed to be out to enjoy the sunshine, she seemed so unexpectedly vulnerable that, rightly or wrongly, Frankie gave her back what he hoped was a reassuring rub. Underneath the fitted cotton vest top, her skin felt warm and firm and Frankie snatched his hand away, probably too quickly. But Alex didn't seem to notice.

'It all hinges on this sodding launch,' she murmured, and Frankie leaned forward to listen. 'If only I can pull this off. Oh! I don't know what's wrong with me!'

'You mean the women's apparel thing? What's up with it? I thought it was going brilliantly.'

She looked at him in puzzlement for a moment, then tutted and said, pointedly, 'Oh, of course. I keep forgetting. You have the advantage, don't you? After all those notes I left you when I thought you were someone else altogether. Well, you've missed out on the latest instalment in my thrilling life, I'm afraid. Due to a series of absolutely elementary mistakes by none other than yours truly, the whole thing keeps unravelling every time I turn my back, and now my job is on the line because my boss thinks I'm incompetent – and just when I really need a promotion and a huge pay rise.' She lapsed back into silence, scowling straight ahead of her and shaking her head occasionally as though trying to work something out.

Frankie kept quiet, hoping to convey sympathy without actually saying anything. If Alex wanted to confide in him, it would have to be on her terms. So he waited. And waited.

'The thing I just don't get is, how?'

'Sorry?'

Alex had spoken as if to herself, but she continued, turning to him so preoccupied by what she was enumerating on her fingers that she'd forgotten her resentment. 'I know this is going to sound crazy, but it's almost as if someone is messing with my arrangements on purpose. At first, I thought it was all just coincidence or me being too busy that I didn't have time to check on things. But it's not like me. The one thing I am is thorough – it's my greatest failing, according to my mother.' The undisguised bitterness in her voice took Frankie by surprise and he looked sideways at her, wondering if it was quite genuine. An expression of abject misery on her face told him all he needed to know, and besides, Alex was not the sort to fake anything. Looking at her now, Frankie wasn't sure she would be capable of it even if she had to.

'How do you mean? Messing with your arrangements? Do

you think someone is trying to sabotage your plans?'

'Oh, I know it sounds paranoid, believe me. That's why I haven't mentioned it to anyone. But things are going so pear-shaped, that's the only conclusion that makes sense.' Frankie wasn't sure what to say. It sounded such a far-fetched idea. Alex gave him a sharp look. 'You see? Not even you believe me. But it's not like me to be suspicious, or to look for conspiracies. You, of all people, should know that.'

'Ouch! Point taken.' He smiled ruefully. 'But you don't think maybe the whole thing with me and Ella might have made you suspicious of everyone, just for a bit? I mean, have you got any real evidence, or any idea who might do something like that to you? Cos it's quite a risk for someone to take, isn't it? I mean, presumably they could lose their job if they were found out?'

Alex snorted and shook her head. 'The only person in danger of losing their job at the moment is me. And if I can't get the better of whoever it is, I'll be out on my arse – particularly if the launch goes wrong. And at the moment, it's looking horribly as if it might. There's so much that has to be perfect – the model, the styling, the press, the venue, the catering, the security, the transport. It's almost endless. And that means there are almost endless opportunities for him to ...' She trailed off.

'Ah, so you *do* have a suspect! Who is he?' Frankie could feel himself getting interested. 'Why don't you tell me what's happened so far, and I'll tell you what I think?' Frankie had turned sideways on the bench now to face Alex, one leg tucked up under him, as he quizzed her.

Alex looked back at him, unsure at first, then slowly started to list the problems she'd had, hesitantly at first, but with more confidence as Frankie nodded, paying close attention to the details of what she was telling him: '... and then there was the flight. It should have gone from Milan Linate ...

183

Frankie listened, fascinated by her face as she talked. The shapes she made with her mouth and the way she faltered and bit her lip then rushed on as an idea occurred to her. It was all so unaffected and real. 'Well, the first thought that occurs to me is . . .'

'Yes?' Alex was leaning towards him, her lips slightly parted. Frankie forced himself to look away.

'. . . That you could do with an ice cream? If we walk up here a bit, we can get one outside the playground.'

Alex flopped back against the wooden back of the seat and laughed for the first time that afternoon – possibly the first time since Frankie had met her. And the transformation was remarkable. She still looked tired and stressed, but her smile curved her cheeks into little dimples that reminded Frankie forcefully of The Bean in her youth. He judged it best not to mention that, however, and stood up offering a hand to Alex to pull her up after him, which she ignored or didn't notice, and they walked slowly along the Broadwalk, side by side, while they discussed the possibilities. To anyone passing by, Frankie thought, they must look as though they were on a date. Ridiculous though it was, just that thought made him feel taller and he experienced a protective surge towards Alex, who was gesticulating as she explained the complexities of office life, and the various players who featured in her daily grind.

By the time they reached the kiosk by the Elfin Oak, Frankie was struggling to keep up with the cast of this drama, and he stopped gratefully under the awning while Alex chose an ice lolly. From the nearby playground, they could hear the excited shouting of children scrambling over the pirate ship, and hiding among the tepees in the Indian Village. They sat down together at a table under an umbrella.

Frankie shook his head and took a bite of his ice cream.

'If only it were like *Peter Pan*. There's never any doubt about who the baddy is there. I don't suppose there's anyone at your office that wears a black hat and runs away if he hears ticking, is there?'

Alex smiled and shrugged. '*Peter Pan* isn't such a simple story, you know. Captain Hook pretends to be nice to the children at first, and he plays on the fact that their father is a bit mean to trick them. The children have to work out who really has their best interests at heart. And there's that whole thing between Wendy and Tinkerbell, too. Wendy trusts Tink, but she tries to kill her. Surely you remember that bit?'

Frankie was interested in her analysis. 'You clearly have a better grasp of the plot than I do. Of *Peter Pan* and your office dynamics, I mean. I'd really love to get in there and watch, like a fly on the wall. That would be fascinating.' Frankie sat back for a moment, watching the passers-by. Gradually, an idea started to take hold. Yes, of course. It was obvious, but would she agree? Saff's comment about Alex's fearsome independence replayed in his head. He sat forward and clasped Alex's wrist. She simply had to agree. It made perfect sense. 'Alex,' he said, his voice hoarse with excitement. 'I could help you with this. I could. Hear me out then tell me what you think.' 'I am an actor. Allegedly!'

Chapter 31

By the time Alex got back from work the following evening, Frankie was sitting on the wall outside the flat as they'd arranged. She could see his tall figure as she rounded the corner, he was scuffing something on the ground with his foot and in his hand was an ice lolly. She slowed down for a moment before he spotted her. Was this really such a good idea? They had gone from confrontation to collusion in the space of twenty-four hours. Could she really trust him?

He smiled as she approached him and held up the lolly rather apologetically. 'Sorry, I'd have got you one, only I wasn't sure how long you'd be.'

Alex dropped her bag on the doorstep to dig out her key. 'What a lovely idea – but, frankly, I could murder a glass of wine.'

Frankie put his hand inside the small backpack he was carrying and whipped out a bottle with a flourish. 'Ta-dah!' He followed Alex up the stairs and she found herself holding her bag behind her to cover up her bum. She'd been in work so early this morning she'd thrown on a pair of her most comfortable but most unflattering cotton trousers.

'Um – I'm just going to change,' she said, as they both sidled into the hallway. 'Why don't you open the bottle. The corkscrew—'

'Is in the left-hand drawer?' Frankie smiled cautiously and Alex felt herself smiling back.

A quick wash, a brush through her hair and a fresh T-shirt and comfortable shorts later, she joined him. He had opened the windows to let in the warm evening air – an over-familiar but still rather touching act – had poured two glasses of wine and was waiting, looking down at some papers she'd left out on the table; ideas she'd scribbled down late last night when, again, she'd wrestled with sleep. She went to cover them up, but Frankie put out a hand to stop her.

'You're clever, aren't you?' He looked at her, an inscrutable smile on his face. 'I mean, this is a great idea – a range for older people. That's what it is, isn't it? Did you come up with that?'

'Well, yes. It was after seeing Mum look so much better for getting out and walking.' Alex paused. 'I suppose I have you to thank for that. But it was something she said about not being seen dead in sportswear. The way it was all young stuff – tight Lycra and crop tops. Anyway ...' She scooped up the papers into a pile. 'It's very hush-hush at the moment so I'd be grateful if ...'

'Alex, I know you have no reason to, and it's an odd thing to say after everything, but you *can* trust me, you know.'

Alex sat down on the sofa, reminded once again of why they had made this arrangement to meet. This was one hell of a risk they were taking. The atmosphere in the office all day had been cagey and suspicious. Gavin had been over every few moments checking up on progress, Peter seemed to be hovering around and quizzing her about issues which weren't really his field, and Alex had even found herself talking on the phone to the dentist's receptionist in hushed tones. 'What's up?' Camilla had asked at one point, and Alex had laughed.

'Oh I'm just being a bit paranoid. Ignore me!'

'Nothing to worry about is there?' Camilla had looked over her shoulder alarmed.

'Just being a bit careful – that's all.'

Alex took a sip of the cold wine now. Proper stuff, not Rajesh's best this time, and she let the fruity flavour roll over her tongue. 'Frankie, I have to be able to trust you.' She realised she was leaning forward earnestly to him in the seat opposite. 'This job, and especially this launch I am coordinating, means everything to me. And it's not just because of the need to bankroll my mother. It's mega in terms of sportswear marketing because it's a whole new concept in apparel. It's like …'

'Getting a part in *Eastenders*?' Frankie enquired gently.

'Oh, more than that! Hamlet at the RSC at least! Put it this way, this business is so incestuous that if I fuck up the launch everyone will know and the only marketing job I'll get will be selling tea towels door to door.' She tucked her hair behind her ear, shuddering at the thought.

'So, what can I do?'

Alex glanced up into his face. He was looking right at her with an expression of such open honesty that she wondered why on earth she hadn't employed him in the first place to look after The Bean instead of his airhead sister. She wasn't surprised he and her mother had got on so well. 'Tell me – just by the way. What sort of things did you and my mum get up to? I haven't … well, I've been too bloody cross to ask, to be honest.'

Frankie looked surprised and he started to jiggle his knee, clearly uncomfortable admitting to what went on behind Alex's back. 'We would go to the park or walk by the river. We did the Tate modern, the Wallace Collection and shopping of course … And we went to Brighton one day.'

'That would explain the shells.'

'You found them?'

'Yes, she left them on her dressing table. So, did she regale you about her glorious youth?'

'Yes, quite a bit. Does that annoy you?' He didn't sound accusing.

'No, Frankie. It doesn't annoy me, but I've heard it so many times, I could probably have taken you there and given you the tour myself. You see, people don't seem to understand that it's no great shakes being the child of a famous person. The adoration just passes you by – she's just my mum – and when I was little I never really understood what all the fuss was about. I mean, wasn't everyone's mother on the front of magazines and in the paper? I suppose it had its good bits though. I've met some pretty amazing people over the years. Anyway … let's get on. Do you really think you can carry this off?'

Frankie shrugged and put his empty glass on the table. 'In my time I've acted Malvolio, a naked drug addict in a New York alley, a banana, and a central heating system, so I should be able to manage this. Who do you want me to be? Don't make it too highbrow though because I still call trainers "pumps" and playing five-a-side is only an excuse for a pint afterwards.'

It was hard to tell what sort of shape he was in when she only ever saw him in baggy T-shirts but he might be able to convince people he was sports-aware. 'Well.' She rolled the glass in her hands, uncertain about what she was going to say. 'I've been mulling it over all day. Obviously I can't bring you in as an expert because they'd rumble you straight away, especially Peter who is the world expert on airflow trainer systems. It needs to be something he's not familiar with.' She ran her fingers through her hair thoughtfully.

'Does your photocopier need an overhaul?' Frankie asked brightly. 'I did Xerox maintenance for a while around Bexley Heath when I was resting after doing Pinter in Weston-Super-Mare.'

'Sadly not! I think it's on contract,' Alex laughed. 'What other highly skilled work have you done?'

'I sold tea towels door to door.'

'You didn't!' Alex put her hand to her mouth in horror.

'Not exactly but not bloody far off at times.'

Alex felt ashamed. The worst job she'd ever done was to work behind a bar when she was a student. 'I'll pay you for this, you know?'

'No, you won't,' he said firmly. 'You have enough demands on your resources at the moment, and besides, it's the least I can do after the last few weeks.'

Alex smiled. 'Yup, you're damned right! Now, how about this: you work in events coordination, and you have taken time out to do an MA or a thesis on corporate marketing. I'll have to check you can do that.'

'Alex, these days you can do a thesis on chicken shit.'

''Spose so. OK, so you have contacted me, and me being so forgetful and all, I forgot to tell anyone you were coming in. So you have come to shadow me and the department in the build-up to a big event. That's it! What do you think?'

Frankie looked thoughtful for a moment. 'Yup, I think I can do that. Give me some phrases can you? Keywords to drop in.'

Alex sat back in her seat, beginning to enjoy herself. 'Well, of course there's the venue, and we talk about apparel not clothes. Let me see, we have brand design, brand awareness, and the lot putting it all together – the hammer and nails people – is our Travel and Events Team. There will be press packs – well, you know about them already – and we're going to give the press memory sticks with all the information on. You'll need to ask about volume and feedback, and look earnest.'

Frankie stood up and pretended to hold a clipboard theatrically. 'Does this look right?'

'No, it looks ridiculous.' Alex realised she had giggled and blushed. Get a grip woman, this was important. She sat up. 'No, you need to ask lots of questions, about delegation, and guest follow-up et cetera. If you are doing a study, that gives you the excuse to talk to everyone about their job and their role. You'll have to follow up a lot of red herrings. By the end you'll be an expert! Camilla will help you about who to talk to. She's my assistant and she's great. She doesn't know about this yet, but I don't mind if you tell her. The one I really want you to keep an eye on is Peter. He's got most to gain by undermining me and if I were fired, he'd be right up there to take over my department too.'

Frankie sat down again but sat forward listening intently. His eyes sparkled. 'OK.'

'I will be in and out of meetings for the next few days, but they are mainly with outsiders so not much help in finding out if Peter is trying to put an almighty spanner in things. You are better staying in the office.'

'Where and when's the big launch?'

'At that big dance venue in Brixton. Do you know it? The one where all the hip-hop artists go. Very "now" apparently – though not my kind of place – and it's ... God! Next Tuesday, and at nine in the morning to give us half a chance of getting a mention in the lunchtime press.' A flood of things she still needed to achieve gushed into Alex's head. 'There's no time and so much to do!'

'Don't panic. I'll be there in the morning. Scribble down the address for me.' Frankie dug into his backpack again and pulled out a thin black diary. Alex gave him the address and the nearest tube.

'Now, what do I wear?' he asked.

'Wear?'

'Yes.' He smiled as if it was obvious. 'If I'm playing a role I need to have the right costume. I mean, this won't do will it?' He indicated what he was wearing.

'Well, we all sort of dress down really but perhaps not as down as you look – no offence!' She laughed at his outraged look. 'I mean, it's all about sportswear so no ties and jackets. Very American I suppose. Jeans, chinos, a T-shirt. You saw what I came home in. Well …' She looked away, out of the window, embarrassed. 'You know what sort of clothes I wear anyway.' She could sense Frankie looking at her hard.

'Yes, yes I do and I'm sorry about that. I realise it must have been an imposition.'

'I don't usually let men look at my underwear unless invited to.' There was silence. Did that make her sound like some kind of tart? Frankie knew about Todd so it wasn't as if – Todd! His shirt would be perfect. Alex jumped up. 'I think I have something that might be right. Todd left it but he won't mind.' She went to her wardrobe and pulled the shirt down from the hanger. It was crisp with sharp creases and must, ironically, have been ironed by Frankie before he left. 'What about this?' She held it up as she came back into the room and his eyes lit up in surprise.

'I didn't think that was yours.' He took it from her and held it against himself. 'Mmm, should be the right sort of thing.' He started to take it off the hanger. 'I was wondering – sorry, rude of me to ask I suppose but that … that green organza dress in your wardrobe. I couldn't help seeing it. Have you ever worn it? It looks new.'

Alex laughed. 'Oh that! My mother made me buy it for a first night we were invited to *years* ago. No, I only wore it once. Shame really because in true Mum style it cost the earth. I think it's by someone posh.'

'Ungaro, I think,' said Frankie quietly.

Alex shrugged. 'I'm not very good at those sort of labels. Actually, I can't remember the last time I wore a skirt.'

'That's a shame too,' said Frankie even more quietly. 'You'd look beautiful in it.'

There was a very loaded pause between them, and, unable to stand it any longer, Alex jumped to her feet. 'Now, if you'll excuse me, I have to get on.'

Frankie stood up slowly and picked up his bag. 'Right, I'll see you tomorrow. Do you think I should give myself another name? Miles – or something?' They both laughed at the random choice.

'I'll only forget and call you by your real name. There's enough to remember as it is.'

Frankie nodded and turned to go, but stopped, his hand on the door knob. 'Alex, I have to say it's odd being with you.' He didn't look up. 'Spending time with you, I mean.'

Alex felt her face become hot. 'Is it?'

'Only, I've been so ... familiar with you and your things without knowing anything about the real person. For what it's worth, it's been fun.' And with that, he left the flat.

Chapter 32

'Come on then.' Ella picked up the basket off the kitchen table. 'Let's go and tickle the taste buds of the deli owners of South London. Show them what real baking should taste like.'

'Oh God, I'm not ready!' Saff could hear herself squeak. She felt sick with nerves.

'You'll be fab. That banana and pistachio is to die for. Good on his ex's mother – at least it wasn't a total waste of Frankie's time. The flapjack is divine too and the Florentines. Well, if we don't get going I'm going to eat them. They will love you. Grab my phone will you?' Ella made for the door and Saff, grabbing the mobile off the table and her bag, scuttled after her. She felt exhausted, having spent the last hour trying to keep up with Ella's random thought processses. She could jump from subject to subject with more agility than even Millie and that was saying something. While Saff had baked and Ella had 'helped', a process which involved asking where everything lived and sticking her fingers into bowls, they'd covered topics ranging from nail polish, to Mike her old boss, to softball, subjects which had somehow blended seamlessly together.

Before getting into her little car, Saff repacked the basket and secured it more firmly in the boot than Ella had, who was now sitting in the passenger seat and going through Saff's CDs, cataloguing them as 'good', 'crap', 'never heard of them'. It made Saff smile. Oh the ignorance of youth. She did however declare her Fat Boy Slim CD to be 'bangin' so Saff didn't let on it was actually Oscar's.

'Right, where first?' Ella turned in her seat, her lime-green dungaree shorts, striped T-shirt and outrageously over-the-top dark glasses making her look like a cross between Dame Edna Everage and a latter day punk rocker.

'Well, looking at you, I don't think Harrods, do you?'

Ella pulled down the sun shade to squint into the little make-up mirror. 'I don't know. I think I look totally cutting edge. The new face of cakes.'

Saff snorted. 'OK, where do *you* think we should start?' The car was stiflingly hot and beginning to fill with the smell of baking. If they weren't quick, the chocolate on the Florentines would begin to melt and her offerings would trickle off the plates.

'What about that lush-looking place on Northcote Road? The ones that sells those yummy sandwiches and criminally over-priced crisps. How can anyone charge that much for fried potatoes? And the chutneys! Have you seen them? These guys are charging about six quid for something my gran used to make! Bollocks, I call it.'

'Quite,' said Saff, and pulled out into the traffic. She felt racked with uncertainty. Ella, who wasn't really the one putting herself on the line, was so confident and had talked all morning about how all the local delis and cafés would demand her baking and in no time: 'Just you wait, you'll be rushed off your feet and Max will have to make do with a Pot Noodle for dinner'. At first her enthusiasm had rubbed off a little bit on Saff, who began to believe it was entirely possible that she made the best flapjacks 'on the planet', but now, the reality of what they were doing hit home and she felt stupid. These people would think she was some homely, bored wife trying to make a bit of pin money selling the odd cake. And they'd be right. She wasn't cut out for this.

'Sorry – it's Max's car that has the air con,' she sighed, opening the windows front and back.

Ella pushed her sunglasses on to the top of her head. She looked flushed and pretty. 'It is scorching isn't it? I had a holiday job once in one of those farm parks. You know, the ones with rare breed sheep and cafés called the Granary or some nonsense. Anyway, it was boiling that summer and I had to rub sun cream into a pig.'

Saff smiled. 'You'll be ideally suited to marriage then.' She looked sideways at Ella and they both snorted with laughter.

'Oh, your Max isn't too bad. Look at him for example.' Ella pointed to a fat bloke on the pavement wearing a white vest, football shorts, sandals and socks. 'You could have ended up with that in bed next to you every night. Ladies and gentlemen, I give you the great British male. Rock god and babe magnet.' Winding down the window she put her fingers between her lips and wolf-whistled so loudly everyone on the pavement stopped what they were doing to turn and stare at the two women shrieking with laughter in the small blue Renault.

Round the corner, Saff pulled into a parking space and turned off the engine. 'Right, we're here.' She let her hands fall into her lap and looked in terror at the racing-green painted shop front of the deli, with its luscious baskets of fruit and vegetables outside, small bay trees in wooden tubs and an A-board sign advertising organic ice cream. On the window was written in white paint a mouthwatering list of goodies sold inside. The whole place had an air of such confidence and conviction.

'Ella, it was sweet of you to be so encouraging, but I don't think I can do this.' She turned beseechingly to the girl next to her.

Ella looked at the shop for a moment, then turned back to Saff. 'The thing about life is, Saff, if you don't make the opportunities, no other sod is going to give them to you. That place is probably run by some ex-public schoolboy with a double-barrelled name and a tiny todger. You could run rings around him. What's the worst he can say? No? Go on Saff. Give it a go. And if he turns you down, we'll eat the lot and go to the pub.' And leaning over Saff, she pulled the handle to open the car door.

Chapter 33

Frankie thought he could probably get used to this kind of life. If he'd been able to relax about the audition, he might even have enjoyed it. The air conditioned offices, constant meetings, conference calls and working lunches all had a kind of glamour because they were so unfamiliar. He had been shadowing Alex closely for the last two days and the more time he spent with her, the more amazed he was by her command of the endless stream of figures that flowed over her desk and by the agility of her thoughts, and her confidence in covering every facet of the launch. What he was less confident about though was that there was someone out to get her. As hard as he tried, he could find no evidence of it. If anything she was treated with respect.

In the lunchbreak, Frankie had started cultivating friendships with other employees, hoping to gauge their attitude towards Alex. It hadn't been too hard, because as far as anyone knew he was completely new to the company with no prior connection with Alex at all. The intricacies of office politics were not so unlike the jockeying for position he'd sometimes encountered in the theatre, although it seemed a bit more subtle here. He was suspicious of everyone, despite Peter being Alex's Suspect Number One but, so far, no one had come into work wearing a black hat. Accordingly, he rolled his eyes just a little when Alex asked him to do a batch of photocopying, smiled wryly when she sent him to retrieve her notes from another office and hesitated just long enough when she got up and expected him to follow her out of the room, hoping to flush someone out. He had to look willing, as a student would, to acquaint himself with every part of the business but he had to give just a hint that he felt some of what Alex was asking him to do was beneath him. The hardest thing, so far, had been treating Alex with polite indifference. That was almost beyond him, and he feared he might be going a little over the top by way of compensation.

Late last night on the phone, they had analysed the day's events, raking over them for clues but Alex had seemed distant and a little distracted. It was too much of a risk for them to be seen together, though, so they arrived and left separately, and never ate together at the office unless someone else was there. Frankie was pouring coffee in the small kitchen when Gavin zipped in. Alex's description of him as a hyperactive, spoilt toddler was absolutely spot on.

'Ah, good! Making yourself at home, I see. Got your feet under the desk all right? Bit of a busy time for us so hope you don't mind if we just let you get on with things. Just observing aren't you? How's Alex treating you? Not too much of a slave driver?' God, this man spoke in nothing but clichés.

Frankie smiled warmly and prepared himself to speak the same lingo. 'Yes, thanks Gavin. I'm really enjoying the challenges of working in this environment. Everyone's been very welcoming. I really appreciate the opportunity to be a part of the team, especially at a time as crucial as this launch.'

Gavin paused significantly. Any pause had to be considered significant with Gavin. 'Yes, yes. How's Alex today? I haven't seen her yet. I need her to give me the heads-up on how things are going. If you see her in the next few minutes, can you ask her to drop by? Nothing major, nothing major. Just want to touch base, y'know. Actually, I'll go and see her now.' And he darted out again.

Frankie picked up both mugs and wove his way through the desks to give Camilla hers. She smiled warmly at him and indicated a pile of print-outs. 'Thanks Frankie, you're a life-saver. Those are the running times Alex prepared for the meeting today. I've just tidied them up for her and done a spread sheet. I think she wanted them distributed beforehand so everyone could look over them. Do you want to grab a copy?'

Frankie frowned at the pile. 'Bit short notice, isn't it? Did you have to come in early to get those together?'

Camilla shook her head, setting her blond ponytail wagging. Her pretty face reminded him of a girl he'd been in love with at primary school. 'Oh, only a bit, and it's no trouble at all. I think Alex wanted the very latest data and that's fair enough. Alex is so on the ball. So thorough! Here, can you drop a copy in to Peter as you're going past? He's just over there.'

Frankie gave her his best smile. 'Course I can. Anyone else on the list? I'm heading thataway.' He indicated the corner conference room with the double black doors.

'Oh yes, if you don't mind. I've labelled the copies. Thanks, Frankie. That'll save me a few minutes.'

'No worries. Hey, what are you doing for lunch today? I thought I might go out and get a coffee that didn't come in corporate polystyrene. Whadya say?'

Camilla tilted her head on one side and considered Frankie for a moment, then smiled slowly. 'Yeah, why not? In fact, I'd like that. But it'll have to be a quickie. I shouldn't be away from my desk for too long. Actually, maybe I'd better check with Alex first, OK?'

Frankie smiled and nodded, then walked briskly away with the copies. Peter put the phone down quickly and stood up as

Frankie stuck his head round his desk partition. 'Yes? Are you looking for someone?' He looked tanned and fit. Alex had said he looked 'hungry', and she was right. There was something nakedly ambitious about him. Too obvious a suspect?

Frankie grinned disarmingly. 'You! I've got the details for today's meeting. Alex thought you might like to look them over first.'

'Oh, did she now? And who are you? Her new messenger boy?'

'No!' Frankie hoped he didn't sound too defensive. 'I'm doing a thesis ...'

'Oh yes?' Peter's eyebrows were raised. 'Another professional student. What's this one about then?' He crossed his arms and waited.

'Strategic planning. New European model.' Frankie tried to sound assertive.

'Sounds like bollocks to me,' Peter snorted. 'Who's it for?'

Frankie blanked. 'Er, The Beckett Institute. I'm studying under Professor Godot.' He held his breath, aware his eyebrows were frozen someone near his hairline. Please God don't let this man know anything about the theatre. There was a long pause.

'Right.' Peter extended a hand. 'Well, let's have a look.' Peter scanned the sheet rapidly, ignoring Frankie. 'Mmm.' He frowned. 'Doesn't seem very thorough to me. Perhaps our little friend is spreading herself too thin these days.' After a moment of casually turning the pages he looked up, almost surprised to see Frankie was still there. 'Something else I can do for you?'

Frankie shook his head, grinned cheerfully and left. Tosser. But maybe a dangerous tosser. He'd be best off acting the village idiot around Peter to try to break through that supercilious shell.

Godot indeed!

Chapter 34

On the whole he was managing to keep up, thought Alex to herself as she saw Frankie around the office, chatting with people. He did have a natural ability to do that, engaging people and talking about their favourite subject – themselves. When she could lift her nose from her desk, she'd seen him a couple of times approach people and within minutes he'd have them laughing and chatting back animatedly. That was a valuable gift.

It was Frankie's new look that alarmed her most. When he'd arrived through the doors on that first morning, she'd done a double take. He really had taken the clothes thing seriously, playing the part as he should. Gone were the baggy T-shirts and jeans, the loose resting-actor look. Here was a tall, and, she had to admit, good-looking man in Todd's pink striped shirt. Just right for the part of conscientious academic. But on Frankie, whose frame was so much leaner than Todd's, it looked comfortable and casual, so different from its owner. On the following morning he had appeared in a polo shirt, and she found herself rather pathetically looking at the muscles on his tanned arms until she'd caught him staring with a quizzical expression and she'd looked quickly away. Everywhere else too he was playing the role with almost alarming conviction. At one point she'd whispered 'how's it going?' outside the lift, and he looked her in the eye as if he hardly knew her and replied very politely that he was very much enjoying being with the company. She'd looked at him questioningly and the slight rise of his eyebrow had been almost imperceptible.

It was becoming increasingly clear though that the idea of sabotage was a stupid one. The last couple of days had passed without any glitches Alex could see, and she'd clearly been deluding herself. Any recent cock-ups and mistakes must all have been hers because, when she was concentrating on the job, things weren't going wrong. She didn't really want to explore why looking efficient in front of Frankie was important, but, she thought irritably as the running order meeting for the launch was about to start, it was pointless him being here anyway.

Her mobile bleeped with low battery and she cast about for her phone charger on her desk, lifting papers and moving boxes. Where had it gone? She pushed aside her notes on the meeting with Donatella and the choreographers she'd had yesterday, but it wasn't there either. She started to pull open her drawers to look for it. Yes, the meeting had gone well. For all her demands the woman was obviously a pro. She'd arrived in a gingham bodice and a black puff ball skirt and sashayed across the floor towards Alex's desk. Frankie's eyes had nearly popped out of his head. Weren't men predictable? Well, if he found that sort of in-your-face slavish dedication to fashion attractive that was his look-out. But more importantly, where the hell was her charger?

Chapter 35

At eleven o'clock, everyone was in the meeting room with the exception of Alex. After a moment, Frankie made an excuse and slipped out. He found her on her hands and knees under her desk.

'I can't find the charger for my phone,' she muttered. 'I'm expecting a call on it from Donatella with an update of some of the issues raised yesterday. Oh, sod it!'

'Alex, everybody's waiting for you. Can't you look for that later? Maybe someone else has the same charger.'

'What?' Alex emerged, her hair sticking up and her eyes wild. 'I thought it was at eleven.'

'It's five past now. Come on. Hurry up. I'll come in after you.'

Alex threw an uncomprehending look at the wall. 'But my clock! It says ten to. It's slow. Someone's changed it this morning. They must have.'

Frankie shoved the pile of papers neatly piled up at the end of her desk into her arms. 'Never mind that now. Go!'

The meeting went well – considering. But there was a distinctly cold atmosphere when Frankie re-entered the room and slipped into his place after Alex. She seemed nervous, although he wondered if the others realised. She was trying hard to cover it up but he was sitting close enough to notice that she had her left hand clenched, as she had the other day at the park when he'd told her the bad news about The Bean's spending.

He noticed her swallow hard a couple of times, and he gently pushed a glass of water towards her. She barely glanced at him but picked up the water straight away to moisten her lips.

Frankie was supposed to be gauging the reactions of the other people around the table. He'd felt sure that whoever was responsible for Alex's troubles would give themselves away at this meeting by some subtle clue in their body language. He glanced around as Alex spoke, hoping to catch someone out, but saw nothing unusual. He glanced at each face one by one. All were turned towards Alex, all were listening attentively. But once Alex started describing what she had in store for the launch, he found himself being mesmerised by her passionate descriptions, and had to keep remembering not to stare at her. Even though much of what she was explaining went over his head, time and time again he felt his gaze returning to her face – and eventually staying put. Frankie frowned. He wasn't even really concentrating on what she was saying any more. He was just watching the way her body moved when she talked, the way she tucked her hair behind her ear when it flopped forward over her cheekbones.

He sat up straighter in his chair, shocked at the way his thoughts had drifted. This hadn't been part of the plan at all. She wasn't even his type. He normally went for the petite bubbly sort, intense and flighty. The emotionally demanding. And they were ten a penny in the theatre. He had to force his attention back to what she was saying.

He found himself willing her to succeed, to blow their socks off and he realised, as he watched her, that she was actually giving a pretty good performance. As she drew their attention to one item on the running order after another, he smiled to himself. Gradually, she seemed to be winning her audience over. She seemed in perfect control, and she clearly loved what she was doing. If only The Bean could see her like this.

In the end, Gavin grudgingly nodded before jumping to his feet. It was some tribute to Alex that he'd stayed put this long. 'Yes, yes. Well, that all seems fine. But it's got to be more than fine, as we all know. It's got to be perfect. More than perfect. So – well – keep on the case, Alex. No foul-ups. If it ends up looking as good as it sounds then maybe … Well, just stay on the case, all right? And I want a constant update from now until kick-off. Understand?' He bolted off into the open-plan area, leaving the others to clear away. Everyone else stopped by to ask Alex for clarification on one point or another, or to congratulate her on how well it had gone. With Camilla standing just behind her, Alex looked more comfortable than he'd seen her in days. Maybe everything was covered now.

Frankie stayed at a safe distance for the rest of the day and, after he had seen her go past him to the door with a stack of files clutched against her chest, wishing him a good weekend, he started to tidy away the papers from his desk too. The recycling bin was almost full, so he lifted it to shake down the loose sheets on top before adding his contribution. It was then he heard something heavy drop to the bottom of the bin. Someone had probably knocked a stapler in there by mistake. He reached down inside but his fingers encountered a wire. Pulling it out carefully he realised he was holding a phone charger. And it couldn't have got there by accident. He looked around cautiously, then pulled it free and slipped it into his backpack. Alex would be pleased to see that.

Frankie's steps slowed as he got closer to Alex's door. Maybe he should have called. Would she think it was odd for him to just turn up like this? Well, if she did, he'd just hand over the charger and go straight away. Todd might even be there. He rang the bell.

She was alone, thank goodness, and her hair was wet from the shower. She seemed pleased enough to see him, but she was certainly delighted to get her charger back. She immediately plugged her phone in and checked for messages, spoke to Bettina Gordino's agent and made some notes in her folder. Then she'd offered him a drink. It felt strange to be waited on in this flat, but it seemed like another lifetime when he'd been here with The Bean, tidying, preparing meals. But now, alone together in the flat, they could stop the office charade and it felt like a liberation. Alex seemed to feel the same too. She looked relaxed when she returned from the kitchen with two glasses on a tray and a chilled bottle of Sancerre, plus some peanuts that Frankie was pretty sure he'd put in the cupboard a few weeks ago. She passed him a large glass of wine then sat on the sofa, her long brown legs tucked under her and looked up at him. 'Well, don't just stand there. Make yourself at home.'

Frankie smiled and sat down opposite her. 'Cheers. It went well today, I thought. Your presentation.'

Alex seemed to reflect for a moment, then a shy smile crossed her face. 'It did, didn't it? I really thought Gavin was going to bawl me out in front of everyone, but the print-outs looked so efficient, it really started things off well – in spite of me turning up late. So tell me, where did you find my charger? I looked everywhere for it.'

Frankie hesitated. 'Actually, it was in the recycled paper bin. I only found it by accident and I don't think it walked there by itself.'

'Who on earth could have put it there then?' She leaned forward, looking concerned. 'And what would be the point?'

Frankie shrugged. 'It seems petty, I agree. But now I'm

convinced you are right. Added to everything else, Alex, it points at someone with a monster grudge against you, who just wants to undermine you in any way they can, big or small.'

'This is just making me even more determined to get everything right, you know,' she replied, her eyes glinting. 'I'm checking every detail at least twice. You know, I really think I've taken care of everything. There's only four days to go now, and all the details are in place. Bettina's apparel is being delivered from the factory first thing Monday and I'm going to bring it home with me so I can keep an eye on it overnight. I got Camilla to run through the final details with the caterer today. I'm living from lists, I know.' She laughed hollowly. 'I've hardly stopped to eat in days – apart from standing up at the fridge, but if I can just hold it together, I really think it's going to be all right.' She took a long sip of her wine and sighed, closing her eyes for a moment. She looked ready to drop. Frankie watched her face relax in the early evening light. What he really felt like doing, he realised with a jolt, was taking her in his arms and telling her everything really *was* going to be all right. Should he? Shouldn't he? She opened her eyes again and the moment passed.

Frankie looked down at his hands. 'Have you still got any pasta? I haven't eaten either.'

In the kitchen, Frankie looked through the cupboards while Alex leaned against the units and carried on chatting about work as he put together some ingredients. Everything was pretty much as he had left it so Alex couldn't have cooked a single meal for herself since The Bean had moved out after they'd been rumbled, and it showed. She was looking thinner and Frankie could see the hollows of her collar bones clearly as she filled her glass with wine again. As he snapped down the switch on the kettle, Alex seemed to rouse herself. 'Here, let me do that. You shouldn't be doing all the work. How much pasta do we need?' Frankie let her take the packet from his hands.

'How hungry are you? I mean, if you do the lot, you can just add some pesto and put it in the fridge then reheat it tomorrow with some bacon or something,' he suggested.

'Right, I'll do it all then.' She poured the boiling water from the kettle into the pan Frankie had got out and set it on the stove, taking a little time to get the gas to ignite. Without waiting for it to come to the boil again and without even adding oil, she poured in the pasta, then jumped back when the water splashed up and burned her. 'Ow! Shit, that hurt!'

Frankie turned on the cold tap. 'Put your hand under here, quick.' He tried to take her hand but she pulled away.

'I'll be all right!' she snapped. 'I can do it myself.'

'Why do you do this?' Frankie demanded.

'Do what? What are you talking about?'

'Why do you push everyone away? I only wanted to help. I wanted … you hurt yourself. You're tired. You're not eating properly. For God's sake, can't you just let me look after you? Just for tonight?'

Alex stared at him and Frankie wondered for a moment if she was going to cry or shout or throw him out. But she did none of those things. Quietly and gently, she held out her burned hand to him. He took it in both of his and examined it closely, holding it up. The burn wasn't serious but the skin was a little red. Frankie carefully raised her hand to his mouth and kissed it softly, then waited, not daring to look at her. She didn't pull away. He paused, then looked into her eyes and kissed it again, grazing the skin with his lips and turning her hand over so he could kiss the inside of her wrist. He heard her sharp intake of breath and gently he pulled her towards him. At first their lips just touched in a brief, tentative kiss, then he buried his hands in her still damp hair as the kiss deepened. She made a small noise in her throat and reached up to touch his cheek. Almost instantly they were devouring each other and her response was as passionate as his. They pulled apart, both breathing hard, and stared in complicity until finally Alex reached past him and turned off the stove.

Frankie wasn't sure whether it was him or her who pulled the other towards the bedroom but, without a word, she turned to him and started to unbutton his shirt. He pushed her hands away and held her face for a moment, seeing his smile reflected in her eyes before he started to undress her. Her body, long and strong, such a surprise under the baggy clothing, enthralled him and her skin was softer than he could have imagined. He threw off his own clothes now, casting them carelessly to the floor, and took her in his arms again, feeling her respond with an energy and passion that took him by surprise. Together, they sank on to the bed.

Later, much later, they fell apart. Frankie could feel his heart pounding and they were both out of breath. They lay side by side, both looking up at the ceiling, not touching and not saying a word. The silence stretched out between them. Frankie didn't know what to say. He was almost relieved when the phone rang and Alex bolted from the bed and out of the door, grabbing a dressing gown as she went. He didn't know what to do now. Would she come back to bed? Or had the moment gone? His body felt alive and new and he could think of nothing better than spending the rest of the night making love to her, but was that what she would want? Maybe he could make her breakfast in bed in the morning? He could hear her voice from the hallway. She sounded a little bit strained. Was it bad news?

'Yeah, sure. When are you arriving? Will you go straight

there from the airport, then? Fine. Me? No, just a quiet night in, working, as usual.' The launch is on Tuesday, remember?

Frankie, hating himself, got up and went closer to the door. 'Well, you don't have to ... no, I'm fine, really. Just a bit tired, you know. No, there's nothing wrong at all. Just ... just missing you. Yeah, see you soon. You too. Bye Todd.'

Frankie felt sick. He heard her replace the receiver quietly. He got up and reached for his clothes, dressing quickly. She was in the kitchen, and he could hear her moving around, putting the pasta back on to cook. He laced up his shoes and took a deep breath before going to face her. She pulled her dressing gown tightly closed as she heard him come in. She was looking down.

'I couldn't help ... I heard ... I think I should go now.' Her only reaction was to nod silently as she prodded at the pasta with a fork.

'Aren't you hungry? We could still eat something, if you want.'

'No thanks. I think it would be better not to. I'll – er – see you on Monday.' Christ, his hands were trembling. Were they just going to leave it at this?

She looked up, there was something in her eyes that he couldn't read. 'Look, sorry about the call. I couldn't ... well, maybe it's better this way.'

'Sure, no problem. It's cool, Alex. I'll be off then.'

She nodded and looked back down at the saucepan as he turned away and left. Out in the street, the night was cool and he shivered. He didn't know what to think, what he should be thinking. It was very quiet away from the main road and the moon was almost full. He didn't even know how he felt. He wanted to be angry with her, but he couldn't be. Not really. He'd known about stupid sodding Todd all along. If he was angry with anyone, it should be with himself, for not just putting her hand under the tap like any sensible man would have done. It had just been one of those spontaneous, spur-of-the-moment things. And it wasn't like it had meant anything. Anything at all, really.

Chapter 36

Alex spent the weekend in a totally distracted state, one minute horrified by what they had done, the next lying in the bath looking at her body and remembering how he had run his hands over her skin and how his body felt next to hers. Not bulky and taut like Todd's, but firm yet soft to her touch. She barely remembered if they had spoken to each other, except when he had whispered if it was safe and when they had both cried out.

She wanted to tell someone, and at one point had her hand on the phone to call Saff but snatched it away. After all that had happened between them, it would be a strange way to pick up the pieces. To admit she had slept with Frankie, when it was his presence that had caused the rift. She knew she ought to call Saff anyway, respond to her messages but a small part of her still felt childishly angry. And then there was Todd. She'd pushed any thought of him from her mind, knowing what she was doing was wholly wrong but exactly what she'd wanted to do. She should have left the phone to ring; the sound of his voice had made her feel sick with guilt. What a mess.

Anyway, she reasoned, as she attacked the bathroom with the bleach and then sat at the table with her notes, running through catering details for the launch, she should feel ashamed for acting like a harlot and having sex with a man she hardly knew. Frankie would probably be thinking of her now as some kind of soppy female who just jumped into bed with any bloke that showed her sympathy. And that's basically what it amounted to, so she deserved nothing more.

She woke on Sunday morning feeling resolute. She'd done something very stupid and she had to get a few things back under control after her momentary lapse so, retrieving her bike from the communal shed behind the flats, she set off for her mother's. Already it was hot. People were lying out in the park with the papers or walking small dogs. Windows were wide open and through them she could hear the crashing of plates and people shouting at their children. Around her was the constant hum of the city and in a couple of hours the heat would be unbearable. The wind against her face was cooling as she bolted over the river.

She chained up her bike outside her mother's mews house and knocked on the door. She'd never had a key and had never asked for one. This was her mother's place, bought with some of the proceeds of the sale of the cottage off the King's Road where Alex had grown up. The rest had gone towards settling her father's legacy of debts.

'To what do I owe the pleasure?' The Bean asked haughtily as she walked back through to the sitting room. Alex cast her eye over the mess – newspapers everywhere, last night's supper on the side in the kitchen, the inevitable pile of post. Ignoring the barbed comment, designed to lob blame right back at Alex, she asked how she was, only to get a sulky response about being bored and someone vaguely interesting having died. Alex picked up the pile of post.

'Are you talking to me now then?'

'Yes, of course,' Alex said as patiently as she could. 'But it's not an easy thing to just forget, when you find your mother holed up in your flat in cahoots with your best friend and a virtual stranger it turns out you are employing. These, however, are clearly easy to forget.' She shuffled through the envelopes, knowing that besides the junk mail and catalogues sent in advance from galleries, she'd find the windowed envelopes. 'We need to talk.'

The Bean sighed and slumped down on the sofa. 'Do you want tea?' She vaguely indicated the kitchen.

'No thanks. You've been at it again, haven't you?'

Her mother looked out of the window, defiantly ignoring her. Annoyed, Alex sat down beside her and blocked her view, ready to shout at her for her stupidity and her irresponsibility.

'It can't go on like this, Mum. I simply don't have the money.' Alex ripped open the envelopes and pulled out the red final demands, the shirty letters: 'Small watercolour, original, signed. £400. Hold until collection arranged.' She opened another. 'Bronze hand. £250. Hold until collection arranged.' Tucked between the envelopes were two more receipts for a pair of Russell & Bromley shoes and a dress from Jaeger for £230. There was even one from a firm of solicitors. But it was the last letter that made Alex's pulse race: William Curtis. Turf Accountants. Bets made by telephone. Final demand for payment.'

She turned to her mother, her stomach aching with dread. It was even worse than Frankie had said. 'What the hell are these? What are you expecting me to do? Bail you out *again*? Even if I could, why should I, Mum, why should I? I work as hard as I can, and I try to pay for what you need, but this …' She waved the envelopes and letters in her mother's face. This is just extravagance. You can't maintain this lifestyle any more. You couldn't even then, but definitely not now, Mum.' She realised she was shaking her mother's bad arm and pulled away quickly. 'I'm right up against it, Mum, and there'll be nothing left if I'm not careful. How can you be so selfish?' The

Bean turned her face towards Alex, her eyes filled with tears. Alex held up her hand. 'Woah there! Oh no you don't. You're not doing the tears thing on me again. I've had that too many times.' She started to read the letters, determined to ignore this familiar chain of events, waiting for the usual 'I'm so sorry, I won't do it again.'

'It's all over, isn't it?' The Bean said quietly.

'Too damned right it's over. This can't go on.'

'It's over, isn't it?' Alex looked up at the repeated question. The Bean was sitting straight backed, almost proud, her hands resting elegantly in her lap, but tears were pouring unheeded down her face. 'My time is over, I mean. All those glorious days. The parties. The adoration. It's gone hasn't it? I'm nothing now, am I? Just a nuisance to you.'

Alex watched for a moment, waiting for the usual sidelong look to check that the blubbing was having an effect. But this time it never came. The Bean just looked down, the tears falling on to her hands. This question was new, thought Alex. Could that mean it was genuine? Slowly, she put her hand on top of her mother's, something she wasn't sure she had ever done. 'Yes Mum, those days are over,' she said gently. 'But nothing will ever take them away, though. Nothing will ever change what you did and who you were.' The Bean lifted beseeching eyes, the sadness in them so deep that Alex felt her chest lurch in sympathy. 'But Mum, you can't go on spending like this. Look at what you have here. Look what you are surrounded by.' They both looked about them. 'So many lovely things already. So many pictures and beautiful dresses. Do you really need more?'

'But it makes me happy, darling,' she sniffed, wiping her nose most uncharacteristically on her sleeve. 'I don't think you understand. You're not like me, or your father really. Sometimes

I wonder where you came from, with your sensible attitude. Never doing anything rash without thinking about it first.' She smiled tearfully and Alex winced. If she only knew. 'I just can't seem to stop myself,' she went on. 'I see something and I want it. I love the smell of the shops and the price tags. I love seeing a red sticker on a picture and knowing it's mine.'

'And the betting?' Alex asked quietly.

'Oh Alex, it's the thrill of the chance. The hope. You know how much your father and I adored the races and the excitement. The clothes. Watching the horses in the paddock. Do you remember how we used to go to Ascot?' Her eyes were alive and animated now. If this was all a performance it was a very convincing one. But Alex had been fooled before.

'But you can't afford to spend at this level! I can't go on supporting both of us, and your trust fund is empty, Mum. It has been for years, I've told you before. I can do the bills and the odd holiday, but not this.' She indicated the pile of letters again.

'I miss all that. I miss your father and I miss the past. I miss being important, because I'm not really important to you, am I?' She looked at her daughter searchingly. 'You don't need me. You never have, you funny independent little thing, in your busy world.'

'Oh Mum,' Alex sighed, rubbing her eyes. 'Don't be like that. Of course I need you, but we need to sort out this money issue'.

The Bean tapped her leg and stood up gingerly. Alex realised with a jolt how much her mother had aged. It had happened so gradually Alex had barely noticed, but here she was, slightly stooped, the famous beauty now changed to the wrinkled elegance of age. Had she been too harsh with her when old friends were dying and the life that had once been hers had disappeared for ever? The thought of losing Saff flitted into her head but she quashed it quickly, not wanting to explore her own loneliness. She looked around the crammed little house that her mother had bought 'for a lark' because it reminded her of the place where Stephen Ward had lived in the days when Christine Keeler used to stay. 'It's a silly little house but it'll do!' she'd laughed carelessly when she'd seen it.

'Do you love this place?' Alex asked suddenly.

The Bean looked round from her position over by the open window that looked down on to the mews. 'What do you mean?'

'What I said. Do you love this house?'

Her mother took in the room as if she'd never seen it before. Then she shrugged. 'I suppose it's quaint, and quite convenient for things. But it's not *that* special, I suppose.'

'Then let's sell it.' Her mother looked startled. Alex ploughed on. 'Let's sell it and you can move somewhere nearer me, and Saff, and the park. With the proceeds – well, let's face it, this will go for a mint if we spruce it up a bit – we can pay off these debts and then you can have a wonderful time buying things to make the new place nice. Take Frankie on a shopping spree with you.' Why on earth had she mentioned Frankie?

There was a long pause, as the word 'shopping' sank in. 'Mmm, he'd quite enjoy that, the lovely man.'

Alex looked down, suppressing a smile. She'd pressed the right button.

'Well …' The Bean began, sniffing and wiping her nose more daintily now on her handkerchief. Alex felt a sudden surge of affection for her as she bravely composed herself and took control of the situation again. 'Let me think about it. Now darling, Grace Fernshaw has asked me for lunch – can't think why. I haven't seen her for donkey's years but thank God her pompous arse of a husband has finally fallen off the perch. Perhaps she wants to celebrate!' She laughed uncertainly.

Alex stood up, knowing she had sown the seed and that it was best left until her mother could bring it round and make the idea her own. 'I've got to get on too. Lots of work to be done. Anything you need?'

'No darling.' Her mother put her hands on her daughter's shoulders and looked into her eyes. 'You are a good girl, Alex Hill.' She brushed a strand of hair out of Alex's eyes. 'And you keep your mother in order. But you have to learn to enjoy yourself more. Relish everything you have and everyone you love now, because soon it may be gone'. Then she kissed her goodbye on the step, but Alex could have sworn her mother held her for a fraction longer than usual.

Chapter 37

Ella flicked through the local paper, but without much enthusiasm. Nothing she'd seen in the Situations Vacant interested her even slightly. Compared with the buzz of working at the radio station, everything else paled into insignificance, even trying to help Saff. She sighed and threw the paper down irritably. She'd just have to call Mike again and see if any of her latest ideas might work. He hadn't yet responded to that string of emails she'd fired off. Maybe she should have waited and sent them in a nice, orderly, professional way, instead of at random as they entered her head. Oh sod it! Maybe he just wasn't interested. She wandered over to the fridge and ignored the remains of the chicken Frankie had roasted the day before.

That had been a dull meal. He hadn't been in the mood for conversation. Just stared into space while she gabbled on and was non-committal when she asked anything. She finally persuaded him to come to the pub to meet up with mates, but he'd even ignored Dan's tedious quips about Frankie being a domestic god. The only time he'd reacted was when Carlo, the perpetual hanger-on, had asked Frankie, winking broadly, whether he missed having his hands in Alex's drawers. Frankie had turned on the little man, scowling, and told him to sod off.

Reaching her hand past the chicken carcass, she went straight for the Angel Delight she'd whipped up and decorated with Smarties. Lost in thought, she took out the bowl and dug straight in with a tablespoon. She was starting to consider an investigation into the changing fashions of puddings in South London when the doorbell rang. She answered it, still clutching the bowl. Standing on the doorstep was Mike.

He peered hopefully into the empty bowl. 'Oh! Why didn't you save some for me? Oh, hang on. There's plenty left – all over your face.' He extended a finger and carefully ran it along the edge of her lower lip, then licked it clean. Ella's mouth dropped open in astonishment. Mike went on, oblivious. 'Anyway, sorry to drop in unannounced, but my computer started belching black smoke. The IT guys say it has overheated, something about an excessive number of emails – and from this address, apparently.' Theatrically he stepped back to look at the number on the front door.

'Oh – right. Yes, sorry about that. I just had a few ideas.'

'A few! I'd hate to be in the way when inspiration really strikes. Anyway, there were some great ideas there. Some completely crap ones too, of course.' He was looking quite hard at her now and, self-consciously, she wiped her mouth with her hand in case there was more chocolate on it. 'But I was wondering if you'd like to go out and talk about doing something else for me – for us. I was going to suggest lunch, but it looks like you've already had pudding.'

Ella caught the twinkle in Mike's eye and felt herself start to smile. 'Yes, but I haven't had a main course yet. I could really murder a kebab. Er, if you like, that is ...' She trailed off, aghast at her own audacity. A few days ago he had been her boss and now this was looking scarily like a date. A proper lunch date, even though her stomach was beginning to feel a bit funny. She held her breath, but Mike smiled in satisfaction.

'Oh yes, I think I do like. Can you recommend anywhere round here? Somewhere suitable for a high-level business meeting?'

Ella put down the bowl and spoon on the hall floor. 'Absolutely. The café round the corner. They do great bacon sarnies too.' She darted back in to get her keys, and to check her face for Angel Delight. Just in case. She walked past him, pleased he couldn't see the silly smile on her lips, and very, very aware of him right behind her. They turned on to the street and he took her arm, as though it were the most natural thing in the world.

'Yes, you certainly had some original ideas there,' he said earnestly. 'I was particularly impressed by that one about people who've trained their pets to talk ...'

Chapter 38

The Bean's parting words about relishing everything before it's gone rang in Alex's ears the next morning as she arrived at the office. Alex wasn't sure any of this was worth enjoying and she had the definite feeling that soon it would all be gone. She'd hoped she'd be the first in to the department, and to be hard at it when Frankie turned up so she wouldn't have to speak to him. She wouldn't know what to say. How he'd feel after their love-making and his sudden departure. Despite busying herself over the weekend, she'd kept checking the phone for messages from him. But why would he call? She'd virtually kicked him out in her panic when Todd called.

Of course with only a day to go, she wanted to get ahead of things anyway, and she was disappointed to see Gavin's dark head already bent over his desk when she arrived. He glanced up at her but didn't acknowledge her raised hand of greeting. On her system were a couple of emails from Camilla sent late Friday evening – gosh she must have worked late – both confirming details about Bettina Gordino's arrival time later today and the hotel booking. At least that was sorted.

She was on to the *Express* arranging a private room for their journalist to talk to the massive Malcolm Sanferino for their American Football special when she finally spotted Frankie. She saw him before he saw her and, as he swung through the doors chatting animatedly to Peter of all people, Alex slipped further down her seat and hid behind her computer screen.

'I think Arsenal will do the double next season,' Peter was saying as they came close to her desk. 'That new striker will be worth every penny of the obscene fee they paid for him. Mind you, he's wearing my trainers so that's my bonus sorted!'

'Good call, mate,' Frankie replied cheerily, slapping him on the back. 'Catch you later!'

Mate? Alex frowned. When did Peter become his 'mate' for God's sake. And 'catch you'? Where did that come from? Had Frankie forgotten what she thought of Peter? Or maybe he didn't care now. You could never really tell when an actor wasn't acting. Alex sighed. And now she'd made things so much more complicated. Perhaps she should try to lose herself in meetings all day.

'Hi.' She started as she heard Frankie's voice close now. She composed her face into a nonchalant smile and looked up. But it wasn't to her he was speaking. Instead he was perched on Camilla's desk and smiling down at her.

Alex's phone rang but as she answered, she had half an ear on the conversation going on at Camilla's desk. They were talking too quietly now for her to hear, their heads close together, one so blonde and one so dark. Frankie then threw his head back and laughed at something Camilla said and they both looked Alex's way.

Alex ducked her head smartly and said 'Sorry, what?' a bit too abruptly down the phone.

'I told you,' came the heavily-accented English of Bettina's agent down the line from Milan, 'that she would only accept the Brook Penthouse, Miss Hill. I said it very clearly during my meeting with you here in my office but my people have checked the reservation to find what? Nothing!. My client is an extremely important woman and frankly she is doing you a favour with your little event.'

For a moment Alex forgot the flirting couple at the desk next to hers. 'Mr Corniani, I can assure you there is nothing little about this launch. There will be more press there than at the Collections, and it will guarantee excellent publicity for your client.' Alex saw Camilla's head pop up with interest. She raised her eyebrows.

There was something that sounded like 'hurumph' in Alex's ear. 'There will be no client unless she gets the right hotel room. She is very particular.' I'll bet, thought Alex.

'I can assure you we have requested that suite and will ensure she gets it. Leave it with me, Mr Corniani.' She put down the phone. 'Camilla.' She sounded sharper than she had meant to, and Frankie stood up and moved away from the desk, not without glancing at Alex, a totally neutral look on his face. To her intense irritation he then *winked* at Camilla before walking away. 'Cam, you did book the Brook Penthouse, didn't you?'

Camilla flicked through her pad. 'Er no, I've just got written here "penthouse". No specific name.'

'But I definitely said the Brook. Are you sure?'

Once more Cam looked back through her pad. 'Absolutely – I would have written it down because I have the Claridges number here and I'd have put it next to that.' She looked up with a horrified expression on her face. 'Oh bugger, Alex. Have I made a cock-up?' She picked up her phone. 'I'll call them now and see if it's free, shall I?'

At that moment Peter swept past her. 'Problems?' he asked over his shoulder, a broad smile on his face, as he headed for a meeting room.

'No no. Nothing. Everything's fine,' Alex called, but he had shut the door firmly behind him. 'Yes straight away please. I'm sure they can change things for someone as important as her. I need a coffee.' And she bolted for the kitchen where she put on the kettle and fussed over preparing coffee, her mind racing.

'You OK?' Frankie said quietly behind her. She jumped and turned to find him leaning back against the worktop, his arms folded. Alex went back to her preparations.

'Yup thanks. Want some?'

'No thanks. Cam made some for me earlier.'

'You're very matey.'

'Does that bother you?'

'Good heavens no. No! Not at all.'

'She's a nice girl.'

'Very nice.'

'Alex?' Camilla stuck her head around the door. 'Bad news, I'm afraid. It's booked already. Some Arab apparently. Immovable. I'm so sorry.' She looked very sheepish.

'Shit.'

'Oh Alex, and on top of everything else.'

'Have you offered an inflated rate?' Alex kept her fingers crossed that she hadn't – that would be the final bye-bye to the budget.

'Yup but apparently this Arab gentleman is very ... strong willed. Want me to call Bettina's agent?'

Alex thought for a moment. 'No. What's the name of that hip new place in Kensington? The one we thought about for the accessories press launch in December?'

'The Stanfield?' said Frankie helpfully.

'That's it. See if you can get her in there. They'll love a name like that staying, and I'll tell her agent it's the best thing ever and makes Claridges look like the Holiday Inn.'

The Milanese gentleman, however, wasn't convinced and it took several phone calls between agent and client, client and agent to get Bettina to reconsider. Alex did her best to reassure and pacify, all the time her stomach cramping. If she lost

226

Bettina Gordino over a bloody hotel room then she might as well hang up her airflow trainers now. Then, at eleven o'clock, Gavin came back from wherever he had been and within five minutes of sweeping through the doors had been informed, thanks to Peter no doubt, about the Brook botch-up.

'You are joking, of course?' He started speaking just outside his office door loud enough to have everyone sitting bolt up-right. It was obvious who his question was aimed at, but Alex still looked away, hoping to God it was meant for someone else. She just hoped too that he'd have the grace to take her somewhere private when he fired her. 'I mean,' he continued at the same volume, 'we are only talking the hottest model around. We have only briefed every publication from the Chipping Sodbury parish magazine upwards that she will be at the launch, and we can't even get her the ruddy hotel room she wants. What does it take, Alex, to get things right?'

'Oh Gavin, you can't blame Alex on this one. It was probably down to me.' Alex looked up, startled at Camilla's voice. 'I probably didn't hear what she said about the penthouse but she has been rushed off her feet with Italy and all that.'

'How could I forget? Wasn't it the wrong airport that time?' Gavin turned to Alex, the hostility obvious in his face. 'Camilla shouldn't take the rap for this – it's up to you, Alex, as the one in charge, to double-check these things. So are we going to get out of *this* one?'

'Yes, I think so.' Alex pulled herself up tall. This was her last shot at self-preservation. 'I've found her somewhere even better, she will be here and the press will love her. I've already had loads of interest and secured an exclusive for Wednesday's *Mail*.'

'And?' he asked, not about to let her get away with any-thing.

'Well, I'll lay on entertainment for her obviously.' Alex made a mental note to sort that. 'And best of all, she'll be thrilled with what she's wearing. It's being altered just for her and it's due to arrive any minute – I'll show you as soon as it gets here.'

Someone must have been watching over her because Gavin's mobile went before he could respond and he went back to his office, waving her away and chatting animatedly, hand to his ear. Alex breathed out.

'Cam, can you please call the couriers and check the stuff *is* on its way – and Sanferino's too of course? It should have been here by now.'

'Sure thing.' Camilla picked up her phone.

Alex slumped down in her seat feeling achy, almost as if she had flu. Frankie sauntered slowly over to her desk.

'Things looking pear-shaped?' he asked quietly. She could smell his skin. She looked down.

Big time. Any ideas?' she muttered.

'Not really. Peter's holed up in the meeting room on a conference call. Or at least that's what he said. If it's him, he's playing things very close.'

Alex fiddled with the seam of her trousers. 'Then it must be me and I must be crap.'

'Sorry to interrupt,' Camilla came over apologetically. 'Er, Alex, the couriers say delivery is due on the twenty-first.'

'Twenty-first? That's ... Thursday. What?' She bolted out of her chair. 'That's no bloody good. Have you looked out the order? I did it online. There must be a confirmation.' This *had* to be a mistake. It could be sorted.

There was a pause as Camilla leaned over her desk, her hand on her computer mouse searching her email inbox. 'Here we are. Yup, hang on, confirmation. Oh. Oh dear.' She clicked off the screen and came over to Alex. 'Er,' she said quietly. 'It clearly says the twenty-first in response to your email. Do you remember doing that?'

Later Alex would describe the feeling as if all the blood ran out of her body. She could feel goosebumps on her arms and suddenly she was finding it hard to breathe. 'It can't be,' she whispered. 'It can't. I *know* I told them the eighteenth.'

Camilla took her arm. 'Oh Alex, are you all right? Is there anything I can do?'

'Shoot me?' She slumped into her chair and started to look back through her own emails but there were so many. So much communication, so many messages about the launch. It would take her ages to find the confirmation.

'Sorry to interrupt,' Frankie muttered. 'But where exactly is this apparel?'

'In a factory in Istanbul,' Camilla replied. 'Oh dear.' She too sat down hard on the corner of Alex's desk.

'What time do you need it by?' Frankie persisted. Alex wished he would be quiet so she could think. She rubbed her temples where her head pounded. The whole room seemed to have receded, full of tiny people going about their normal day, oblivious to the fact that her world had just collapsed.

'First thing tomorrow morning at the latest ready for Gordino to put it on when she arrives in Brixton, but it will take ages to clear customs.' Alex could hear her own voice sound monotone. 'It's pointless. Oh fuck.'

Frankie crouched down beside her. 'Are you sure?' he asked quietly.

Alex ignored him. She was thinking fast. How long did they have? Was it ... could she? 'Something like this happened once before,' she said slowly. 'Not to me, but I remember there was a delay with some zips. They all had to be changed, and we sent someone over to pick the garments up personally.'

'Oh Alex, there's no time!' Camilla gasped.

'I'll go.'

Alex looked at the expression of determination on Frankie's face. 'Where?' she asked.

'Istanbul, of course. It'll be like *Midnight Express*.'

In contrast to her desperate mood, Alex found herself smiling. 'Oh Frankie, don't be daft. You can't possibly!'

'Alex is right.' Camilla stood up. 'It's madness, and besides if anyone should go it should be me. I work for the company and, do you know, I think I might even have my passport in my bag.' She began to rummage. 'I needed it to pick up a letter from the post office the other day.'

'No, I can do it. I'll go.' Frankie moved to get his things, prepared to leave already. 'You're too important to things here, Cam. You can't be spared. I'm the obvious choice. If I get on a flight this afternoon, I can be there for this evening and back latest first thing tomorrow. OK Alex?'

'But—'

Frankie put his hand on Alex's arm and looked hard at her. 'Trust me, Alex. For once?' And he turned to Camilla. 'Let's keep this from Gavin, hey? Let's do Alex a favour? Now give me the details will you, Camilla, and can you let them know I'm on my way?'

Chapter 39

Frankie did up his seat belt. He was breathless from the dash back to the flat for his passport, the race to Heathrow, the haste to buy some currency and the run across the concourse to the plane, which now started its whiny roar as it began to move. He smiled thinly at the large woman sitting next to him and attempted to squeeze further against the wall of the cabin.

'On holiday are you?' the woman asked comfortably. 'We're meeting up with some friends and going sailing for a week. Turkey's wonderful. Have you been there before?'

Since she didn't really seem to need any answers to her many questions, Frankie allowed the one-way flow of conversation to give him the space to ask himself what the hell he was doing here. He hated flying, he hated being too hot, he hated not knowing what was expected of him and he hated unexpected changes to his routine. All in all, he couldn't have dreamed up a worse undertaking. And for what? But he knew the answer already. Alex.

Something, he wasn't even sure what yet, had made him as certain as he could possibly be that he had to do this for this tall, complicated woman with the endless brown legs. And he knew he was the only person who could do it for her. So much depended now on the garments being there safely and on time for Gordino and, unqualified though he felt, he knew that no one else could be trusted to do what was right for Alex and her launch.

Dinner came and went, and he ignored it, willing the plane to go faster. The woman sitting next to him had a little nap, her mouth falling open to allow the sound of soft snoring to escape. Frankie looked out of the window at the light beginning to fade, the clouds framing the sunset like a proscenium arch. When they started their descent, Frankie was almost on his feet before the tyres touched the runway, and he barged people out of the way to be off the plane first and through customs and arrivals, with his virtually empty holdall in his hand.

Frankie's only images of Istanbul airport had been indelibly marked into his memory from watching *Midnight Express* but now it looked westernised – cool, shiny and marbley. He could have been anywhere. Bolting out of the sliding doors into the warm evening air, he jumped into the first available taxi and showed the driver the address for the warehouse, urging him to hurry. They swung into the traffic and Frankie realised he was leaning forward impatiently. His driver, when he wasn't turning round to converse with Frankie in fragmented English with a strong American accent, swerved wildly from lane to lane, sounding his horn constantly. The string of worry beads hanging from the mirror swung like a pendulum ticking away the seconds and Frankie held on tight. How had he managed to find the only psychopathic driver in the whole of Istanbul? He glanced around, terrified, at the other cars and vans. Which one were they going to collide with? Because it was only a matter of time, that much was obvious. But, he noticed in horror, the other cars were being driven in exactly the same way. They were all covered in dust, all dented, and were hurtling along at breakneck speed.

It was quite dark by the time the taxi driver deposited him in a wide street with tall buildings on one side, a park on the other.

The trip had only taken ten or fifteen minutes and Frankie handed over a muddle of coins and a couple of notes, before the driver waved a cheery. 'See ya around, pal', and screeched off into the darkness.

Frankie was alone. He compared the address that Camilla had printed out for him with the number above the large wooden gateway. So far, so good. But why was the whole building in darkness? Frankie glanced at his watch. Almost eight o'clock, British time. He'd been on the plane for nearly four hours, but it was around two hours later here – closer to ten. Of course the place would be locked up! Why hadn't he thought of this? He studied Alex's scribbled sheet of phone contacts she'd pressed into his hand with an awkward 'thanks' before he left the office, and, pulling his phone from his pocket, started dialling. He was beginning to panic by the time the third number he tried was finally answered, with a gruff 'Alo!'

'Hello? Do you speak English?'

'Yes, of course I speak English. Who is this?'

Frankie sighed with relief. 'Right. You don't know me, but I've got a problem …'

Twenty minutes later, a battered Peugeot braked abruptly at the other end of the now totally deserted street and a short, compact man got out, looking round. He returned Frankie's questioning stare, pointed at him and gestured incomprehension then waved his hand up and down, palm downwards. Frankie walked cautiously towards him.

'Frankeee?' he called. 'Is this you? What are you doing down there? The warehouse is here. Come.' Relieved, Frankie hurried to meet him. 'I'm Melik,' he said abruptly, clasping Frankie's hand. 'This is very strange! Why did you not call me to say that you were coming?'

Frankie sighed in exasperation. 'I thought someone had.

Well, let me explain …' As he told him what had happened, Melik's face first cleared, then fell.

'So no problem with the special apparel. That is good. But this is not regular. I don't understand this, why you are coming in the night? We can always deliver when you ask us. This should not be necessary.'

'I'm afraid you may have been given the wrong information,' Frankie explained diplomatically. 'But the problem is, the launch is tomorrow morning. If I can't get back in time with the clothes, it's going to be a disaster.'

Melik thought for a moment, then raised his head sharply and clicked his tongue. 'No! There will be no disaster. I have met Alex Hill. She has been here to visit our operation and she knows she can rely on me.'

The stocky man led the way to a modern building on the corner and took a large bunch of keys from his pocket. After a complicated series of operations, he swung open a door and darted in to switch off the alarm. As he did so, a loud swooping wail rose into the air around them. Frankie looked around in fright as the amplified sound came at them from all directions. Melik smiled. 'It is the call to prayer. Welcome to Istanbul, Frankie!'

The building must have been air conditioned all day, because it was still cool inside and stepping in from the heat of the street was a blessed relief. Frankie followed Melik through a series of darkened offices into a huge, high-ceilinged hangar of a building that hadn't been visible from the street. Metal racks stretched in every direction, stacked with boxes, and metre after metre of neatly hung garments covered with clear plastic lined the walls. Melik walked over to a computer terminal and booted it up. 'You are new to the company,' he stated, rather than asked.

'Is it that obvious?' Frankie asked. Melik just smiled pityingly and turned back to the computer. He searched the screen, nodded and walked off into the semi gloom.

'Come with me, Frankie,' he called over his shoulder.

Melik had located the consignment straight away, and he tapped a few keys on the computer until a mechanised arm slid along a gantry on the ceiling that Frankie hadn't noticed. Smoothly, the bundle was lifted from the rack and lowered gently to the ground, where Melik unhooked it and checked the numbers on the labels against the screen of a palm-top scanner, then he ran it over the bar codes and nodded slowly.

'Yes, you see. The dates have been changed. First it was for Monday, then for Thursday. But we have it all on the computer so we can change the day it goes out. This is very efficient for us. You see? The email comes in – we can change straight away!'

Frankie was staring at the little screen in disbelief. 'Hang on, Melik. Do you still have the email on your system? Could I see it?'

'Of course! Look – here it is.' Melik stepped to the side and showed Frankie the screen. The email was from Alex all right. It had her name on it. Frankie frowned in puzzlement. But Alex had claimed not to know anything about it. What on earth was going on?

Melik pointed to the screen proudly. 'You see! Only Friday night, she changed her mind to Thursday. But with our computer, we can change straight away. What a shame she get it wrong this time. But now I drive you back to airport. But here. Before we go, take a couple of T-shirts from the new range. Slight seconds but free and off the house! One for you and special for your lady. You have a lady don't you?' He roared with laughter from the belly. 'Come on, Frankie! No time to waste!'

Frankie folded the clothes carefully and zipped them safely away in the holdall he'd brought with him, then walked ahead of Melik, retracing their steps to the offices. Something was gnawing at him. There was something ... Then he stopped and Melik cannoned into him. 'What is wrong, Frankie? What is it?'

Somewhere in his head a penny very slowly started to drop. On Friday night, Alex had certainly not been in the office, sending emails. She'd been in bed with him.

Chapter 40

In between weighing out flour and butter, Saff kept trying to call Frankie but each time she was told his phone was switched off. All she wanted to know was if he'd got the part. Did the lack of response mean good news or bad? She tried to imagine both scenarios – Frankie still drunk after hearing he had the part and Frankie dead from suicide having heard he hadn't. She'd call The Bean. She'd know.

'No, darling, not a dickie bird,' Alex's mother breathed down the phone. 'In fact, I've tried him a couple of times too. I'm dying to know myself. The poor boy must be beside himself waiting.'

'Have you heard from Alex?' Saff asked lightly. It had been days now and Saff had given up trying to leave messages. It was her birthday soon so perhaps Alex might get in contact with her then. They always tried to share a bottle of wine at least, if Alex wasn't away. It was a tradition really. A birthday without Alex and a bottle of bubbly wouldn't be right.

'Yes, dear, she came over at the weekend. She's frantically busy of course and I thought she looked awfully tired poor dear. But she is so terribly independent she just won't show a chink of weakness. She really could do with someone to care for her. Not that twit of an American who's no use to her being on the other side of the Atlantic and who's more interested in his rippling muscles. No, she needs someone to make her feel like a woman. Every woman needs to be made love to, to be worshipped – and often.'

Saff giggled. It was about the last thing she could ever have imagined her own mother saying.

'Now how is the cooking going dear? Have you had any orders yet?'

Saff sighed and looked at the chaos of muffin trays and mixing bowls on her kitchen table. 'It'll never work. The delis Ella and I tried were enthusiastic enough – when Ella finally bullied them into tasting things. Crikey, she's formidable when she wants to be. She told one chap that I'd cooked for Princess Diana for goodness' sake! But the minute they found out I was doing it at home, well they started going on about health and safety and how I couldn't just bake cakes in my kitchen.'

The Bean snorted loftily. 'Perfect codswallop. Think of all the things we ate during the war when I was a child. All fit as fiddles. Never even heard of salmonella. Alex grew up eating mud pies. Never did her any harm.'

'Exactly,' Saff replied, thinking about her great career plan which had now disappeared down the pan. 'So now I'm making forty muffins for sports day on Thursday. At least the headmistress is grateful for my efforts.'

The Bean said a warm goodbye and promised to let her know if she heard from Frankie. Saff was wiping flour from the table and thinking about starting supper when Millie strolled in, her feet slipping out of her sequinned pumps and her chubby little tummy peeping out between a pink ra-ra skirt and stripy top. She had white beads around her neck and had obviously been experimenting with the free make-up from the cover of a magazine.

'Hi, darling. What you up to?'

'I'm bored.'

'I'm just about to start supper. I'm doing your favourite pasta. Want to help me? You love doing that.'

Millie contemplated for a moment. 'Nah thanks. My friend Lydia says domestic chores demean women,' she said and she strolled out of the room.

Max stood back in the doorway as she passed. 'Did I hear that right?' he said as his daughter walked upstairs.

'I think so!' Saff started to chop an onion. 'Glad to hear feminism is alive and kicking!'

'She'd better ditch that idea if she wants to find herself a husband,' Max tutted and sashayed out of the way to avoid the tea towel his wife flicked at him. Saff laughed as he left the room, but a shadow of sadness crept over her. That was it then. The days had gone when Millie would have pulled up a stool next to her and helped by tipping ingredients into a bowl or stirring a pan. Now she was a tweenager, a woman-child who didn't need the silly ministrations of her mother. Even Millie seemed to know that a woman should find more to life than baking. Tipping the chopped onions into the heated olive oil, Saff stirred them more vigorously than she meant to.

It wasn't until later that the phone rang. Saff was cleaning up the dirty dinner plates and Max was chivvying up the children to get ready for bed when she heard him pick it up. 'Saff?' he called downstairs a moment later. Saff went into the hall and he held out the handset to her over the banisters, his hand over the mouthpiece. 'I don't know who it is,' he whispered, 'but they sound terribly distressed.'

'Hello?' Saff asked cautiously.

'It's me.' A voice howled down the phone.

'Alex? Is that you? Whatever's the matter?'

This was the most extraordinary noise Saff had ever heard. It seemed to come from deep in her chest. It was all the more remarkable because she hadn't heard Alex cry since they were both about fourteen when Ross Eardley had sent her a Dear

John letter. 'Calm down, sweetheart and tell me what's happened.'

After a few moments Alex spoke again, this time her voice a little more recognisable. 'I'm so sorry.'

'Sorry? What for?' Saff sat down on a kitchen chair, waving away a concerned looking Max at the door.

'For being a bitch and for not speaking to you,' Alex sobbed.

'Oh Alex, it doesn't matter. I deserved it. I did a terrible thing.' Saff smiled with relief. Nothing mattered now that Alex was talking to her again.

'But I have been and I was still angry as hell and was being stubborn and wasn't going to ring you.' There was a deep sniff. 'I've been such a fool, Saff. So proud and so stubborn. I know you were only trying to help, and I just wasn't there enough. All I could think was that you were all tricking me, laughing at me.'

'Oh Al.' Saff was so pleased to hear her voice. 'It wasn't like that at all. But we were wrong. We should have owned up about Frankie. He's such a lovely bloke, Alex. He didn't mean any harm.'

'I know, I know I should have trusted you,' Alex sobbed. 'And now I need your help and I'll understand if you say no. Oh Saff, I'm in such a mess. Can you help me, Saff?' Her voice sounded desperate.

Saff's heart contracted. 'Of course. Anything. What do you want?'

'It's huge Saff.'

'Shoot. If I can do it, I will.'

Alex sniffed again. 'Can you produce breakfast for three hundred people tomorrow morning?'

Chapter 41

Frankie quickly stashed his bags and holdall on to the back seat of Melik's old Mercedes and struggled to get his phone out of his pocket. Climbing in the front, his nostrils were filled with the smell of leather, aftershave and strong cigarettes. 'Is it OK if I make a quick call?' he asked and Meliks raised his black caterpillar eyebrows.

'Of course, my friend,' said the Turk as he screeched away, crunching the gears.

There was some delay as his phone searched for a signal and he scrolled through the options hurriedly. Eventually, he jabbed the button for the recently called numbers. Oh hell! He hadn't bothered to program in the international prefix for Ella's number. What was it again? He listened to the silence, the seconds ticking past, then the ringing tone. Where would she be now? What time was it at home? Please let her pick up.

'Hey, bro! Thanks for the text. Are you still in Istanbul, you jammy old sod? What's it like? Have you got me anything? You were a bit quick to volunteer, for someone who hates flying.'

'Listen, never mind all that now. I've got a taxi waiting and I'm about to come back. I've got all the stuff. Ella, I need you to do something for me, now listen carefully. This is really important ….'

Chapter 42

Alex rubbed her eyes and delved into her bag to try and find something to cover up the puffiness. Of course, there was nothing in there except a lip salve so, grabbing a handful of tissues, she ran them under the cold tap and held them to her eyes. She read in a magazine she'd picked up at an airport that it worked with cucumbers, so perhaps wet tissue would do the trick.

Not much improvement, she decided, as she peered into the mirror. The blackness of the paint on the walls of the Ladies and the intense light around the mirror revealed more detail than she could really cope with at the moment. For the first time in ages she took a moment to look at herself. I'm thin, but not in a good way, she thought. Pulling down the skin around her eyes she looked at the pale colour inside her eyelids. The shadows under her eyes were purple and she could see the veins. What could Frankie have possibly seen in her? She pushed her hair off her face. Perhaps he hadn't. Perhaps he'd just tried his hand and got lucky. Where was he now? She pulled out her hairbrush and tried to tidy herself up, pulling her hair back into a ponytail at the nape of her neck. It needed cutting. Perhaps she'd treat herself when this nightmare was over. She'd probably have plenty of time while looking for another job. Briskly she put her hairbrush back into her bag. Well, at least she had her model, even if what Bettina had to wear was on the other side of Europe. And, after a fashion, she had the catering sorted. Alex threw her bag over her shoulder and made her way up to the lobby of the hotel, sniffing and smiling a bit to herself as she remembered Saff's reaction to her absurd request.

'Three hundred?' she'd said after a pause, and Alex had explained briefly how Maurice had called her on her mobile at six and screeched dramatically how he was on the verge of a nervous breakdown and how he couldn't get the right strawberries and how his boyfriend's cat had been run over and that really he couldn't see how he could get everything done on time. Alex had been too shocked to react at first and had simply said OK and put down the phone, but it was in the taxi to meet Bettina Gordino at the Stanfield that the sheer extent of the disaster this represented sank in. Three hundred people, top sports and fashion journalists from all over the world, arriving at nine o'clock tomorrow morning and not so much as a bread roll to feed them on. She knew how Jesus must have felt. Ignoring the black leather, chrome and white lilies in the hotel's retro lobby, she'd bolted for the Ladies and had sat on the loo for ten minutes howling and sticking her fist in her mouth every time she heard someone come in. Her finger had hovered over Saff's number for ages before she'd finally called her. It was a ridiculous thing to ask. How could one woman single-handedly produce food for that number in the middle of the night? But it was Alex's only chance and, true to form, Saff had swallowed hard and simply said 'leave it with me'.

'Can you tell Bettina Gordino that Alex Hill is here please?' The thin receptionist, his hair gelled forwards as if he'd been in a wind tunnel, ran his finger down the computer screen to check the room number.

'Mmm. Senorina Gordino. Are you her publicist?' he asked sniffily.

'No no. She's doing a show for my product launch tomorrow. Is there a problem?'

'Well dear,' he sighed. 'She's been here about half an hour and has called down to reception five times already. The bath towels are too small, the pillows are too soft, can she get MTV, the air conditioning wasn't cold enough, oh and could we find her some bendy straws'? She wants red Jelly Babies and has asked that we fill the mini bar with Diet Coke. In glass bottles only.' He leaned forward conspiratorially. 'We're on the case with the Jelly Babies.'

'Thank you,' Alex breathed. 'I'd really appreciate it if you could ... look after her.'

'We'll do our best. Miracles may take a little longer. This isn't Claridges you know.'

'Indeed not.'

He picked up the phone to call Bettina's suite. 'Have you noticed,' he said as he waited, tapping his long thin fingers on the blotter, 'that Royalty try to behave like us these days – with their baseball caps and visits to the supermarket – and celebrities behave like royalty. This one,' he indicated the still ringing phone, 'would make Marie Antoinette blush.'

By half past eight, Alex was ready to admit the guillotine would have been too good for her. After frantic and begging calls to a leisure club where Alex had once been a member, she had managed to procure the diva a masseuse and someone to give her a pedicure, with a generous wedge of cash and the cachet of Bettina's name finally persuading them to cancel any evening appointments and come running. The hotel came up trumps with the right coloured Jelly Babies but they, regrettably, turned out to be the wrong make, and a bell hop was despatched to buy every type and make he could find until she approved.

'Otels in dis country are so terribull.' Bettina pouted, as she sat back against white silk cushions in her suite, draped in a thick hotel dressing gown, having her toenails painted by the beautician. 'You ave no idea ow to treat peoples. Now give me New York or Los Angeles. Nossing is too much trouble. What ave you lined up for me this evening?'

Alex swallowed and crossed her fingers behind her back. 'What did you have in mind?'

'Oh dear dear, dat's up to you. Dis city is so dismal. What on earth do you do for fun?' Get an Indian takeaway? Shave my legs? thought Alex dejectedly. 'I want to see the real London,' Bettina gasped, smoothing her hand over her perfect, unlined forehead. 'I don't want any of your tourist London.' She waved her hand expansively. 'So boring and so dirty. I want to see the London no one else sees. That,' she announced determinedly, 'is what *I* have in mind.'

'Right,' thought Alex quickly, discarding the faint hope that Bettina might be tired and wanting an early night. 'Would you like dinner somewhere?'

'Dinner? I don't eat dinner before a show!' she screeched, pulling her foot out of the beautician's hand. 'It makes me bloat up and spoils the look of the clothes. Didn't my peeeple tell you? Incidentally where are the clothes?'

'Here any moment,' Alex fluffed quickly. 'No dinner then. How about a show?' She couldn't think what, and time was running out but didn't good concierges boast they could get any theatre seat in London?

'What do you think I am? A child! I don't want one of your tacky musicals!'

'No, of course you don't.' Alex had run out of ideas and looked at her watch. Perhaps her friend on reception might have some brainwaves. How much would an exclusive pod on the London Eye be? she wondered. 'Just give me a moment. Relax and enjoy your pedicure and I'll be back.'

Ignoring the lift, Alex dashed down the stairs to the lobby but behind the desk now was a young girl who simply shrugged when Alex asked her for some pointers. The last thing Alex needed tomorrow morning was a disgruntled supermodel who'd had a shitty night in watching *Newsnight*. Her mobile buzzed in her pocket. Alex sighed.

'Hi Mum.'

'Just thought I'd wish you luck for tomorrow, dear. I hope it all goes well.' Alex couldn't stop herself and let out an hysterical cackle that made the head of the girl behind the desk shoot up, a look of alarm on her face. 'What's wrong dear? Are you OK?'

'Absolutely and completely not OK, Mum, to be honest.' She could hear the hysteria rising in her voice. 'I should be at the venue with Camilla, checking everything is ready for the biggest launch I have ever had to handle. But here I am standing in the lobby of the Stanfield, one of London's more pretentious hotels. I have a caterer who's had a hissy fit and pulled out. I have Saff producing breakfast for three hundred, though God knows how she'll achieve that. I have a diva of a supermodel upstairs who will only eat red Jelly Babies of a certain brand and whose outfit for the show is in Istanbul. I have Frankie trying to get it out of the factory, through customs and on to a flight so he's back here by nine a.m. tomorrow. And the aforementioned model is throwing a wobbly about the fact that she is bored and wants entertaining and anything I suggest isn't good enough. And to cap it all, I have someone at work who is determined to put the spanner in whatever I do out of some odd vendetta against me.' Alex stopped, exhausted.

There was a long pause at the end of the phone. 'So, for once,' said her mother eventually in a soft and rather teasing voice, 'my oh-so-independent daughter is admitting that she needs a bit of help?'

'A bit of help?' Alex knew her voice was raised. 'I need a sodding miracle!'

'Well, darling, for a start you need to trust people. If Saff says she can help, then she can. Let Frankie sort out things his end. He is a very capable man and if anyone can get the clothes out of Turkey he can.' Alex smiled to herself at the absurdity of what her mother was saying – how could she possibly know? – but it was sweet of her to try. 'I don't know anything about sabotage, though it sounds nasty. I remember someone did slash one of my dresses once before a show out of jealousy, that's usually the reason. Now, as you know, I am something of an expert on entertaining and being entertained. I'll be there in …' She paused, presumably looking at the delicate gold watch on her wrist. 'Twenty-five minutes.' She put down the phone before Alex could say anything else.

Fifty-five minutes later – after a delay while Bettina tried on and discarded ten different pairs of shoes – Alex experienced one of the more remarkable moments of her life: the sight of her 68-year-old mother in a floaty pink kaftan and white trousers, jewellery jingling, strolling out of the Stanfield hotel chatting animatedly to one of the world's highest-paid models. The expression on the younger woman's face was a mixture of awe and disbelief. From the moment The Bean had arrived, promptly, for the first time in her life, Bettina had been putty in her hands. For once, the model, who was probably paid more in a week than The Bean had earned in her lifetime, was cowed with admiration at this icon of the film and modelling world.

Alex smiled. Yes, perhaps having a famous mother had its compensations. She hailed the next taxi and headed for Brixton.

Chapter 43

The last place Ella imagined she would ever see someone like Alex was in a hip hop club in Brixton. But Frankie had been so insistent on the phone from Turkey that Ella had got in touch with Alex straight away. Alex, her voice frantic, had explained that she would be at the venue until late for the lighting and sound check and could she come there? She'd naturally sounded quite confused at being hounded by her erstwhile housekeeper but, when Ella had explained that Frankie had contacted her, Alex sounded keener to cooperate.

The space was huge and painted black, dominated by lighting gantries and engineers climbing over them attaching lights. Men in black T-shirts with headphones were rushing everywhere and chippies were banging nails into a catwalk that ran down the centre of the room. Thirty-foot high Zencorp logos in silver covered the walls and the whole place seemed to glisten and throb with excitement and expectation.

Ella almost had to run to keep up with Alex who was alternately talking to people and trying to get through to someone on her phone. 'Is he on his way?' she asked over her shoulder to Ella as she headed towards the green room. 'Has he got the stuff?'

'He'd just left the factory when I spoke to him last,' Ella panted. 'I didn't have time to find out more because he had no battery on his phone.'

'Oh bugger.' There was deep concern in Alex's voice. 'Oh God …'

Ella put out her hand to stop Alex and get her attention. 'Alex, he's the most reliable man I've ever met. Trust him.' Alex was looking hard at her. 'He once drove from Birmingham Rep to Carlisle just to change the wheel on my car on the M6 because I couldn't afford to go to a garage. He's always there when he says he's going to be.'

Alex sighed. 'I really want to believe you.'

'You must, Alex, which is why you've got to listen to me now. If Frankie says you need to wear an earpiece, then you need to wear it.'

Alex still looked sceptical. She had a sheaf of papers in her hand and was shuffling through them with a worried frown on her face. 'Look, Ella, do we have to talk about this now? I can't find where I've written down the phone number for Bettina's driver. I keep getting unobtainable and that can't be right. I have to double-check it.'

'Look, I can see you are busy – let me take care of this. I can get the equipment from a … a friend of mine. He works in radio and he's got access to everything you could ever need. I'm sure he'll lend it to me. I'll call him straight away. Please, Alex,' Ella pleaded. 'Frankie said it was vital.'

Alex seemed to reflect. An odd expression crossed her face and Ella wondered if she'd gone to far, but Frankie had sounded so urgent. Finally, Alex nodded, her face serious. 'OK, Ella. Do it. If Frankie says it's essential, it's essential. I trust him. And God knows I don't trust many people at the moment. Go for it.' And she turned away and continued rummaging through her papers.

Ella walked off in triumph and jabbed out the number on her phone. 'Hi Mike. Are you still awake? Don't go to bed yet, sweetheart, I'm on my way home. She's agreed to the earpiece so we need to get to your office to pick it up with the radio mikes. Put the kettle on, will you?' She smiled at his reply. 'Mmm, me too but we'll have to wait till later for that. I'll make it worth it though.' And she snapped her phone shut with a grin.

Chapter 44

The bright lights of the airport came into view. Even in the short space of the journey, Frankie was now Melik's new best friend. He'd had chapter and verse on his entire family and Frankie had invited him to stay in London with him sometime next year. They began warm farewells as Melik screeched up to the setting-down area and Frankie was about to slam the car door, his arms full of bags, when Melik suddenly slapped his forehead.

'Frankee, we have a problem. Where's your customs clearance?'

Frankie faltered. 'My what?'

'Well, when we send products out of the country they have to be cleared for export ...'

'Oh bugger. What am I going to do?' He could just hide them in his bag, but that scene from *Midnight Express* came into his mind once again. They'd find it and he'd be face down on the tarmac, guns trained on him, and what would Alex do then?

Melik shook his head. 'There is one thing you could do, but it wasn't my idea OK?' He smiled tooothily.

Chapter 45

Alex managed exactly thirty-five minutes of sleep. She didn't leave the Brixton club until gone 2 a.m. and was back, standing in the same spot, four hours later, the only difference being clean knickers and the company T-shirt. The time in between had involved ticking off lists, pacing, drinking coffee and worrying. Worrying about people turning up, worrying about models letting her down, worrying about food being hopeless/late/inedible. She worried about power failures, stylists making a hash of it, speakers blowing and seeing Todd now that she'd made love with Frankie. Had they made love? Is that what you call a moment of madness, even if it had been well … electrifying?

And she worried about Frankie. She worried about Frankie failing entirely. Somehow she knew he would do what he could – Ella had been insistent about that – but what if everything else conspired against him? She went online to check the Heathrow arrivals and then realised she actually had no idea where he had flown from and back to. It could be Inverness for all she knew.

The number of people bombarding her with questions kept her rooted to the spot and she peered over their heads to see if she could see Todd arriving. He'd texted to say he was on his way from the airport and was due any time. She wanted to see his face to be sure he didn't suspect anything. When he scooped her up in his arms it would wipe the slate clean. It would be as if sex with Frankie hadn't even happened. Wouldn't it?

'So, it's your big moment?' Alex started as Peter nudged her elbow painfully. 'Hear it's going to be the food-free breakfast. Innovative idea, Alex! That'll impress the hacks!'

But before she could answer he had sped away towards the flurry of activity by the door, and the arrival of the enormous figure of American Football hero, Malcolm Sanferino; one of the biggest names the company sponsored and Peter's pet project. He had to dip his head as he came through the door, but when he stood to his full six foot nine again he was head and shoulders above his sunglassed and menacing entourage. His black face had a broad smile and, before he could really take in the room and certainly before Alex could move towards him, Peter was on him like a bluebottle, with Gavin not far behind. Alex watched as they both fawned and scraped, necks craned up at the athlete who simply smiled back benignly. As they fussed over him and moved him towards his dressing room, a familiar perfume filled Alex's nostrils. Donatella, resplendent today in gold lamé and Burberry, was beside her.

'Donatella, do you have the exact running time for Bettina?'

She tapped her teeth with her perfectly sharpened pencil and consulted her schedule. 'Yes, but I need her here. What time is she due?'

'Seven-thirty. She wouldn't come any earlier. She said it was the earliest she had got up. Ever.'

'And her clothes? They're out back in her dressing room?'

Alex looked about her, hoping Frankie would swing through the doors any minute. 'Er, not exactly.' She leaned in closer. 'In fact, to be honest they aren't here at all yet.'

Donatella went white under her tan foundation. 'You *are* kidding?'

'Oh trust me, they are on their way with our special courier but they have had to be done so exclusively for her that there's been a delay.' At that moment and like an angel of salvation, Camilla came towards her, her eyes bright, holding in her arms a pile of the new range for the dancers, all bagged up. She looked fresh and pretty. How did she manage it?

'Morning!' Camilla smiled brightly. 'I'm just checking off the clothes against my list. Donatella, do you want to come with me? We can go through it all together? Alex, I've put Jelly Babies in Bettina's dressing room and some of that special water she likes. That should keep her happy for a while at least!'

Through the swelling mêlée of company press people, all of whom had flown in from all points of the compass, Alex finally saw Todd's head. He was taller than most and he scanned the enormous room to find her. He had a frown of irritation on his face and from nowhere she felt a sudden urge to turn away from him. Where had that come from? She didn't have time to think about it, but pushed aside a strong feeling of disquiet. Instead, she put up her hand and waved. His face changed to recognition when he saw her and he made his way purposefully towards her.

'Hi there,' he said as he reached her, slightly out of breath. 'Goddamn taxi couldn't find the place, and there were hold-ups at the airport. Now, is Sanferino here yet? And I've got *Vanity Fair* wanting to do a British hip hop piece. You have lined me up a spokesperson, haven't you?' He cast about him to assess the situation.

'And hello to you too!' She could hear the forced cheer in her voice. 'Don't I even get a kiss?'

He looked at her as if he only just remembered who she was. 'I don't think that would be very professional, do you?'

'Oh, right. No. Perhaps not.' Feeling stupid, she looked

down at her papers and told him what time his interviews were scheduled, and he walked off briskly towards one of the people putting out press packs near the door.

'Alex?' Someone else came into her eye line now. 'Gordino? She here yet?' It was the make-up girl. 'I need her soon. Where is she?' Alex looked at her watch. Shit. Nearly eight o'clock. Less than an hour before the doors opened. She gasped. 'I had no idea it was that late.' She pulled out her phone and pressed redial on the driver's number. Unobtainable.

'Where do you want the juices?' A short man in a logoed T-shirt that said The Organic Smoothie Company was standing in front of her now holding a heavy box.

'Juices?'

'Yupo. Juices. I've had an order from …' He balanced the box on his knee and looked askew at his delivery sheet. 'Saffron, I think it says. Three hundred and fifty bottles of our very best smoothies. Ordered last night. Where d'ya want them, this is kinda heavy?'

Alex's face lit up. God bless her. One thing had arrived at least. 'Yup, over there.'

'Gotcha.'

Alex's mobile then buzzed. 'Alex, it's me.' Saff sounded so breathless Alex could barely hear her. Had something gone wrong? 'We're just coming down Acre Lane. Can you make sure there is someone at the door to help us unload?'

'Will do! Are you OK?'

'Bit tired but fine. See you in a mo.' And she hung up.

Alex collared one of the events team who was sound-checking the music system to stand and wait by the door and, as she went to show him where, a large and flash-looking limousine pulled up. Relief flooded through Alex and she opened the rear door. But what stepped out was not the long lean supermodel she had been expecting. It was a long white-trousered leg closely followed by the pink-kaftaned body of The Bean.

'Good morning, daarling,' she said expansively and opened her arms as if she was stepping on to the red carpet at an award ceremony.

'But where's Bettina gone, for goodness' sake?'

'I'm here. Stop your fretting!' She popped her head out, her long brunette hair tumbling over her shoulders. 'I haven't had a minute of sleep, but …' A broad grin swept over her face. 'I've had sooo much fun.' Before she could elaborate, Donatella tottered out of the main doors and scooped her up with a broad arm ushering her into the building and away from the crowd of onlookers who were beginning to gather behind the security barricades.

Alex turned to her mother. 'What the hell have you been doing all night?' she asked, not sure whether to be cross or relieved.

'Oh, I can hardly begin to remember.' Her mother had a rather self-satisfied look in her eye. 'We had a cocktail at the Ritz. Do you know, Alphonso *still* works there and was thrilled to see me. They served us on the house of course. You know, I don't think I've ever paid for a drink at the Ritz.' She started to walk in through the doors as if invited and Alex hurried after her. 'Then we did the French in Soho – or was that next? Anyway, I found the most charming cabbie – right about my age, late fifties, and a great fan apparently – and, bless him, he took us on a tour of the places I'd filmed with Terence and Alan. That Bettina girl was enchanted. Completely mad apparently about all that Quant stuff. Made her scream with laughter when I told her we wore paper dresses! Well, after that, let me think, we stopped by at the National to say hello to some friends – they gave her a super tour back stage and we joined in the after-show party, and then New Covent Garden … some lovely man showered us with lilies – they're in the car – followed by a splendid breakfast at Smithfield. Gosh, for a little thing, she can pack away bacon and eggs. Are we late? Only we thought we might be, but the driver didn't turn up until seven forty-five. I did ask him but he said he'd had a call changing the pick-up time.' The Bean turned to Alex. 'I did think that was a bit odd dear. Do you think it's that saboteur again? How exciting!'

The Bean entered the huge hall and took in the stage, now festooned with suspended logos, the company motto adjusted to Live For Your Life not Play For Your Life, writ large and, against the back wall, a giant screen showing a visual montage of great sporting moments intertwined with hip hop and R&B videos, the singers gyrating provocatively. The crew were practising training lasers on the ceiling. All it needed now was people.

'Alex, a moment?' Todd was by her side before she could respond to her mother's monologue. 'Hello, Mother dear,' he said. 'I just need to speak to your daughter.' Taking Alex by the elbow, he steered her away, though not before she spotted the outraged look on her mother's face. 'Mother dear' would not have gone down well. 'Alex, I'm not happy with the short time you've given me for the *New York Times*. They have been on the phone—'

'Alex.' Ella's voice came from behind her. 'Can you just pop this in your ear?'

'Oh, Ella, I've got too much to sort out …'

'Just do it, Alex?'

Grudgingly Alex took the little earpiece and slipped it into her ear where it hummed quietly. 'Now, Todd, I've given you what I can. I promise, you have more interviews lined up than anyone else. Is there any sign of Saff?'

'Saff? Your friend? That little thing? Why on earth would she be here? First your mother, now Saff. Is this some kind of family get-together?' His voice sounded sneering and spoilt.

'Yup, Todd,' she said, looking directly at him. 'It's looking very much that way. They're here to help me.' Turning on her heel, she went towards the door. It now thronged with people all holding clipboards and talking into walkie-talkies. Alex glanced at her watch: 8.50 and still no food and no Frankie. This was a nightmare, especially as she could see Gavin out of the corner of her eye. He was clearly getting an update from Camilla, who was looking at her watch anxiously then putting her hands to her mouth with an expression of deep concern. Behind him Ella was hovering, virtually jumping from one foot to another, and she was holding something in her hand and trying to get his attention. What on earth was wrong with the girl?

Then at that moment the group at the door parted like the Red Sea and they all looked up, startled by the vision that came between them. Framed in the doorway was Frankie, but the only thing recognisable about him was his red face. The rest of him looked as though it had been inflated like a balloon. On his legs, just peeping out beneath the enormous Sanferino-sized livid yellow American Football shirt, emblazoned with the company logo, was a pair of long baseball shorts which came halfway down his calves, and on his face was an expression of excruciating pain.

Chapter 46

Frankie struggled over to where Alex was standing, her face a picture of incomprehension. He didn't think he could hold out much longer.

'Frankie! Thank God you made it! Where's the stuff? And what on earth is wrong with you?'

'Am I in time?' he squeaked. 'Where's Bettina? Can you point me to the nearest loo?'

'What? What are you …? Oh, my! Frankie! You're not?'

'Yes,' he gasped. 'Yes, I'm wearing it all! It was the only way to get it through customs without the documents. I had to put it on in Istanbul airport. I'm wearing all Bettina Gordino's outfits under this, as well as a couple of T-shirts Melik gave me as a gift.' He gestured awkwardly at his padded body. 'You might have mentioned she had more than one change of clothes. You wouldn't believe how uncomfortable I am! What size is she, for God's sake? This stuff will only stretch so far!'

Alex burst out laughing, almost doubled up with mirth. She pointed over to the corner where the loos were and he waddled hurriedly towards them, stiff legged, like a huge duckling but, as he turned away, he was almost sure he heard her say, 'Frankie, you're the best!' Frankie shrugged off the odd looks he was attracting from the ranks of cool hunters, journalists and photographers and shouldered his way through into the relative peace of the Gents, followed closely by Ella, who he heard before he saw.

'Yes, I do know it's the Gents, thank you very much!' she snorted, pushing a man out of the way. 'I've got urgent business in there – no, not that kind! Don't be disgusting! Frankie! Are you all right?'

Frankie was grappling with the first layer of clothing. The trouble was Bettina's outfits were so tight he could barely flex his arms to pull anything off. In fact, he seemed to have lost all sensation in his buttocks. Ella set to at once.

'Right, can you bend over at least? OK, I've got it, now puuuull!' Off came Sanferino's T-shirt. 'Oh my goodness, Frankie. What do you look like?' Ella was gaping at the tighter than skintight tops and shorts that he'd crammed himself into over five hours ago.

'To be honest,' he croaked. 'I'm past caring what I look like. I'm baking hot. My nuts are killing me. And I'm desperate for a wee. That Turkish coffee's strong stuff. Just get me out of here, would you?'

Tugging and heaving, Ella gradually eased him out of a zip-up jacket, two hooded tops and three crop tops, sympathetically rubbing the red marks the seams had left on his skin. Then she started tugging down the waistband of a pair of cropped leggings, leaning back to pull at them with all her weight while he lay on his back on the floor. As Frankie shed each layer, he felt himself expand to his normal size and shape again and, as she dragged off the last pair of shorts – especially made to cling to Bettina's slinky form – he dashed into a cubicle in his pants and socks to relieve himself.

Ella rubbed the tears of laughter from her eyes and set about shaking out and folding each item of discarded clothing. 'Oh Frankie!' she called. 'You've really changed! You've become so … so random!'

'I hope to God that's a good thing because I'm not going

260

through that again.' Frankie stretched his arms to check everything was working again.

'Oh yes,' chuckled Ella as she passed him his own clothing from the holdall he had trailed behind him. 'A very good thing. You'd never have tackled anything as mad as this before. You're like a new person. I'm really proud of you.'

Frankie buttoned up his polo shirt and glanced at her reflection in the mirror. 'Now I really am worried! Oooh! That feels better. But I'm not sure my tackle will ever be the same again. Come on, now. Let's get those mikes sorted. Deliver the clothes to Sanferino and Bettina – thank God for Lycra but give them a squirt of air freshener maybe – and Ella, leave Melik's T-shirts in the changing room too will you? I'll collect them later. I might even let you have one.'

Chapter 47

Saff didn't think she had ever known Max drive so fast. He already had six points on his licence but he seemed oblivious to that as he hurtled along the road and she, Oscar and Millie, all squeezed in beside him in the Offcut Productions van, simply swayed one way and another as it lunged. Saff did mutter 'watch the food', but that was all. He had been so fantastic over the last few hours that she didn't want to say anything else. She knew that she'd suffer for the children not having slept all night either, but for the moment the whole family was running so high on adrenalin that it didn't really matter.

'Right,' she'd said as soon as the enormity of Alex's request had sunk in last night. 'All hands to the oven, and I mean all.' Barking orders like a field marshal, within minutes she had Oscar manning the mixing bowls, Millie on the weighing scales and Max on his way to the all-night supermarket under strict orders to buy every muffin, brioche, pain au chocolate and croissant he could lay his hands on. He'd arrived back at 3 a.m., having visited eight supermarkets, while she and the children had used up every ingredient she could think of to make more cakes and muffins, including one batch of coconut and raisin invented by Oscar. It had been Max's idea to commandeer the company van to transport the food and now every tray and baking tray, plate and chopping board Saff possessed was lying in the back, the breakfast offerings on them covered in cling film. She'd let her imagination run wild, customising the shop-

262

bought muffins exuberantly with icing or sweet garnishes until they looked unrecognisable. She just hoped they didn't taste that way too.

'Pimp my muffin!' Oscar had shrieked at one point, icing tube in hand.

'It's just here on the right. Where all those people are standing.' Saff pointed. 'Can you move please!' she shouted out of the window only to have Millie dig her in the ribs and tell her to stop being so embarrassing. 'My darling, we are the A-Team today and nothing must get in our way,' she smiled, curiously elated by the last frantic hours. It must have been light-headedness from lack of sleep.

'Are you Saff?' A tall man in a black T-shirt ripped open the door. 'Alex tells me you need a hand?'

'Sure do!' Saff hopped out of the van checking vaguely that she didn't look too hideous. There had just been time to change her food-splattered T-shirt before they left home but a hair-brush had been a detail too far. She pulled open the rear doors of the van and they began to unload, the large plates from her wedding dinner service going in first to act as serving platters. Well, you can't offer a muffin to the leading fashion journalists from around the world on a baking tray, can you?

As she entered the hall for the first time, Saff's jaw dropped as the scale of the event hit her. In the cosy atmosphere of her kitchen, a breakfast for three hundred seemed like a joke, but this was serious. The décor, the lighting effects and the industriousness of the people rushing about, even before the arrival of the press, was on a level Saff could not have imagined. With the children's help, she laid out the food on the serving table they were shown by the tall man, while Max went to park the van somewhere it wouldn't get a ticket. There was no sign of Alex, though Saff did spot Todd who didn't seem to notice her wave of greeting. He must be busy.

'Wow, Mum – this is amazing. Can we stay?' Millie was beside her, suspended in motion and gaping at the room, a tray of tiny Danish pastries in her hand.

'Of course not! The last thing they need is us knocking about. We'll just set up and make ourselves scarce. Come here and put those down.'

'Wow!' Saff turned at Alex's voice and spontaneously they rushed into each other's arms. 'I can't tell you …' Alex began, wiping her nose with the back of her hand.

'Then don't,' said Saff laughing. 'It was fun. Now we're outta here.' She brushed some fallen icing sugar from the side of a plate, and put her hands on the children's backs to steer them out. They were oblivious to her, having spotted a hugely tall black man in livid yellow kit. Their mouths gaped open.

'Mumm!' Oscar hissed. 'That's only Malcolm Sanferino. Please can we stay for a bit? He's mega!'

'I hope you *are* bloody staying.' Alex turned sharply from the person who had collared her about a translator. 'I need waiters. Any size will do. Do you think Max might help? I'm going to ask Frankie if he's willing, though the poor man has just flown in from Turkey.' She stood on tiptoes to see if she could spot him. 'But I think he may be permanently disabled from wearing several pairs of women's shorts!'

'What are you on about? Has he been on holiday? Only he never said.'

'Don't ask – I'll explain later.'

'But.' Saff was confused. 'I thought he was waiting to hear about the audition?'

Alex's hand went to her mouth in horror. 'Oh God, I've been so self-absorbed I didn't even think to ask about what he was doing. Is it a big one?'

'Pretty huge, yes. And he's nervous as anything about it. Crikey.' Saff watched in horror as people began to take up their positions around the room and at the door in readiness for the event to get underway and the show to start. 'We can't waiter like this.' She tried pointlessly to brush down her clothes.

'Wait there,' cried Alex rushing off backstage only to come back a moment later with four company T-shirts. 'Do this for me you lot and I promise Sanferino autographs and a photo opportunity if I can nab him. Is that enough pay?' Oscar and Millie laughed in excitement and promptly took off their tops to replace them with the T-shirts.

'Er,' said Saff hesitantly. 'Is there somewhere I could go to change? Otherwise you'll end up with a topless waitress.'

'Now that *would* guarantee us press coverage!' quipped Alex and they both roared with laughter relishing the fact that they were communicating again.

'Alex,' someone said, taking her arm. 'You're needed over here urgently.'

Chapter 48

'What's the problem?' Alex looked in the direction the roadie who'd interrupted her was pointing.

'I don't know, but the girl over there was very insistent that I got you over as soon as possible.'

Alex made her way across the room. The tension of expectation in the place was palpable now. Last-minute wires left on the catwalk were being whisked away by crouching chippies and electricians. The company's PR managers, including Todd, were glued to mobile phones or briefing translators. Donatella was in and out of the backstage door like a ferret in high heels, checking lighting angles so she could brief her models and dancers on their routine one more time.

Alex sighed. The girl was Ella and now she gestured to Alex frantically. 'Ella, what in God's name is this all about? You have been hassling me since last night! I don't even know why you are here and this bloody earpiece is driving me mad! Besides, you have a bit of explaining to do to me—'

'I told you, Frankie asked me to be here. Now listen,' I need to get you somewhere quiet.' Ella was pulling her by the arm away from the noise of people arriving.

'But it's about to start!' Alex was stumbling behind her, looking back over her shoulder at the room that was poised and ready. Ignoring her protestations, Ella careered through the swing door to the backstage area, almost colliding with the crowd of models and dancers waiting to go on to the catwalk and all dressed in the new range. Alex just had time to register that they looked breathtaking before Ella did an about-turn and pulled her down a corridor in the other direction to an area where it was quieter, and pushed her firmly behind an air conditioning vent.

'Sssh, now listen.' Ella was barring any escape route.

Alex wasn't sure what she was listening for. All she could hear was the chatter of the dancers in the distance and the hum of the earpiece in her ear. Perhaps Ella was going to tell her something. Though, judging by the deadly serious expression in her face, it looked more likely that Ella was going to beat her up. 'What for?'

'Just wait.' Ella was panting and out of breath.

At that moment there was a rustling noise in Alex's ear and the muffled tap of someone putting their fingers to a mike. 'Alex, it's Frankie.' His voice came deep and clear through her earpiece and she jumped. 'I know you can't say yes or no so I'm just going to have to assume you can hear me.' Alex nodded then felt stupid. 'It's crap timing I know,' he began and for a moment Alex thought he was going to talk about what happened on Friday night. Then he went on. 'But I need you to listen to something.' All she could hear then were footsteps, his presumably, going down a corridor and the squeak of a door opening. It shut with a quiet thud behind him and she could hear his footsteps, though more lightly now and the faint noise of the fabric of his clothes rubbing as he walked. What was going on?

'Ah!' he said loudly and suddenly. 'Camilla? What on earth are you doing?'

Chapter 49

Frankie stared at the pale figure in the shadows. From out on the dance floor he could hear a hum of expectation building. The whole thing was about to start. He would have to be quick.

Camilla had jumped when she heard his voice and turned round to face him. She was smiling and he wondered for an agonising moment if he'd made an awful mistake, but then he noticed that she was concealing something behind her back and saw the way her eyes kept darting to the side. 'Frankie! There you are. Alex has been looking for you everywhere. You're in big trouble! You'd better go and find her, quick.'

Frankie moved closer, hoping the mike Ella had clipped to his shirt would be sensitive enough to pick up Camilla's words as well as his own. 'I don't think I'm the one in trouble, am I, Cam? What have you got there? Show me.'

She side-stepped towards the door, keeping her back to him. Frankie glanced at the floor and there were what looked like the T-shirts Melik had given him. They were slashed to ribbons. 'Did you do that, Cam?'

'What? What are you talking about?' Her expression was almost childlike, her eyes wide with innocence.

'The outfits there. They're ruined. Did you slash the outfits, Camilla?'

Her eyes flicked to the pile on the floor and she looked almost manic. Frankie tried to sound gentle as if talking to a frightened animal. 'Did you do it so that Bettina couldn't go on? So that it would look like Alex had messed up, Cam?'

'Yes, I did!' Camilla hissed slowly, her teeth bared in an ugly snarl and she produced a long pair of scissors from behind her back. 'I did, and I'm glad I did. She doesn't deserve this job. She'd be nothing without my support. Gavin's realised it at last and now everyone else will too.'

'You've been very clever, Cam,' Frankie said, more calmly than he felt. 'All those other things you did – hiding the phone charger, sending the email to Melik changing the delivery date.'

Camilla shook her head dismissively. 'That was nothing. Just the icing on the cake, you might say. I've been working on this for months. And she never suspected a thing!' she laughed shrilly.

'Oh, but she did, Cam,' said Frankie but Camilla didn't seem to be listening.

'You don't know the half of it, Frankie,' she went on triumphantly. 'There was the Power Point presentation in Toronto, the flights in Milan. I even knew Maurice wouldn't be able to cope with the catering and would back out. His references were crap! He couldn't make a bacon sandwich. But Alex was so trusting! She made it so easy. She even let me take her computer home with me. I deleted files, changed dates, sent all kinds of emails. What a fool she is! And now this! I was so disappointed when you arrived with the clothes, Frankie. I thought giving you the wrong address would stop you. It wasn't very nice of you to mess up my plans. But I've taken care of that too.'

'Ah, but you haven't, Cam. That's the thing. Bettina has the clothes. What you've just shredded was a present for me from Melik. I left them around as bait. You're not so clever after all.'

Camilla's smile faltered. 'Listen!' They could both hear music getting louder above them. 'You've failed, Cam. And Alex has won – through sheer hard work and talent, Alex has beaten you.'

The drumbeat above them was firm and rhythmic. 'But,' Camilla faltered. 'I don't understand. You don't even like her. I thought you were on my side?'

Frankie took in her pretty face turned ugly now with spite and envy. 'Well, you've got it all wrong. I like her. I like her very much. It was Alex who asked me to come in and help. She suspected someone was out to get her. She just didn't know who.'

'You bastard!' she hissed. 'You stupid, interfering bastard!' And she hurled the scissors at him and fled through the open doorway.

Frankie let out a sigh of relief. 'Gavin, if you can hear me you'd better alert door security. I hope you all heard that, cos I'm not doing another take.'

Chapter 50

Blissfully unaware of any drama backstage, Saff made her way amongst the growing crowd of people who had arrived, offering around the plate of muffins in her hand. The guests, if that was what you called them, didn't seem as friendly as those at the parties she'd waitressed during sixth-form holidays. This lot were sour faced and had the world-weary expression of people who had done this many times before. The range of nationalities was extraordinary; there were Oriental and Mediterranean faces, American accents, and languages Saff didn't recognise being spoken at high speed and even higher volume. As she approached with trays of food, several gave her a look as if she'd crawled out from under a stone. She only hoped they weren't treating Millie and Oscar with such disdain. She peered around the various groups to see if she could spot them, but the crowd was too thick now. Max swept past at one point and pinched her bottom surreptitiously. 'Hey cutie,' he leered into her ear. 'Doing anything after breakfast?' She giggled at him and moved on to wave Danishes under the nose of the Japanese delegation. Tentatively they picked them up and peered at them suspiciously, not sure if they were meat or pastry and then slowly tasted them. Saff waited, holding her breath, until they nodded their heads in fervent approval and took more.

Oscar came up beside her. 'We're clean out of coconut and raisin, Mum!' he squealed. 'I told you it would be a winner.' Then he was off again to collect another tray.

The volume of noise in the hall increased, helped by the constant thud of music from the huge speakers. Lasers began to flash across the roof and a deep and rhythmic drumbeat began. As the tension was cranked up, the gathered audience began to focus their attention on the stage. The lights over them were dimmed and Saff began to search more seriously for Millie. There had been so much movement of people, she was worried she might have got lost. Over the other side, Saff spotted Alex coming through a swing door to the backstage area. Her eyes were on the stage but her expression was blank. Saff squeezed her way across to her side.

'I know you don't need this right now, but have you seen Millie?'

Alex started and looked down at her friend. 'Sorry?'

'I've lost Millie.'

Alex waved her hand vaguely. 'She'll be fine. The staff on the door wouldn't let her leave.' Her eyes looked completely startled.

'Are you OK?' Saff put her hand on her arm. 'Has something gone wrong?'

'Yes, but I think it's sorted now.' Alex looked at her and smiled. 'It's fine. In fact everything makes sense now. It's all falling into place. And Saff ...' She gave her friend a warm kiss on the cheek. 'You've been wonderful.'

Anything more she may have said was drowned in the sudden gust of sound from the stage and they both turned as the show burst into life. What followed was so awe-inspiring that Saff forgot that she had been awake all night, that she hadn't sat down since seven o'clock yesterday evening and that it was breakfast time in Brixton. Accompanied by a pounding beat that Saff recognised from one of Oscar's CDs, a swarm of dancers cascaded on to the stage in a mass of colour and clothing that cleverly mixed sportswear, casualwear and what Saff imagined people called Urban. They spun and cartwheeled, swayed and strutted, all flat stomachs and legs up to their armpits. Some of it was so sexually electric Saff looked about quickly to see the children's reactions, only to spot Oscar's face lit up in wonder. It was not as awe-struck, though, as his father's behind him. Max was almost dribbling.

Images of the Zencorp logo, swooping and diving, lit up the screen behind the dancers, ramming home the branding. The words Urban Active flashed on the screen. This, thought Saff, was unashamed hard selling and she watched as the assembled audience scribbled on pads and flicked through the press pack looking for more information. Flashbulbs momentarily lit up the catwalk even more, and photographers crawled about to get interesting positions and angles. Then on to the stage came figures dressed entirely in white. No skin was showing, not even their faces which were hidden behind fine white mesh, but on their feet was a glorious array of footwear in the colours of summer fruit. Not trainers exactly but not fashion shoes either. Something in between, in pink and lemon, mango and lime green. So delicious you would want one pair in each colour. Saff spontaneously clapped her hands in glee and then realised she was the only one doing it. Alex put her arm around her gratefully and to cover her friend's embarrassment.

Next came models – boys and girls, black and white – wearing alternately jeans or beautifully cut trousers, skirts and even business suits together with items from the new range. Saff could almost see herself in them, though she might be ten years too old.

'What do you reckon?' Alex bent down and whispered loudly in her ear over the music.

'It's so clever, Alex. So clever. Millie will be nagging me to death about it. The punters will love it!'

'How can you tell?' laughed Alex nervously. 'This lot seem to be distinctly underwhelmed.' Saff looked at the amassed journalists and Alex was right. They were all staring at the stage, that was for sure, but their expressions were unreadable. One small woman in black with short bobbed hair and half-moon glasses was talking into some kind of dictaphone. It could even have been her mobile. At an enormous whooshing sound Saff's attention was snatched back to the stage where a fountain of silver fireworks had gone off at the back, and through the smoke came Bettina Gordino.

'God, isn't she gorgeous?' Saff gasped, as the rake thin model made her way like a pedigree feline up the catwalk. The photographers went mad, catching every angle of her beautiful face made up now with the lightening-like flash of the Zencorp logo, her back-combed hair transformed with gold and bronze highlights. The crop top she wore clung like cling film and on her hips were the briefest, belted white shorts cut somewhere between athletics shorts and a fashion item from the sixties. They looked like they had been sprayed on. Saff nudged Alex. 'How in God's name did she get into *them*?'

Alex snorted with laughter in reply. 'She didn't have as much trouble as Frankie did!'

More dazzling variations on the theme pranced on to the stage including a hip hop posse who danced to a jerky track, the climax of which saw the enormous Sanferino strolling on to the stage in livid yellow. He was clearly not used to appearing as a model but, despite his size, he managed to be graceful and exude an almost intimidating presence. Bettina followed, transformed again by another outfit. The energy coming off the stage was extraordinary and Saff could feel herself dancing along to the beat. The models and dancers seemed to be enjoying themselves, Bettina even managing to wave at someone in the audience but Saff couldn't see who. Then, as the music reached a massive crescendo, there was another explosion of fireworks and lasers and they all froze, their arms held out in a position of celebration.

There was silence. Saff glanced up quickly to Alex whose face was a picture of tension, her eyes trained on the audience. It occurred to Saff then just what this meant to her. Just how important this event was. Then there was another explosion but this time of thunderous applause. People stamped their feet and whooped and Alex threw her arms around Saff in an embrace that almost stopped her breathing.

'Fantastic. Bloody fantastic!' Saff yelped, and watched as Alex then made her way into the crowd to talk to the astonished journalists. As the groups parted, Saff could see a smallish black man in shades and a loose jacket and trousers. On his fingers were a mass of rings and there were chains around his neck. Surrounding him were huge men in suits who had to be minders, and a growing crowd of photographers and onlookers, but he was too deep in conversation with the small girl standing beside him and chatting animatedly to notice. Saff could sense Max standing beside her. 'Who is that Millie is talking to?' she asked in horror.

'I am reliably informed by Oscar, who is pea green with envy, that it is a character called Dizzy Zee who, Daaad,' he mimicked, 'is only like the coolest hip hop singer in the universe.'

'Crikey, that's a coup. Was he invited?'

'I believe not. He slipped in during the show. A friend of Bettina's apparently. Alex looks as surprised as anyone.'

'Well.' Saff looked about her as the crowd began to mill about, some being escorted by press reps for interviews, others beginning to leave. 'Do you suppose they all want some more breakfast?'

'There's not much left for them to eat. I think we're virtually cleaned out. A woman from some snooty magazine asked me which company I worked for because they had a magazine event coming up.' He put his hand in his back pocket and pulled out her card. 'Here you are.'

Saff took it and laughed out loud. 'Jeeeze. That's a biggie. Shame. That would be fun!'

'But why's it a shame? Why can't you do it?' Max insisted.

'Cos I can't, silly. This was just a one-off emergency to help Alex.'

Max put his hands on her shoulders. 'Darling, I have never seen you look so excited by anything as you were last night putting this together. You were loving it, weren't you?'

Saff looked down, a bit embarrassed. 'Yes, I was really.'

'Then why not think about doing it more seriously? We'll get the kitchen all up to standards – even rent you a little unit if you like – and you can cater events at Offcut and we'll get your name out there. Alex will help I'm sure. And you can do it when you want so you can still be there for the children.' Saff watched the excitement in Max's eyes. 'I've been worried about you, but I didn't know what to say. What to suggest. Then, when I watched you last night I realised you were missing a challenge. How about it?'

So he *had* noticed, and for once this was about her, about what *she* wanted to do, about what she *could* do. She threw her arms around Max's neck, tears in her eyes.

Chapter 51

Alex had waited behind a while at the venue to answer questions and make sure all the promised interviews had been completed – *The Times* took ages – and she'd seen Bettina off back to her hotel, accompanied by Dizzy Zee who'd kissed Alex and declared the show to be 'awesome' and could she send some stuff over to his hotel? Sanferino had shaken and almost dislocated her hand and, with a deep rolling laugh, had announced he could quite 'dig' being a model. Of Frankie and Ella there was no sign.

'Have you seen them?' Alex asked The Bean who was at her side. 'Only I need to say thanks.'

'Perhaps they've gone home, darling. The poor boy must be exhausted after his midnight flit and then he was holed up with Gavin and Camilla and a very tall security guard for quite some time. How exciting! He told me all about it.'

'Did he get to see the show?' Somehow it was important to her that he had.

'Oh yes, he stood with me. Quite the strangest outfits but I suppose they have a certain charm. I'd quite like a pair of those shoes in nectarine.'

'Then Mum, you shall have a pair. And in fuschia and lemon and anything you want. I am so grateful to you.'

'Not bad for an old Has-Bean am I?' Her face was questioning, searching Alex's for reassurance.

'Certainly not. You are my favourite Bean.' She brushed back a stray hair from her mother's face. 'I think I have realised

I can't do all this on my own. You know, be Miss Independent. Sometimes it's good to let people help. I know I couldn't have managed without you.' She could feel a lump in her throat. 'Now get yourself off to bed before I get all soppy.'

The Bean kissed her daughter on her forehead. 'And that wouldn't do, would it, Alex, my dear? I'm so proud of you, my clever little girl.' And she laughed and walked away. Suddenly Alex felt her feet go from under her as she was scooped off the floor.

'Babe, you were brilliant. Awesome!' Todd spun her round. 'The *New York Times* is enchanted. *Vanity Fair* are nagging for show pics and Miss Ice Cold from the *LA Times* even smiled!'

Alex returned his kiss, but his mouth tasted stale. 'So you managed to keep them all happy? Nagging me paid off then?'

'Oh, come now. I've gotta do my job. It's publicity you want, isn't it?'

'Yes, Todd, it is.'

'Now, how about dinner later? Let me follow up all these requests …' He held up his file. 'Then you and me will go somewhere lovely and celebrate.' He leaned closer and whispered in her ear, 'Your bed would be a good start.'

She pulled away slightly and there, over Todd's shoulder, she could see Frankie disappearing out of the building. Alex flinched as Todd nibbled her earlobe. 'Er, perhaps not tonight hey? I'm very tired and there will be loose ends to sort out.' She smiled weakly at his puzzled expression. 'I'll call you some time.' And almost barging him out of the way, she dashed for the door after Frankie, shaking off people trying to stop her and shake her hand. She needed to see him. To say thank you. To say anything. Just to see him. Which way had he gone?

As she heaved open the swing doors, she was faced with a pavement full of people and crowds pushing against the security barriers for one last celebrity gawp. And through the crowd she could just make out Frankie and Ella's heads through the back window of a departing taxi. Suddenly the exhaustion of the last few hours caught up with her and she could feel herself slump.

Back at the office things were not as she had left them last night. As they all poured back in from the launch there was chatter and laughter. Phones rang incessantly and people called their colleagues across the room for information, more details on prices, earliest dates for supplies. People slapped Alex on the back as she arrived. Even the receptionist seemed to have heard it went well and smiled warmly. As she approached her desk, there was a small crowd gathered around it.

'Is this the welcoming committee?' she laughed as she dropped her bag, but none of them appeared to be smiling. Alex followed their gaze to the top of her desk. Her laptop, or at least what was left of it, was strewn across it, the lid smashed and twisted, the contents spewing out like road kill. Papers had been ripped and hurled about, save one on which was written 'Fucking bitch'. Alex looked over at Camilla's desk, which was completely clear because anything on it had been swept on to the floor, and its surface had been scratched deeply with something sharp. 'Oh dear,' Alex said lamely. 'I take it she's not here.'

'No. She came back to clear her desk and went beserk.' Gavin approached from his office. 'We had to call the police, though I probably should have done so straight away. She's with them now – I'm sorry you had to see this, Alex. Come on, people.' He turned to the crowd and put on a cod American accent. 'There's nothing for you here. Go back to your lives. Alex, in my office?' She followed him, leaving the carnage behind and Peter who, ironically, was beginning to pick up papers from the

279

floor. Gavin shut the door behind him, but didn't sit down. Instead he did his characteristic twitching, moving papers and fidgeting. 'Did you have any inkling?' he asked without preamble.

'About Camilla? Not a clue. I thought it was Peter, to be honest. How do you know about it?'

'Some girl, I think you know her, made me wear an earpiece, so I heard what you heard. Who was she and how was Frankie involved? I thought he was just a post-grad student.'

'They're friends of mine. Good friends, and I asked them to help me because I had suspicions.'

'They were great. I think we should employ them. I have to say I'm staggered though and I think I owe you an apology.' This time he did sit down, and leaned back in his seat. 'You have been stitched up by that girl.'

'I should have noticed.' Alex walked over and looked out of the window at the river. 'I should have got suspicious earlier, but she was so clever, always making things appear as if they were my fault and then offering helpfully to sort them out. I've been thinking about it in the taxi back from the show. When she looked at her old emails when I asked her about the timing of the Turkey courier, she can't have been looking at anything at all. She must have sent an email changing the time as if it was from me and then deleted it.' She leaned her head against the glass. 'I've been such a fool! Frankie must have realised when he got to Turkey.'

'Frankie went to Turkey?'

Alex explained what happened and Gavin raised his eyebrows in amazement. 'What a man! We'd better make sure we pay him handsomely for that. And what about the newspaper exclusives – and *Scorch*. Did she screw that up too?'

'Must have done. And delaying Bettina's car this morning.'

Another thought occurred to her. 'And maybe even the Claridges' suite mess-up. I should have thought it a bit odd the way she kept wanting access to my laptop.' Alex paused, her head filling with clues now. 'The screw-up with the press pack – I wonder if that was anything to do with her?' She sighed. It was incredible really. 'I've been too trusting and all the time she was after my job. But hell, Gavin, she was my assistant. I had to delegate.'

'Of course you did. And that's how it should have been. If it's any consolation, there is no way I'd have given her your job. She wouldn't have been right. Camilla didn't have a tenth of the initiative and motivation you have, Alex. Today was superb and the feedback already is magnificent. We're looking at a significant raise for you, and let's not see if we can't get you a wider brief, hey?' He smiled. 'Maybe Europe? Though I'd hate to lose you in the UK. Better still, give me some more ideas? What have you got up that sleeve of yours?'

'Well.' Alex looked at Gavin, about to share her idea for the senior sportswear range but something made her hesitate and she felt anger rise. It made her rash. 'You know, Gavin, you haven't really been very supportive of me during all this, have you? But that doesn't seem to matter now it's all gone well.'

Gavin's eyebrows were raised in astonishment. 'Well, you ...' he blustered.

She ploughed on. 'But it matters to me. You were so quick to think the worst of me. So keen to undermine and discredit me in front of everyone, shouting at me across the office. You didn't give me time to explain, you just piled on the pressure.'

'Yes, but you came through. That's what matters.'

Alex shook her head slowly. 'It's pretty sloppy management, I think. Let's see shall we? I've got some mulling over to do, then I'll let you know what I think of your offer.' And she walked out of the office leaving Gavin with his mouth hanging open.

Alex fielded calls for the rest of the morning, even during a celebratory crayfish and rocket sandwich and small plastic beaker of bubbly someone had produced at her desk. IT had swooped and were attempting mouth to mouth on her laptop hard disk. In the meantime she took and made calls of congratulations, including one to Donatella and an interesting one from a headhunter who would 'love to take her out to lunch when the dust has settled'.

'Guys, get this.' It was Peter who burst through the door brandishing the *Evening Standard*. He let out a whoop of delight and within seconds people were round him, but he held up the paper so Alex could see. 'Get a load of this!'

There, on the front page, was a colour picture of Dizzy Zee, all teeth and bling, with his arm around an ecstatic Bettina in crop top, the company logo in full view. 'Zencorp's new look set to go mega', shouted the caption. 'Full launch story page 3'.

'Wow, and look at my trainers! This has to be worth a hundred per cent raise for both of us,' laughed Peter smugly. 'And a company Beamer!'

Alex felt her arms goosebump with excitement. This was the very best she could have hoped for. It had been not just a success but a triumph. Her future was looking great.

So why was Frankie the only person she wanted to celebrate with?

Chapter 52

Ella finished her Ricicles then washed up her bowl and spoon. She paused and listened. Still no sound from Frankie's bedroom. He'd disappeared in there when they got back from the launch and by the time Ella had got home again, after returning the equipment to Mike and taking him out for lunch to thank him, and then going out to supper with him after a delicious afternoon in bed so he could thank her for taking him out for lunch, Frankie was fast asleep in his room. She'd found the cold remains of a pizza which she polished off, an empty bottle of red wine lay on its side next to the sofa and his glass stood unwashed on the draining board. It was all looking very bad. Worst of all, *The Deer Hunter* was in the DVD player. When he put a heart-tugger on like that things were serious. Ella had shrugged sadly as she'd cleared up after him.

Should she sneak out quietly and leave him be, or wake him with a cup of tea? The phone rang. She answered quickly, to give him a chance to sleep it off, and a voice she recognised sounded in her ear. 'I need to speak to Frankie, please. Urgently. Is he there?'

'Oh hi, Marina. It's his sister, Ella. Er – he's not available at the moment, I'm afraid. Can I get him to call you back?'

Ella could hear loud tutting. 'Well, can I get him on his mobile? I've got to get back to them as soon as possible, you see.'

'Hang on. Who? What are you talking about?'

'Darling, I'm the agent, not you. Just get him to call me back straight away, will you?'

'Oh hang on,' Ella bluffed. 'I think I hear him coming back in. Hold on a moment, can you?' She laid the phone down gently and crashed into Frankie's room. God! It smelled like student digs. 'Frankie!' She shook him urgently by the shoulder. 'Frankie! Wake up you old wino! That agent of yours is on the phone. She says it's urgent. Come on, Frankie!'

He rolled out of bed and on to the floor, squinting at her with bloodshot eyes. 'Wha? Whasa? Eugh! If you're winding me up I'm gonna wring your neck. Hand me the phone.' He cleared his throat with difficulty and she ran to the kitchen to get him a glass of fresh water. He nodded his thanks, then took the phone. 'Marina. Whassup? Yeah, it is me – honest. Oh, just a virus, I think.' He took a long swig of water. Ella hovered by the door, watching him cautiously. He suddenly looked awake. 'Yes? Yes? Yes? NO! You're kidding! I thought … Well, yes, absolutely. Of course! When do rehearsals start? You bet! Yes, I can come in later. Well, what can I say? That's terrific news. Thank you very much. I will. I will. Bye!'

Ella looked questioningly at him, not daring to ask, when he leaped to his feet, grabbed her hands and started jumping around, still dressed in yesterday's underpants and socks. 'I've got it! I've got the part! I'm gonna be Joel. We're starting rehearsals in three weeks! How bloody fantabydoozy is that. Eh?'

Ella laughed and laughed as they cavorted around the room. 'You clever old thing. I knew you'd make it! I just knew it. Oh Frankie, I'm so proud of you. I didn't think anything could be as exciting as that launch, but this is even better.'

Frankie paced the kitchen muttering 'I can't believe it, I can't believe it' and clapping his hands together, then doing a funny goal-scoring jig. Ella fully expected him to pull his T-shirt over his head any minute.

'Right!' Ella grabbed the kettle and started to fill it. 'Today you are a star, and must be treated in the manner to which you'll probably become accustomed. I'll make the tea. I'll even make your toast. And I'll even spread it all nicely for you. Are you going to call The Bean?'

Frankie stopped pacing and frowned. He rubbed his un-shaven chin for a moment. 'Yeah, course I will, when I've had my tea. And the boys. And Saff too, of course.' He paused for a moment. 'Gosh, this is what I've always dreamed of. And now I've got it. I've done it, Ella.' He smiled at her. 'Funny, isn't it? I thought ... well, never mind.'

Something wasn't quite right, but Ella couldn't put a finger on what exactly. She looked at him anxiously. This didn't look like a man who'd just achieved his life-long ambition. She placed a mug of tea in front of him. 'And will you tell Alex?' she asked gently.

'What do you mean? Oh! I need this.' He took a long swallow and sighed with contentment.

'Are you going to call and tell her?'

'Yeah, probably. Well, maybe not. She may not even know I was going up for it, so it'd be a bit pointless. Maybe Saff will say something to her.'

'Frankie ...'

He took the plate of toast and marmalade from her hands and looked her straight in the eye. 'Not now, Ells. Just drop it, would you?'

Chapter 53

Alex held the painting up over the fireplace. Yes, it would look good there. The bright slashes of colour looked even more dramatic against the plain walls. It was just what the room needed. A bit of life. As the phone rang, she leaned it back up against the sofa.

'Hi, it's Saff. Whatcha doing?'

Alex smiled. 'You're not going to believe this, but I'm trying to hang a painting.'

'What? A new one? A real one?'

'Yes, a real one. Actually, I've just done something a bit reckless …' And she told Saff how she'd passed the gallery on her way home, something she'd done hundreds of times before. 'But it just caught my eye, Saff, and before I knew it, there it was wrapped in brown paper and under my arm, and my credit card is two hundred quid lighter. I must be turning into my mother.'

Saff giggled. 'You could do worse. Good on ya! You deserve a reward for yesterday.' There was a shriek of children from down the phone. 'Anyway, can't talk long – Oscar is off to tennis – but I wondered if you wanted to come over for lunch on Sunday. Nothing special. Just us. We might eat in the garden?'

Alex felt a surge of love towards her friend. 'I can't imagine anything nicer. See you then. I'll bring the plonk as usual.'

'Oh please don't!' laughed Saff. 'Must dash.' And they hung up.

Alex sighed and picked up the hammer and the hook, then looked at the painting and put them down again. It was too bloody difficult trying to hang a painting on your own.

Chapter 54

Friday night. Date night. Frankie smiled wryly and adjusted his collar as he stood outside The Bean's front door. He'd phoned straight away to tell her about getting the part, but she hadn't been free until now, so their celebration had been deferred. The Bean had told him on the phone too that, after much thought, she'd decided to sell her mews house and that it was time to move on. She fancied being nearer the park, she'd said, but to Frankie it felt like the end of an era. He'd been feeling like this for the last few days though. In fact, it had been a strange, anticlimactic week since his mercy dash to Istanbul and the launch. In spite of the fantastic news about the part, he felt mopey and down, and Ella hadn't held back from telling him how miserable he looked. He shook his head irritably. This should be the happiest time of his life, but he just didn't feel right. Maybe he'd picked up something in Istanbul?

The Bean took slightly longer than usual to answer the door. Perhaps she was titivating. He smiled to himself and thought about the evening ahead. The Bean would cheer him up. She'd been delighted when he told her the news on the phone – not surprised, as he had been – but thoroughly delighted and she'd said straight away that he deserved the part, and that she'd known all along he would get it. Frankie wished he could share her confidence. To him, it still felt like a fluke, or at least the hugest stroke of luck. He'd just been in the right place at the right time. That was how it felt, anyway.

At last The Bean opened up. It had been worth the wait; she did look amazing, in narrow trousers and a kind of brocade frock coat. She looked like a Regency dandy. 'My darling boy!' she exclaimed, giving him a bracing hug. Then she stepped back and looked him up and down, an expression of satisfaction on her face. 'Don't you look smart! I'm so delighted. Isn't this thrilling. Come upstairs, won't you?'

She'd been busy. A great deal of the clutter, the stacked up canvasses and knick-knacks had gone – probably forcibly removed by Alex. Frankie felt suddenly uncomfortable again and looked around, puzzled. The table was laid for two and there was a bottle of red wine open on the sideboard. From the kitchen, a delicious smell of food wafted. He hadn't realised The Bean could cook.

'I thought we were going out, Bean. I've made reservations. Have we got our wires crossed?'

A slightly furtive look crossed her face and she glanced at her watch. 'No, darling. Not at all. This is just what I had in mind. Did you reserve somewhere? Oh dear. Perhaps you could call and cancel.'

'You're looking very dressed up for an evening in. I'm honoured. And you've cooked! This is so sweet of you. I thought it was against your principles.'

Again the slightly guilty look. The Bean went over to the windows and looked along the street, then turned to him, an almost pleading expression on her face. She seemed in a hurry to speak. 'Frankie, I'm so pleased for you, and so proud. I ... I couldn't be prouder if you were my own son, you know. And you have so much talent. So much to give. Please don't let it go to waste. You're a very special young man. And if ... if you think I've stage-managed things a bit, well, don't be cross with me. Because I have your interests at heart, you know. And whatever happens, please let us always be friends.'

'What on earth are you talking about, Bean? You do sound melodramatic. Have you robbed a bank?'

There was a ring on the doorbell and she hurried down the stairs to answer it. Outside, Frankie could hear a large, well-tuned motor purring and went over to the window to look out. A white stretch limo with tinted windows was waiting outside and a large uniformed man with dark glasses was holding the door open. Frankie ran downstairs to the front door. 'What on earth's going on? Are we going out after all? Why didn't you tell me?'

From inside the car, he heard a deep, languid voice. 'Hey Bean? How's it hangin? So this is the famous Frankie, huh?' A short black man dressed all in black with intense mint-coloured, untied trainers – ones from the launch – stepped out on to the pavement, then leaned into the car and offered his hand to … to Bettina! Frankie looked again. The man was Dizzy Zee, the rap artist who had turned up at the launch in Brixton and driven the press into a frenzy.

'Frrrrankie! I 'eard about what you did to 'elp the other day. The Bean says you saved the day for everyone. You are an 'ero, no?' Bettina leaned closed and kissed him fragrantly on each cheek.

Frankie was unable to speak. As Dizzy pumped his hand and slapped his back, he could only stare and try to be polite. What the hell was going on?

Behind the limo, another car had pulled up, and the engine turned off. He peered to see who it was and through the wind-screen he could see someone who looked suspiciously like Alex. Suddenly, nothing else mattered. He watched her emerge and he stared, astonished. She looked as puzzled as he felt, and he couldn't take his eyes off her. Clinging to her slim figure was the delicious green Ungaro dress from her wardrobe, there were dangly gold earrings in her ears, her hair was scooped up on her head in clips and on her surprisingly delicate feet were high strappy sandals. She looked breathtaking but stood there awkwardly, a part of this extraordinary tableau in the mews. Beside her, the supermodel, the rap star, the ravishing, ageing actress, the opulent car and its driver all faded away, and Frankie just stared. Suddenly, everything in his life made sense.

She came up to them tentatively, frowning slightly. 'Mum? What's going on? Bettina? Dizzy? I thought you'd both left for the South of France. And Frankie ...' She trailed off.

The Bean coughed delicately. Darling, you look beautiful. But you know, my dears, I somehow seem to have got my diary all mixed up. I'd quite forgotten that I'd arranged to see both you, Alex dear, and Frankie tonight. And Saffron has cooked up a delicious meal for two, which is keeping warm upstairs. Shame to waste it. And then Bettina and Dizzy are only in town tonight, and I would so love to go out with them so ... I was thinking ...'

Chapter 55

They both stood there in silence as the tail lights of the limo disappeared out of the mews and on to the main road.

'I think,' said Frankie slowly, still looking ahead of him, 'that we have been well and truly stitched up.'

Alex found herself laughing awkwardly. 'Story of my life! The old witch. She knew full well she was going out.'

Now Frankie turned to her. 'Do you mind?'

'Mind what?'

'Spending the evening with me? Look at us – we've made such an effort to dress up.' He glanced at her cautiously, the laughter dancing in his eyes. 'If you don't keep me company I'll feel like Johnny No Mates and I could never eat all that food on my own. You'd be doing me a favour.'

'Well, Frankie,' replied Alex. 'I do owe you a favour. In fact I owe you big time. If it wasn't for you I'd be looking for a job tonight and Bettina would have had to appear stark naked.'

Frankie laughed. 'Nice image.'

They stood in silence. Alex was itching to ask. 'Tell me, how did you know to challenge Camilla? When did you realise?'

Frankie absent-mindedly scuffed his shoe along a ridge in the cobbles. 'Well, to be honest I wasn't sure even until the last minute. Her eagerness to help all the time was beginning to raise my suspicions, and she was so swift to offer to go to Turkey. Then it was Melik who pointed out the email changing the delivery date. It was sent from your computer last Friday evening, but of course last Friday you were, we were ...' He faltered.

'Together at my place?' Alex willed him to look at her. If she could only see his eyes she'd know what he was thinking. That he felt the same way she did.

'Yes.' He looked at her boldly. 'We were, weren't we?' There was a small smile on his lips. 'So the penny dropped finally when I was in Turkey and so I alerted Ella. I realised whoever it was would try something at the launch. It would be irresistible. I was starting to feel like an extra from *Poirot*. I asked Ella to leave some T-shirts Melik had given me in the changing room – he's quite an admirer of yours by the way – and it was mad really! But just by chance I spotted Camilla coming out through the doors carrying them and, well, I followed her – getting Ella to alert you.'

'And wiring up Gavin so he heard it all too?'

'That was Ella's idea. She's very persuasive you know. The poor man hadn't a hope.'

Alex chuckled, thinking of Ella's first call about the 'wife' job. 'You're telling me! And thank goodness she is.' She saw Frankie glance at her questioningly. 'What I mean is, you both saved the day. I owe her too.'

'The launch – it was wonderful. You know that, don't you?'

'I hope so. And so much thanks to you.' She laughed softly at the thought. 'What a lot of debts to pay. I needed people, didn't I? And not just for that. What about all you did for my mother? You've made her come alive and I think I understand her much better now than I ever have. We both have you to thank for that.'

Frankie stepped closer to her and Alex found herself studying his shoes intently. 'I love your mother,' he said quietly. 'She's helped me so much – especially to get this role.' He paused. 'You have more in common with her than you think.'

Alex looked up horrified. 'Oh, I should have congratulated you! It's wonderful news, Frankie. Saff told me about it. I didn't realise Mum was helping you, I'm sorry.'

'It wasn't only your mother who helped me get the part, you know.' He gently put his hand on her cheek. 'It was you for making me feel so miserable.'

What had she done? 'I don't understand.'

He put his other hand to her face and cupped it in his hands. 'You have such perfect skin. Do you know how long I've wanted to do this?'

'About a week?' she teased gently.

'Oh no, longer than that. Even before that time in the park. In fact …' He gently lowered his head and rubbed his nose against the tip of hers. Probably since the first time I ironed your knickers!' Alex gasped with embarrassment and put her head against his chest to hide her face, but he put his hand under her chin to raise her lips to his warm mouth.

Standing on the pavement they kissed for what felt to Alex like ages, exploring each other's mouths and touching each other in wonder, and it wasn't the driving, selfish passion they had felt last week. This was something deeper. Then Frankie pulled gently away and rested his forehead against hers. 'I was right, you look so beautiful in that dress.' He kissed her forehead thoughtfully. 'Alex, what do we do about the American boyfriend? Because if we don't have a future, then please tell me now and I'll go. You don't have to do this out of gratitude.'

Is that what he thought this was all about? Alex almost laughed until she saw how serious he looked. Soul-baring didn't come easily to her but he deserved her honesty. She had to do this right because it felt like he could be the missing piece in her life. And until the last few weeks she'd hadn't even realised anything was missing at all.

This time she took his face in her hands. 'Frankie, I never had anything with Todd that comes close to what I feel for you.' She watched with pleasure as relief flooded into his eyes. 'You were so not part of my life plan. But do you know? I'm beginning to think I'm fed up of being ruled by plans and schedules and other people's needs.'

'My life doesn't even have a plan.' Frankie smiled ruefully. 'We're so different. Could you cope? Could you live with an actor?'

This time Alex did laugh out loud. 'Frankie, I was brought up by one! But at least you can cook!'

Frankie gasped. 'The food! It's probably burnt!' He took her hand.

Alex held him back for a moment and kissed him again. 'Frankie,' she said. 'You are the best wife any woman could hope for.' And they both ran, laughing, towards the front door.